THE JOURNEYS OF McGILL FEIGHAN combine the epic sweep of *The Lord of the Rings* and the tight suspense of the *Dune* trilogy with the wry humor and techno-fantastic imagination of *Stranger in a Strange Land*...

Book III: LAVA

Welcome to a world of unlimited possibilities, in a universe of no escape!

Third in the new series by
KEVIN O'DONNELL, Jr.
Book I: CAVERNS
Book II: REEFS
Book III: LAVA

THE JOURNEYS OF McGILL FEIGHAN

BOOK III:
LAVA

KEVIN O'DONNELL, JR.

BERKLEY BOOKS, NEW YORK

LAVA

A Berkley Book / published by arrangement with
the author

PRINTING HISTORY
Berkley edition / April 1982

ISBN: 0-425-05248-6

A BERKLEY BOOK® TM 757,375
The name "BERKLEY" and the stylized "B" with design are
trademarks belonging to Berkley Publishing Corporation.

PRINTED IN THE UNITED STATES OF AMERICA

I want especially to thank Mary Anne Burghart, who taught me to love plants; Fred Jackson, who taught me about them; and Dave Schlosser, who taught me I could grow the damn things in the first place. I'm also grateful to Mary Kittredge, Mark J. McGarry, Joel Rosenberg, Victoria Schochet, and of course, my wife, Kim Tchang. They all read this novel in manuscript and what they said about it helped me make it better than it would otherwise have been.

To Cherry Weiner,
because I couldn't spare a gastropod
when she really needed one,
and because without her
the lava might never have flowed.

▪ Chapter I ▪

The psychiatric evaluation of Marion Jefferson Greystein disgusted him. "Emotional immaturity and consequent rebelliousness, compounded by alcoholic tendencies." In plain English, Greystein broke whatever rules he pleased. As that anonymous phone call had just made clear.

Davis drummed his fingers on the desk. PsychSection recommended nonsense: comprehension, counseling, therapy. All a smokescreen spewed out to hide its failure to properly indoctrinate Greystein in the first place. If it had done its job—damn the personality damage!—Greystein would never have acted up.

Not one Flinger except Harry Lipsiento, whose Psych session he had overseen personally, seemed to have been indoctrinated properly. Whiners, all of them! Ask them to work overtime, to squeeze in one extra Fling—"I'm too tired," or "Couldn't get it there safely," or even, to his fury, "No." Except for Harry, who was as courteous and as reflexively obedient as any boss could want.

Time to draw a line. Whip the *prima donnas* into shape. Make an example out of Greystein. His roommate Feighan was nearly as bad, but at least Feighan did his job. Greystein thought he was above all that. Dead last on the performance ratings the last six months. Four days out of five he came to work hung over; on the fifth, he came drunk. No therapy for him.

1

What he needed—and would get, if that caller sent the proof—would be a good headscrub.

That would solve the problem. For sure. And forever.

▪ Chapter II ▪

Teetering on the edge of the bathtub, Sam asked, "Why won't the other kids play with me?"

McGill Feighan smiled sadly at his three-year-old ward, then raised his chin to shave beneath his jaw. "Probably because you're different."

"But why does that matter?" Sam blinked all four lids on each eye: the inner pair were transparent; the outer, opaque. He swished his tail. At the scrape of his twenty-four claws on the plascelain, he shuddered. The triangular fins running the length of his spine rippled.

"I think it makes them afraid of you." Feighan tugged a comb through his tousled black hair, but to little effect. He made a face. "That's the way people are."

"I'm a people, and I'm not afraid because somebody's different."

"Well, yes and no." Feighan squinted into the mirror: bloodshot brown eyes peered back at him. *You gotta start getting more sleep,* he told himself. *Next time, leave Gina's earlier.* "First of all, most people can't tell when somebody wants to hurt them, like you can. Second, you're an intelligent being, and you were born and raised right here in New York, but you're still a Rhanghan, and when I say 'people' I mean Terran."

"What's a Terran?"

"Like me and Greystein—we're Terrans." He sighed. He and Sam must have held this same conversation ten times in the last month alone. "Listen, if I don't get a move on, I'm going to be late for work, so—"

3

"Can I come with you?" His magenta tongue flickered out to sample Feighan's forearm. Please, McGill, can I?"

"That's 'may I,' and the answer is no." He pirouetted to inspect himself in the mirrored back of the bathroom door. The black boots and white pants accentuated his height, and the interwoven color bands of his energy tunic set off his muscled frame nicely. "Not today, Sam."

"But there's nothing to do here!"

"Believe me, it'd be just as dull in the Flinger Room— worse, 'cause there's no holo. And you'd have to keep quiet all day long. You wouldn't like that, would you?"

"No, I guess not." His surrender sounded like a snake's hiss. "How come I can't go to school like the other kids?"

"I told you, you start at All Saints in September."

"But the other kids go to O'Toole."

"That's a public school. The law says you have to be five years old to get into public kindergarten, and you're only three."

"That's not fair."

"Hey—why don't you go pester Greystein while I eat breakfast?"

"I wanted to, but he's not home."

"He's not?" Feighan stepped out of the bathroom; Sam slithered off the tub and followed. "Where'd he go?"

"I don't know. His bedroom's empty, though."

"Did you check?"

"McGill, you know I don't have to check—I just *know* it's empty."

"I wish I knew how you did that." Feighan headed for the kitchen. "When did you see him last?"

"The night before yesterday."

He frowned. "I'll bet he's on Canopus Eighteen again, on that beach he calls Hideaway." To the computer that ran the penthouse apartment, he said, "Oscar, query: where is Greystein; answer it now."

A ceiling speaker replied. "No data."

That worried Feighan. His roommate might go off without notifying his human friends and acquaintances, but he almost always told Oscar where he would be. "Oscar, query: when does Greystein's next shift start; answer it now."

"June 4, 2105; 1000 hours."

He checked his watch. Nine-thirty already. Half an hour was time enough, but . . . as he stepped into the kitchen and said, "Oscar, order: plate three blackberry doughnuts; pour one cup coffee, cream three sugars; do it now," he fretted.

You're gonna feel real dumb when he shows up safe and sound, he told himself, but he did have cause for alarm. For most of his life, an interstellar crime syndicate known simply as The Organization had been trying to capture him, for reasons that were still not clear. Over the years of sporadic skirmishing, The Organization's man-hunter, Milford Hommroummy, had killed a number of people close to Feighan—including his parents. And every time Greystein went off on his own, Feighan feared that he had been added to that list.

The chef panel opened to reveal his breakfast. He carried the plate and saucer over to the table, set them down gently, and sat. His stomach growled. Sam wriggled into the seat across from him.

The doorbell rang.

Groaning, Feighan put down the doughnut. "I hope that's not Mrs. Estwund again."

Sam looked offended. "McGill, I haven't bit her dog since the last time! And you know that wasn't my fault."

"Yeah, I know, kid, but she's got you on her rot list now, and anything happens to her beloved Absalom—"

"Gets blamed on me." Sam's spine fins drooped morosely.

Feighan pushed himself back from the table. "Oscar, query: who rang the doorbell; answer it now."

A hum came from behind the grille in the ceiling. "Print ID impossible."

Feighan froze. Building Security was supposed to prevent anyone from reaching the penthouse without authorization. He had too many enemies. "Oscar, order: run visual ID; cross-reference it with police files—"

Sam slipped down from his chair. "I'll check it, McGill." Four legs blurring and tail held high, he whisked out the kitchen door.

"Be careful!"

The Rhanghan threw a disgusted look over his shoulder. "McGill!"

"Yeah." He got to his feet. "Sorry, Sam. I keep forgetting."

At the front door, Sam closed his eyes. He touched the mahogany with his right hand. Cocking his head, he inhaled till his chest puffed up—then nodded with apparent satisfaction. He turned the knob. And jumped back, hissing.

"What is it?" said Feighan.

Silencing his guardian with a raised hand, Sam swallowed visibly. "Good morning. May I help you?"

The raspy voice sounded like a giant cricket: "I seek McGill the Flinger."

Sam turned his head and motioned. "It's safe."

Damn. As his stomach rumbled its discontent, he eyed his watch. He had twenty minutes to get to work, and breakfast sat untouched. Yet he had to be polite. "Tell him to come in."

Sam squinted at the stranger. "Are you a him?"

Feighan winced in embarrassment.

"I am an it," it said in that serrated voice. "May I enter nonetheless?"

"Oh, sure." Sam's tail dropped, and brushed from side to side. Backing away from the door, he let it swing open.

Into the vestibule hobbled a two-meter-tall barrel cactus on spider's legs. "Thank you." It spoke by rubbing four of its longer spines together. A pale, glossy patch of skin pointed straight at Feighan; another ambered its left side. A purplish gourd the size of a cucumber dangled from its top.

The Flinger almost tripped. He blinked—then snapped his fingers. *An Actuni!* He had met one, once, a long time ago. An odd creature, it had been: A diplomat attached to the Flinger Network Control's New York Field Office, it had become addicted to Terran showers; crown rot had hospitalized it within six months.

He walked forward to greet his visitor, wishing he could remember some Actuni customs. He could not. Ordinary politeness would have to do. "Good morning." Checking his instinct to extend a hand, he bowed. "What is it that you wished to see me about?"

The alien, green and bristly, hopped through a quarter turn, bringing into view the third of its glowing ocular aureoles. The middle convexity stared Feighan full in the face. From it jutted a slender spike that quivered at its grey tip. "You are Feighan McGill the Flinger?"

"Yes. Please, come into the living room."

Once the Actuni had tottered all the way inside, Oscar closed the door behind it. "Thank you."

"You're welcome." It moved with a slowness maddening to a hungry twenty-two-year-old whose doughnuts dried just around the corner but who had to be at work in—*Eighteen minutes, now; sure hope this guy talks quicker than it walks* . . . He kept his face stiffly free of impatience, though, because some aliens could read human expressions.

The living room's glass wall overlooked Manhattan; a southern exposure, it received direct sunlight all day long. At 9:45 a.m. on that June day, a wedge of brilliance electrified the blue of half the Chinese carpet. The alien marched all the way into the wedge. The green of its waxy skin came alive. Then it did a dance and a scuttle to turn itself around. "I am called Hngchgck."

Dubiously, Feighan attempted to repeat the sound. The hoarse gutturals tricked him into a cough.

"Your people approximate that as: H'nik."

"I am very pleased to meet you." Bowing again, he gestured to his ward. "And this is Sam."

"How do you do, Sam?" The Actuni's thousands of spines rippled like grass in a breeze. "You are a long way from your home world; are you also a pilgrim?"

Sam nictitated in apparent confusion; his tongue fluttered briefly. "No, I'm a Rhanghan-American."

The alien's noise of response sounded like a dry chuckle. "I have been studying your language for many years, Feighan McGill—"

"It's the other way around," said Sam. "You've got it backwards. It's really McGill Feighan."

"Ah? I apologize. We of Actu, having no parents, are unfamiliar with patronymics; I had thought all names beginning with 'Mc' were surnames."

"Usually they are." Feighan shifted his gaze to check the wall clock. He had twelve minutes left. "But, ah, in this case, it's my given name."

"Fascinating . . ." It seemed very much at ease, with its short thick legs buried in the carpet's pile, and the sunlight rubbing its back. "Your language is a source of constant wonder to me—in part because it has no exact term to describe my vocation."

Ten minutes. "Listen, H'nik, I am sorry to be rude, but I have to report for work in a very short while. Ah . . ." He did not know the diplomatic thing to say. "Why exactly did you want to see me?"

"I do apologize, McGill Feighan. I am slow and verbose. It would take more time than you have for me to explain precisely why I have taken the liberty of calling on you. Perhaps when you are finished for the day, we might talk together, and I could elucidate."

"That sounds good." He glanced at the wall clock again. Nine-fifty-two. *Scratch the doughnuts*. "I finish for the day in twelve hours."

H'nik flexed its legs and wobbled upright, then began to creep out of the pool of sun. "I will wait for you in the hall. Should I not respond to your call, shine a strong light on me for perhaps ten of your minutes; that should activate me."

He looked at Sam, who shrugged. "Activate?"

"The paucity of light, you see, causes something akin to your sleep; it is a natural physiological response, however, and nothing to be alarmed about."

"McGill," said Sam suddenly, "he—it can wait here. On the terrace. There's lots of sun out there."

He wished he could ask his ward if their visitor were on the level—but then, Sam would not have made the offer if he were suspicious of H'nik. "Okay. H'nik—please, make yourself at home until I come back. Sam will get you anything you need or would like or—or whatever."

"Thank you very much. It is most gracious of you."

"No problem. I'll see you both later." He had less than a minute to make it to work. Stepping back, symbolically to distance himself from the other two, he closed his eyes. Summoning his Talent, that inborn, out-of-this-world skill that only one Terran in ten million possessed, he concentrated on himself: tall; broad shoulders veeing into a seventy-centimeter waist; thumbs hooked into the corners of his pants pockets; boots reflecting the glitter of his tunic in their gloss. At the same time, he visualized his destination: the small, white-walled chamber at the Flinger Building on Long Island, the one with the fluorescent lights that hummed and the white-tiled floor that no amount of scrubbing could ever rid of heelmarks. And in the seeing he juxtaposed the two images, feeling how the one belonged inside the other, knowing how to make it so, and—

PING

—he began to teleport. It was instantaneous, but time is relative; from within, a Fling lasts forever. Space explo/lapsed. He grew yet shrank. In one and the same perceived instant, he ballooned to twice the universe's size, yet the smallest subatomic particle dwarfed him. The insanity of shredded time and space came through as pain: a tearing, a rending. It lasted longer than could possibly be endured—almost long enough to sense. And then his sizes changed again, the one shrinking and the other growing, until they merged, and he was, once more, one meter ninety centimeters and ninety-five kilograms, standing on a scuffed tile floor in a small, white-walled chamber in a busy building on Long Island.

The teleporting was done.

Sort of.

He left his private locker room as the second of four musical chimes pealed from the building's public address system. He hurried down the long hall to his Flinger Room; the shift officially commenced in fifty seconds.

"McGill!"

Still moving, he looked over his shoulder. Behind him, leaning half out of a doorway, was his roommate, Marion Jefferson Greystein. Feighan halted in mid-stride. "What the—?"

Greystein wore only a bathing suit, black with silver piping; a wet towel hung around his neck. His curly brown hair was plastered to his skull. Stubble coarsened his long cheeks. A silly grin on his pale face, he rested a shoulder against the doorjamb as though he needed to.

Aw, geez, late again! But Feighan went back. "Where have you been? We were worried."

Greystein drew himself up to his full height, which was nearly Feighan's though he lacked his roommate's bulk. "I have just discovered a magnificent way to get laid."

"You're drunk!"

"And rightfully, delightfully so, McGill my young daffodil. For I have discovered that if you take a cute young thing to a beautiful black sand beach on a planet so distant that its star can't be seen through even the mosht acute of Earth-based telescopes, you can ball that cute young thing to your heart's content. All it takes is to meet her resistance with the shimple sentence, 'If thash the way you feel, then you can walk home!'"

"Greystein, that's rape!"

"Isn't everything?" He blinked owlishly. "But I was only kidding, anyway."

"Jesus, Greystein, sober up."

The other closed his eyes and sagged against the doorframe.

"Uh-uh," he said in a mumble. "If I sh— sober up, I'll remember what a prick I was, and that's something I don't wanna do just yet . . . hey, before you go—"

The speakers mounted in the ceiling boomed: "McGill Feighan, report to your station. William Abernathy Cole, report to your station. Marion Jeff—"

"I have to go," said Feighan.

"No, wait!" He lurched into his Room, and came back proffering a large parcel wrapped in irridescent paper. "Here. For you. Picked it up on Inta Leina."

"What is it?"

"A mirror."

"Greystein, I—"

"When you get a chance, open it up—look into it—then turn it around. Surprise hell out of you, it will, McGill my young daffodil."

"McGill Feighan," said the public address system, "report to your station. Wil—"

"I'll see you later." Feighan took the mirror and moved off.

After him Greystein called, "You can count on it, roomie!"

Safely inside his Flinger Room, he hurried to the Data console. The display screen flashed: THRONGORN II. In the white chamber below the window, four Terrans and one alien, a three-meter-tall Timili that looked like an unhappy lemur, waited on the scale with a stack of boxes. Feighan slid into his chair; the corner of the display screen glared 926 kilograms. He touched the button on his microphone. "Good morning, folks; sorry I'm running a bit late but you know how it goes. You are eight kilos overweight."

The shortest Terran, a pipe-smoking woman with waist-length black hair, said, "How much extra will those eight kilos cost?"

He suppressed an angry rejoinder. People could be so ignorant. The signs, the manifests, the brochures—they all explained it—but people never read the fine print, so this situation arose again and again. One of these days he would start screaming, but until then, he would remember the rules and stay polite to the customers. "Ah, no, ma'am, that's not the way it works. The most I can Fling is 918 kilograms; if the cargo weighs more, I can't get it off the ground. You'll have to leave something behind."

"But I need all this!"

"Ma'am, I believe I mentioned that I'm running late?"

"Yes." Hands on her hips, she stared up at his window. "So?"

"Ma'am, my whole day is scheduled already, and the next cargo is waiting outside. If I don't get you off real quickly, things are going to back up something fierce. So please, cut eight kilos off your load—"

"I'll do no such thing, young man!"

Why were people so difficult? Why did they have to behave as though they could flout the rules with impunity? "Ma'am, you've got thirty seconds to dump the excess baggage or you will lose your time slot for good. Do you want to get a move on?"

She stalked off the scales, raised a clenched fist, and shook it at him. "I am Professor Katrina van der Voort of the University of the North Atlan—"

He could not resist the opportunity. Closing his eyes, he concentrated, visualized, felt, knew—*PING*—and sent the other three Terrans and the one Timili on their way to Throngorn II.

After adjusting the travelers' angular momentum, and setting them down safely on the planet so many parsecs away, he said, "Professor, I really don't give a good goddam who you are. I'm in charge here. You are legally required to obey my instructions in regard to mass and dispersement. You did not. I have sent the rest of your group on. You will have to make another reservation. Good day."

"You filthy bloodsucking pig!" She threw her pipe on the floor and stomped it; shards of plascelain skittered across the tiles. "You can't do that to me; I'll have your ass in court—"

To his computer he said, "Program: Cite overweight option regulations; execute."

The screen displayed a series of numbers and letters, and beneath that, four paragraphs of closely spaced, densely written text.

He skimmed the screen. "Professor, North American Consortium Regulations, Section Twelve, Paragraph 93, subparagraphs (a) through (e) specifically enable me to do what I have just done. I have neither the time nor the inclination to read them off to you. I will simply state that Twelve, 93, (f) empowers me to have you arrested for causing a disturbance in a Fling Booth. You have thirty seconds to leave before I call the police. Counting." With that, he switched off the PA system and leaned back, eyes closed.

People!

Feighan's job was to Fling up to 918 kilograms of mass—animal, vegetable, or mineral; it mattered not—to one of the twelve planets in the Flinger Network to which he was certified to teleport. It was a good job, in the sense that it gave him security, $250,000 a year, a distinctive uniform, and a fair amount of prestige—but it was boring.

He opened his eyes. Van der Voort had gone; the next group had entered. Thirteen Terrans, both sexes; all were young and a bit on the lean and hungry side. The screen's destination segment read: DELURC. The countdown clock gave him forty-two seconds. They weighed in at 917.8 kilograms. He touched his mike. "Is everybody ready?"

A chorus of assent rose up.

"Anybody who wants to change his mind has thirty-five seconds—mark!—to leave the room."

Nobody moved.

He sighed. "Twenty-five seconds, mark! Delurc is not what you think it's going to be, friends, and dream-selling is a lousy way to make money. Fifteen seconds, mark! All ashore that's going ashore." He shut his eyes, concentrating on the group before him while visualizing the underwater domes of the planet Delurc, where lived the fish who bought men's souls. He felt, and he knew, and—*PING*—for one gasping moment thought he had skewed the angular momentum. At the last second he got it right, and Flopped them down safe and sound. "Idiots!" Savagely, he switched off the PA and called up a crossword puzzle onto the screen.

He had forty-six more Flings before his first shift of the day would be over. After four hours off, he would have to report back for another four on.

The phone rang; he picked it up. "Feighan."

"Hi, McGill, it's Sam. Listen, you know that big tub on the terrace, the one the Christmas tree was in?"

"The guaranteed live one that died in a week?" That still stung; he should have seen the brown needles.

"That's the one."

"Uh-huh. What about it?"

"Can H'nik use it?"

He scratched his head. "For what?"

"To, um . . . you know. To sit in. Or whatever."

Feighan shrugged. "I don't mind." Through the telephone came a rasping. "What?"

"He says, do we have any plant food? What was that?" said Sam to H'nik. While Feighan waited for them to settle it, the door below opened. Automated pallets bore in a stack of crates the screen showed were destined for Rii—edsch. Then Sam got back on the line. "He says 5-10-5 is best, do we have any?"

"What is 5-10-5—and I don't think we have any, anyway."

"Can I ask Oscar?"

"Sure, if you know how."

"Thanks!" The receiver clattered down; Feighan replaced his own with a puzzled frown.

He sent the crates to Rii—edsch when the clock down-counted to zero, then called back his crossword puzzle.

Flinging was a lot like driving a bus that went nowhere.

At the end of his first shift, he stepped into the hall. Yawning, and stretching the kinks out of his back, he looked around for someone to talk to.

The long hall was empty, but from the Flingers' Lounge fifty meters down came grumbling voices. That hooked him; he started walking. The Lounge was rarely used: most Flingers found it easier to pop home for their four off.

Inside, fifteen or twenty of the North American Consortium's first-line teleports clustered around an oversized display screen. Jaws and fists were clenched; angry mutters bounced around the room. The anger focused on the text and numbers scrolling up the screen.

"Hi, McGill." A hand touched his shoulder; lips pecked his cheek.

"Hey, great!" He smiled, and hugged Gina Maccari, the staff telepath. "I thought you were on vacation."

She took his hand. "Come on." Leading him a few doors down the corridor from the Lounge, she said, "I hate to meet and run, but there's too much hostility in there—it's starting to get to me."

"Well, listen—" He slipped his arm around her waist. "I know a nice quiet restaurant—"

She snuggled against him. "I'd love to, but I can't. Director Davis wants me in his office quote right now end quote. How about tonight?"

She felt warm and good and he wanted to hold her forever. "I don't get off till ten, if you don't mind a late dinner."

"That's fine, as long as it's an early evening—I got rescheduled. My shift starts at 6:00 tomorrow."

"A.m.?"

"Uh-huh."

"You poor thing. An early evening it will be." He drew her close and kissed her forehead. "I'll pick you up—oh, nuts! Why don't you meet me at my place at ten? I've got a visitor, an Actuni—ever met one?"

"H'nik?"

"You know him?"

She smiled wearily. "I gave him directions to your place this morning." She glanced at her watch. "And I really have to go—see you at your place at ten tonight."

"Let me give you a hand." He closed his eyes—

"No!" Prodding him in the ribs, she winked. "No offense, but I'd rather walk." She blew him a kiss, turned, and ran down the corridor. The hem of her skirt flipped up with each move.

He shook his head and sighed, then went back into the Lounge to see what had so upset his colleagues. Greystein vociferated in the midst of a knot of them, but Feighan did not feel like talking to him just then. He looked around for someone else.

"How do, McGill," said an Arizonan from behind.

He spun. "Hi, Walking Mule." He shook hands with the Senior Flinger who had trained him in interstellar teleportation four years earlier. "What's all the uproar?"

Walking Mule flipped his braids back over his shoulder, then nodded to the display screen. "The honchos dreamed up a new comp plan."

"They're always doing that."

"Yeah, yeah, they are—but this one here is what they call a competitive rating system. The score you get figures your schedule, the number of times you Fling a day, and how much you get paid for each Fling."

Feighan gaped.

"Come on over, take a looksee for yourself." He led Feighan through the crowd by the elbow. "Remember that clause in our contracts, the 'You Get Exactly What You Earn' clause? Somebody finally wrote that—" He pursed his lips in mock-prissiness: "'quality control program to establish norms for Fling-ing.' And they invoked that clause. Here's height above ground and velocity at moment of materialization." His stubby fore-finger tapped a line on the screen. "Point-oh-one centimeters up is now the norm for h-over-g; velocity norm they reckon at one centimeter per second. You hit those numbers bang between the eyes, they'll pay you $7.93 for that Fling. Do better, they pay you more; worse, less."

"Seven-ninety-three a Fling? I never calculated it out—what are we making now?"

"Seven-ninety-two point-seven." He smiled. "Naw, I didn't work that one out in my head: it's right up top there."

"So if you hit the norm, you're making exactly what you are now?"

"You got it. But if you don't, you make less."

"That rots!"

"And that's just for openers. They are listing us in order of accuracy; list changes once a month. High man on the totem pole gets his choice of shifts for the next month, then number two picks his, and then number three, and so on down the line . . . here's the list." He called it up on the screen.

Feighan raised his eyebrows. "I'm Number One, huh?"

"You always were a meticulous sumbitch. But don't let it go to your head, boy—you might get paid more, and you do get to set your own hours, but you are going to have to work a little some harder than, say, your roommate, who came in twenty-third."

"Out of twenty-three, huh?" Then he frowned. "What do you mean, work harder?"

"What I said: See, along with the higher pay per Fling goes more Flings per day." He leaned forward to examine the num-ber after Feighan's name. "See here, now? They cut your rest time to 255 seconds—your daily quota's now a hundred and twelve."

"Uh-*uh*." He peered at it himself, not believing— "One hundred twelve a day!"

"Yup."

He shook his head. "No way. Walking Mule, I can't do that many. I do ninety-six and I'm really tired; after nine days on I'm wiped! Who do they think I am, Superman or something? I can't do it."

Walking Mule tapped himself on the chest. "I know that.

You know that. Everybody in this here room knows that—but Director Davis can't seem to get it through his thick head that Flinging's harder work than riding fence in a blizzard. Which figures, since he ain't got even a trace of Talent."

"We're going to have to talk to him about this."

"We already have, McGill—and he says his mind's made up. This is the way the rain falls. No changes. Period."

"He's crazy."

"Yup."

A hand touched Feighan's back as a familiar voice said, "Then let's drop the bastard in the sun, hey guys?"

Walking Mule scowled at Greystein. "Don't even think that way. That's a real good way to make people think it's something we just might do."

"No sense of humor, Walking Mule. Hey, McGill, what do you think of that mirror I brought you?"

He snapped his fingers in annoyance. "I'm sorry, Greystein—I forgot all about it."

"Well, you check it out, you are going to be so pleased! Those Inta Leinans do not make bad mirrors."

Walking Mule said, "Greystein, I'd reckoned the bosses made it clear you just ain't supposed to Fling off on your own without permission."

For one moment Greystein blanched. Then his smile flashed bright as ever. "What they don't know won't hurt them."

"And what happens when they hear about it?"

Greystein's dark eyes narrowed. "Now how would they happen to hear about it, Walking Mule?"

The older man shrugged. "Word gets around."

Greystein caught his breath, then let it out raggedly. "I do my job and I do it awful damn well, if I do say so myself—"

Walking Mule jerked a thumb at the screen. "The numbers say different."

"Goddam the numbers! I can make any set of numbers say anything I want them to so, so I don't trust those fudged-up so-called facts of theirs. I do my job, and that's all they should be worried about."

Feighan drifted away. Depressed and grouchy, he could too easily imagine himself as overwrought as Greystein—and did not want to achieve that state. So he wandered back to his Room and opened the package. The paper fell away from a double-sided mirror mounted in such a frame as to enable the user to spin it around. He did. It displayed the back of his head. "That's perfect!" With a laugh, he straightened the cowlick at the rear of his skull. "Trust Greystein to find something like this . . ."

He napped through the rest of his break, awoke to the computer's beep, and Flung forty-eight more loads in the next four hours. At 10 p.m. he was done. He tucked the mirror under his arm, and Flung himself home. Greystein was already there, stretched out on the couch with a beer mug in his hand. "Gina, Sam, and the plant are out on the terrace."

"Are you okay?"

Greystein scowled. "I have a headache, a bad one." He hoisted the mug. "Maybe this'll help."

"Until you wake up in the morning." He crossed the room and pushed the gliding door back on its rollers. Manhattan shone like a tiara. The night breeze ruffled his hair. "Hi, everybody."

Maccari hugged him hard, lingering on the release. "I'm sorry, really—I have to go. But I programmed Oscar for dinner. Teriyaki is all right, isn't it?"

"Just fine," he said, bewildered. "But—"

"Honest, I'm sorry, but I'm standby Minder tonight, and they just called me. Please?"

He made a face, a histrionic pout, to mock that which he actually felt.

"Please?"

"Okay." He closed his eyes, concentrated— *PING*— then, suddenly weary, turned to the other two. "How's it going, Sam?"

"Neat, McGill! H'nik's five hundred years old, did you know that? And this is the thirty-ninth planet it's been to, and it met my mother! And she wants us to visit her."

"Really?" It was an effort to be polite. "When did you meet Sahaang?"

The alien's speaking-spines rustled together. "When we first met she barely cast a shadow at all, but fascinated me even then; I returned to visit her recently, and she directed me to you."

"Oh?" Leaning back till the stucco wall bit into his shoulders, he wondered how to deal tactfully with what had to be coming. "What, ah—?"

"I will come directly to the point, McGill Feighan. I am researching the Far Being Retzglaran—"

"Somehow, I knew you'd say that."

"I have been told that shortly after you broke into the world, you had a most curious encounter with an agent of the Far Being, and that that encounter has altered the entire course of your life."

He nodded. "H'nik, if you're researching the Far Being, maybe you can tell me: What *is* the Far Being? What species, what—"

"My studies, even after all these centuries, have barely begun to penetrate the mystery that is Retzglaran; one web of evidence, however, suggests that it is the last scion of an ancient stock of space-farers."

Feighan frowned. It did not jibe with what he had learned on his own. "But I thought—"

"That is one web of evidence, McGill Feighan, or perhaps only a portion of one web. Yet there are many, many others; I would seek your help in determining on which prowls the true Spinner."

He shrugged. "If I can—ask away."

H'nik's spines scraped in apparent agitation. "No, no. I would question you longer."

"Well, you can stay a day or two if you like. I—"

"No, no. I would question you longer."

He sighed. "How much longer?"

"Eight hours a day for perhaps a year."

Feighan blinked, and forced a chuckle. "No, I'm sorry, that's impossible."

Before H'nik could reply, Greystein shouted in the living room. "No fucking way!"

Feighan turned. "What's the matter?"

Greystein joined them on the terrace, a printout in his hand. His cheeks were pale; spilled beer stained his pants. He thrust the sheet of paper at Feighan. "Read it yourself."

He did. It said: "Report to Behavior Modification Center immediately."

▪ Chapter III ▪

"Don't you understand? I don't care!" He slammed the phone down. Psychiatrists! The nerve, criticizing his order to Greystein as "counter-productive: it might trigger an undesirable response."

"Undesirable response." Phaugh! What could be less desirable than drunken lechery? The idiot psychiatrists just did not understand. His half-psychotic employees had to maintain Earth's links in an interstellar transportation web. The only way to keep them working was to crucify anyone who stepped out of line.

He picked up the holocube and stroked it with a fingertip. Thank God *somebody* had his head on straight, and would help him bring those spoiled brats to heel. This clear plastic box, fifteen centimeters on a side, offered enough evidence to justify scouring Greystein's skull twice over.

"Undesirable response." Like what—mutiny? He almost hoped it came to that. The more insubordinate Greystein became, the more severe an indoctrination his behavior would warrant. Even PsychSection would agree to that. So let Greystein flout him. Just let him.

The system had rules so it would run smoothly and efficiently. When people started breaking the rules, they threatened its survival. But the Network was bigger than people, and star travel more important. It *had* to survive. Even if some of them did not.

The obedient ones, like Harry Lipsiento, would do very well.

And the Greysteins would make very nice examples.

• Chapter IV •

Feighan settled gingerly onto the terrace railing. The night wind moaned in his ears; all around gleamed the light jewels of Manhattan. Shock waved tremors through his voice: "Why do they want you?" He gripped the cool wrought iron for support.

Greystein rattled another sheet of paper. "Because of this."

"What?"

"Do you know they put a detective on me?"

"What?"

"That bastard Davis hired a detective to investigate me, and this is what she came up with." It crackled when he passed it over. "She listed all my alleged violations of the FNC Code. You ever seen such crap?"

"Can I see?" asked Sam.

"No," said Feighan instinctively. "This is, ah, this is grown-up stuff here."

"Aw, come on, he's my roommate, too."

"Sam," said Feighan in a warning tone.

Greystein bounced impatiently on the balls of his feet. "Just look at that, can you believe it? The NAC spent good money on a detective just to smear me!"

"Listen, ah—" He glanced from Sam to H'nik. The Actuni's eyespines pointed right at him; Sam had cocked his head attentively. "Let's talk about this inside, okay? H'nik, please excuse us."

"Of course. Sam, perhaps you can point out to me some of the city's major landmarks?"

"Sure, H'nik." He flicked his tongue at Feighan, then turned his back on the two. "Over there is—"

Feighan led Greystein by the arm. "Now what is this?" he said, when they had closed the living room door behind them.

"I need a drink, you want one?"

"No, and—"

"Order, Oscar: Pour one beer; do it now." He stalked across the room to the bar, and tapped its wood-grain panel. "C'mon!" But he had to wait. He rested his elbows on the countertop and lowered his face into his hands. "I don't believe that bastard Davis hired a detective . . ."

Feighan skimmed the legal-sized sheet of paper in his hand. Headed "Surveillance Report: Marion Jefferson Greystein," it was subtitled, "Summary of Violations."

The compiler, one Avis Louder, had numbered the offenses in chronological order. Feighan skipped down the list. "Flinging for Personal Gain" cropped up more often than any other. The last entry, #67, was dated 3 June 2105; it accused Greystein of rape on the planet Canopus XVIII. He shook his head. "Are these true?"

Greystein looked up just as the bar delivered his beer. He downed half the stein before wiping the foam off his lips with the back of his hand. "What do you mean, true?"

"Did you do all these?" He checked the printout. "On May 10, did you charge William N'komo five thousand dollars for passage to Delurc?"

"No, dammit!" He slammed the empty mug on the counter. "Look, McGill, Bill's a good buddy. He came to me, he said his father's on Delurc and they just got a message that the old chief's really sick, and could I Fling him there 'cause the waiting list is four months long. What the fuck was I supposed to say, 'Gee golly whillikers, Bill, I wish I could, but the rules say I can't'? Huh?"

"Did you charge him five kay for it?"

"Christ, no! What do I need money for? Transportation?" He told Oscar to give him another beer, and twirled an ashtray on the counter while he waited.

Feighan consulted the list again. "I know you made all these trips to Hideaway—"

"Yeah, I did." His tone was belligerent. "You wanna make a big deal about it, too? I'm a Flinger, dammit, and if I want to go to Hideaway or Rehma or wherever, I'm going."

"But the rules—"

"Would you get it through your head that I don't give a shit what the rules say?"

Feighan threw down the printout. "You idiot! The only reason we never got called in for behavior modification before was because we pretended we'd already been brainwashed. We followed the rules in public; we made sure nobody noticed the b-mod hadn't taken—and now you go, and you blow the whole thing, and you have the audacity to complain that you got caught? Jesus Christ, all you needed was a little discretion."

Greystein leaned against the counter, a sour smile on his face. "You know, I sort of thought you'd worry more about yourself than me."

"What's that supposed to mean?"

"I'm in a bind and you're worried that maybe they'll notice you."

"Well, what do you think I am, a saint? My head's at stake here, too. For Christ's sakes, Greystein, I never asked you *not* to visit Hideaway, or Fling your friends around, or—or—" He kicked the list of accusations. "Or any of that! All I asked was that you not be so blatant about the fact that you jammed the b-mod program when we were rooming at the Academy. And what do you do? You—"

"No." His hand slashed the air diagonally. "I did not flaunt it. You and Sam and Oscar are the only people with any connections to the NAC who know what I've been doing."

"And Walking Mule and whoever else was listening when you were talking about that mirror."

"But that was the first time, and that was this afternoon!" He raised his hands above his head, imploring the heavens to grant Feighan understanding. "Oh, McGill, McGill, don't you see? I *was* discreet. I *did* behave—in public, at least. And they got me anyway. And I don't have the faintest . . . I mean, look at that. Go on, look at it."

Feighan bent over to pick it up. "Yeah? What am I supposed to see?"

"Let's start with the fact that the detective listed my destinations."

"Uh-huh. So? It's the destinations that make the violations."

"Feighan, I didn't take any detective *with* me. I mean, granted, somebody's watching me, *she* can see when I ping out—but how the *hell* does she know where I'm going? Can you tell me that?"

"Ah..." He frowned. The crisp typescript had suddenly lost much of its authority. "Did she get it right, though? Did you really go to these places?"

"Yes! But how the hell did *she* know?"

"Maybe you bragged about it in a bar?"

"God save me from fools! How many years have you known me? Have you ever heard me brag about that kind of thing in a bar—or anywhere else, for that matter?"

He thought about it. It made no sense. "How—wait a minute. I know how she did it." Then he scowled. "No, that's crazy, too."

"What?"

"Well... one Flinger can follow another Flinger—"

"What?"

"Ah, come one, Greystein, you've felt the pull when I've Flung out—didn't you know you could let it take you along?"

He waved a hand. "Now I know what you mean, yeah. But you're saying the detective is a Flinger, then."

"She's got to be!"

"You mean one of our own spied on me? I can't believe that..." But from his expression as he ordered another beer, it was clear that he could believe it—and maybe did. When the beer came, he chugged it down. "Oscar, order: pour one beer; do it now." He belched. "Jesus, a spy in our midst."

"And she's got you cold."

"Yeah."

"What are you going to do?"

"What do you mean?"

"Are you going to turn yourself in?"

Greystein narrowed his eyes. "You know me better than that, McGill—or at least I thought you did. Do you really think I'd let them brainwash me?"

He laughed with both affection and sadness. "Since you wouldn't even let them do it to you in the Academy, no... although I think, now that things have gotten to this stage, maybe you ought to give the idea some consideration."

"*I* think *you're* crazy!"

Before Feighan could reply, the gliding glass door opened; Sam and H'nik came in from the terrace. Wind swirled through the living room. Feighan winced: he had promised Sam help with the coloring book, and H'nik help in its researches, but he was devoting all his time to Greystein. And yet Greystein was closer to him than any man alive; he could not just say, hey, you worry about your problems, I'll worry about mine. Briefly, Feighan wished that others could manage to need him one at a time—and only about half the time, at that. Then he sighed. *That* would never happen.

"Hey, McGill," said Sam. "H'nik's hungry, and—"

"I am very sorry, H'nik," said Feighan. "I have been a thoughtless host. What may I get you?"

Sam slapped his tail on the Chinese rug to draw his guardian's attention. "It can't eat our food, McGill. Well, it can, but it's not good enough for it."

He opened his mouth and shut it again. He did not know what he could or should say except, after a moment's thought, "May I get you some water, or—"

Again it was Sam who lacked the patience to wait for the alien to scrape out a reply. "It's the fruit thing on its, um-um, head there—*that's* what it can eat, and it's what it wants to eat, and it asked me to get it but even when I jumped I couldn't reach that high, so—" He pointed to the purplish gourd jutting out of its upper body. It had grown to cantaloupe size in the course of the afternoon. "So why don't you pick it for us?"

"Oh, okay. Sure." He reached for it—

H'nik jumped back.

"Ah . . ." Baffled, he spread his hands wide and looked from Sam to Greystein and back to H'nik.

The Actuni said, "Forgive me if my action seemed rude, for it was not so intended. The—" It rasped out one syllable so alien Feighan could not remember it, much less pronounce it. "—is coated with many millions of tiny glochids—barbed hairs—that would penetrate your skin and initiate an allergic reaction; the itching is said to be maddening."

Sam's tongue flickered. "How come you didn't tell me that?"

"Because your physiology, my bud, is different, and your skin is thicker; the glochids would not penetrate your epidermis."

"What's a epiwhatchamacallit?"

Greystein answered that one. "It's the outer layer of your skin, Sam." He finished another beer and shoved the stein back in for a refill.

In the meantime, Feighan had crossed to the bar, where he rummaged around for the ice tongs. They were behind a row of dusty shot glasses. Holding them up to the light, he approached H'nik. "Would it cause you pain if I were to use these to remove the, ah, the—"

"The—" It made that sound again. "No, not in the least."

He closed the jaws of the tongs on the fruit. "Should I pull, twist, or—"

"Twist first, then pull."

Taking a deep breath, he tried it. The fruit popped off easily, but slipped out of the tongs and fell, bouncing once on the thick rug, flustering Feighan immensely. "I'm sorry, I—"

But H'nik scuttled forward until its spread roots straddled the fruit. Lowering its body a few centimeters, it sat on it like a bird on her egg. Its lower body *slurp*ed. The fruit disappeared. *Squish* it went, and *crunch*. Then silence.

In the interim, Greystein had had his mug filled. "That is the goddamnedest thing I have ever seen." Elbow on the bar, he tilted back his head and poured the beer down his throat. His Adam's apple rose and fell again and again.

Feighan wanted to speak to H'nik, but did not know if Actuni conversed during meals. He did know that they hated to be kept waiting, so it impressed him that H'nik had displayed any patience at all, much less calmness. Even a Terran would have been insulted by a fourteen-hour wait.

H'nik's lower body . . . belched. "Thank you. My inner half had grown restless."

"Inner half?" said Sam.

"We are symbiotes, Sam—that is, two life forms who need each other so much that each would die without the other."

"Like me and McGill, huh?"

Feighan's face flamed.

H'nik spared him the embarrassment of having to comment. "Your symbiosis—your mutual interdependence—is of an emotional nature. Mine is physical. I—"

Greystein interrupted. "You're a monk, aren't you?"

H'nik shuffled about to face him. "That is, perhaps, your language's best approximation of my actual vocation. Not accurate, you must understand, but it is approximate."

"Well I got a question for you." He burped; a silly smile spread across his face.

"Then by all means ask it, Marion Jefferson Greystein."

No, don't, thought Feighan. *You're drunk, it's going to be a stupid question.*

Swaying back and forth, Greystein raised a finger to strike a forensic pose. "Do you believe, most reverend vege-table—"

"Greystein!" hissed Feighan.

He blinked owlishly at his roommate. "Whatsh the matter?"

"You're drunk, that's what's the matter."

"In vino veritas, old boy, which is to say that if I weren't a little on the inebriated side I probably wouldn't have thought to ask this question, which is, when you come right down to it, a very serious kind of question indeed, and desh—deserving of the most serious form of reply. Do you, kind sir and honored visitor, believe that intelligent beings should be required to submit their innermost selves—verily, their souls!—to the tampering of temporal authorities?"

"As Actu boasts a theocracy," said H'nik dryly, "that ques-tion is one to which we have devoted little debate."

Sam pulled on Feighan's pants leg. "What's a theocracy?"

"Ah . . . where the church is the government."

"Oh." He made a face. "Can I watch the holo?"

"If you keep it soft."

"Thanks." He waddled over to the set and turned it on. In the background, Greystein looked nonplused. H'nik stood qui-etly, asking nothing, apparently ready to answer anything. The holovision came alive: the cube swirled with light that coalesced into three-dimensional shapes that sharpened into a line of medics kneeling over the victims of a hotel fire. A woman in her thirties with red eyes and a soot mark on her forehead walked straight toward the camera, hands outstretched, crying, "Jim! Jim oh god where are you, Jim?" Her voice rose as she swelled in the cube and filled it and blurred away when she passed through the focal range. The voice-over said, "Mrs.

James Winsocki of Philadelphia outside the Seven-Come-Eleven Hotel in Las Vegas, just minutes after the century's worst fire claimed four hundred and seventy-six fatalities."

In the silence imposed by the camera's slow pan of the bodies in their tagged green bags, H'nik asked, "Have you come yet to a decision, Marion Jefferson Greystein?"

"About what?"

"In connection with your consortium's directive."

"Huh!"

Feighan said, "Maybe you ought to go in."

"What, worried about yourself again?"

His cheeks warmed. "Cheap shot, Greystein."

"So what are you worried about?"

"You, dammit! You're my best friend—"

"I thought I was," said Sam from the floor before the cube. Puzzlement—hurt—pinched his ward's face. "You are, Sam—Greystein's my other best friend."

"Oh." He nodded, wrinkled his scaled forehead, and swung his attention back to the holo, now aglow with the low-slung sleekness of a Kwama sports'hove.

Feighan turned to Greystein. "I don't want you to get hurt."

"Come on, McGill—they can't hurt me! Hell, The Organization's been trying to get you for years, and they've never succeeded for the same reason that the NAC will never be able to hurt me—we're Flingers. We can vanish anytime anybody attacks us—no matter who it is."

Feighan dropped into a black forcechair. What he heard disturbed him; it took him a while to organize a logical rebuttal. "Greystein, The Organization has never tried to *hurt* me—it's been trying to *capture* me, alive and well, so it could use me. There's a world of difference between that and what the NAC will do if you don't submit. They'll Rogue you!"

Greystein burped, covered his mouth a second late, and shrugged. "So?"

"Are you dense or are you just drunk? If they do that, if they Rogue you, anybody, anywhere in the universe except in the psychiatric care section of a Flinger Building, can kill you—and get paid for it!"

"What?" At last Greystein looked shaken.

"That's right. A reward, a bounty. One million dollars, payable in any currency of the Network including fancies."

He raised his eyebrows. "They think I'm worth a million, huh?"

"For God's sakes, man, this isn't a joke! With that kind of price on your head, somebody, somewhere, is going to shoot you just to claim it. Please! Don't let things get that far."

"They won't."

"Not if you report—"

Greystein's eyes cleared, and blazed. "No! I will not be brainwashed. Order, Oscar: pour one—"

"Oh, Jesus Christ, I don't believe you . . ." He looked around the room for support, but H'nik seemed content to observe in silence, and Sam lay rapt before the holo, where a man-sized purple bird, briefcase tucked under one wing, was emerging from the Embassy of Rehma to say, "We have no comment on reports that our government has fallen, and we will have no comments until such time as we are able to contact our capital city."

While Greystein wobbled to the bar, Feighan picked up the phone. Punching the number, his finger shook.

"Yo."

"Walking Mule? Hi, it's McGill. Listen, we've got a major problem here—Greystein's just been ordered to report to the b-mod center, and—"

"Yeah, I heard about that," said the Senior Flinger. "You go on and offer him my sympathies, will you?"

"Doesn't he get a hearing—any kind of chance to defend himself?"

"Nope. He waived that right when he signed his last contract—hell, McGill, the two of you should know that, shouldn't have to ask me about it. First thing Running Bear taught me was to read what I signed."

"Sixty-two pages of fine print? Give me a break, Walking Mule . . . but isn't there something you could do, a string you could pull or—"

"Nope."

"But—"

"I'm sorry as all hell, McGill. It's a damn shame, I agree, but there's nothing I can do to help the boy. This comes straight from Director Davis himself."

"But why is he doing it? I mean, it's not like the charges against Greystein are thoroughly substantiated or anything—

Walking Mule, they're all anonymous accusations. That's unconstitutional."

"Now, I wouldn't talk too fast if I were you," said the older man. "Truth to tell, there was a test case on this twenty, thirty years back—and the Supreme Court held that, given the circumstances, the NAC had the right to impose whatever sort of discipline it felt necessary."

"But—"

"McGill, you're old enough to know that the only reason we Flingers are tolerated is because we're disciplined." Impatience sharpened his voice. "You get somebody like Greystein kicking up his heels, you got bad press—that means a queasy government—that means feuding with the FNC—and the next thing you know, Flingers all across the galaxy are in one heap of trouble."

Feighan winced. "Yeah, but—"

"Look. You tell Greystein to get his butt into the Psych-Section. He'll be out in a week or two. And McGill, I swear this on my ancestors' burial grounds, he ain't going to be able to tell the difference, and neither will you. He just won't be as stupid as he is now, that's all."

"I'll tell him, but I don't think—"

"You just remind him that it's his ass, McGill. Talk to you later."

"Yeah." Feighan hung up. He liked the situation not at all.

He liked it even less when he raised his gaze to the holocube: an oldstyle marketplace with thousands of stalls. Vaguely humanoid figures in masks and breathing tanks moved past racks of glassware and stacks of produce. They paused only to lift another body onto another litter. The voice-over said, "This was the scene this afternoon in Hotu Botai, a provincial capital on Inta Leina. The plague struck with deadly swiftness; authorities—"

From across the room, Greystein called, "Hey! That's where I got you your mirror. What happened?"

"Plague." He leaned forward to hear the announcer.

Greystein tottered over to plop into the other forcechair. "Plague?"

The 'caster said, "It is suspected that the plague was released on the planet by a Terran Flinger who was seen wandering through the marketplace yesterday, our time."

Feighan's eyes widened. "My God! They're blaming you."

"McGill, I—" All color had drained from his cheeks. His voice shook, but it no longer slurred. "I've been there lots of times. The books say—hell, they prove!—that Inta Leinans and Terrans are mutually imcom—communicable. I couldn't have—"

Feighan shushed him with a wave of his hand.

From the speakers came, "—not of Terran derivation, but of Rehmal origin. It is suspected that the Flinger—"

"Oh, sweet Jesus, shut it off!" Hand to stomach, Greystein looked as though he might vomit.

"You took a Rehmal to Inta Leina?" said Feighan in disbelief.

"She—"

"You did?"

"Yeah, but—"

"Jesus Christ, Greystein!" He threw his head back and his arms up. "You stupid ass! You Flung someone to another planet without going through Immigration? Bad enough doing interstellar Flings on your own time, but—but—" He pointed to the cube. "I don't believe you did that!"

Greystein slumped deeper in his chair. "I didn't know," he said softly. "If I had, I never would have—but I didn't. She didn't tell me she was sick. I didn't know . . ."

In a tone equally, incongruously soft, H'nik said, "Your burden is heavy. You should seek to lighten it."

"How?" snapped Greystein.

"I am unfamiliar with your culture's means of expiating guilt, but surely you are not."

"I don't believe in religion."

"It requires not faith but sorrow, shame—do you believe in them? Or do you believe that you have done no wrong?"

"Of *course* I've done wrong!" He made a fist and pounded it against his knee. "But the answer isn't going to the PsychSection and getting my head scrubbed. I know that isn't the answer."

"Then—"

The doorbell rang.

Feighan said, "Oscar, query: who is at the door; answer it now."

As Oscar hummed preparatory to replying, Sam picked himself off the floor and raced for the vestibule. His spine fins had stiffened.

The computer said, "Three Terrans; unfamiliar; NAC uniforms."

"Something's wrong, McGill," called Sam.

"What?"

"They're not nice; they want to—to hurt. But not you or me. It's—" He touched the door and squeezed his eyelids shut. "It's Greystein I think."

"Oscar, order: run ID check; do it now."

Tension mounted in the few brief seconds before the computer came back on-line: "The visitors are Jayeff Washington, P. Thomas Schintrino, and Kay Bechett; NAC Central Computing vouches for them; they are attached to Internal Security. They have been issued an NAC warrant for—"

"Oh, shit," said Greystein. He levered himself to his feet. For a moment, he stood unsteadily, looking from Feighan to Sam to H'nik to the great glass doors opening onto the terrace. He took a step toward the doors.

Feighan said, "Greystein, please: go with them. Walking Mule says—"

"No." He stumbled away. "It's my head, it's my brain, I won't let anybody fuck with it, anybody."

"But who will forgive you?" said H'nik.

"What?"

"To accede—to submit—"

The doorbell rang again, longer, more harshly.

"—is to initiate the rites of expiation."

"I don't need them!"

"But you do. Without them you will never forget those alleyways, those bodies, that guilt. Without expiation your every sleep will raise monsters against you. Every sapient everywhere will hunt you. Go with them, Marion Jefferson Greystein. Only they can bring you peace."

"No, dammit, no!" He took another step, and—

Feighan felt the other Flinger's Talent tug his own as Greystein teleported away. He shook his head. "Thank you for trying, H'nik."

The doorbell rang four times, short and sharp.

The Actuni said, "I only wish I had succeeded."

Sadly, Feighan crossed the room. Sam stood with his tail

cocked and fists raised. "Don't let 'em in, McGill. They're—they're *nasty!*"

"I have to, Sam." He turned the knob.

A shoulder caught him in the chest and bowled him over. A deep voice said, "Shit, I'm sor—" then cracked, and yelped.

Flat on his back, Feighan lifted himself on his elbows. The InSec who had knocked him down was trying to shake Sam loose from his calf, but Rhanghan jaws are strong. The female in the trio was drawing her weapon. The third cop was grabbing at Sam's thrashing tail. "Sam!"

The Rhanghan dropped off and backed away, tail high, tongue waving. He hissed and spat. "He hit you!"

"It was an accident, Sam."

"Little bastard," said the woman. Automatic out, now, she was drawing a bead on Sam's head.

Before Feighan could react, the third guard grabbed Bechett's wrist and yanked it behind her back. "Uh-uh, Kay. Drop it."

The gun thudded onto the floor.

The first guard, the one with J. Washington embroidered above the pocket of his steel-blue tunic, was twisting his right leg into an awkward angle to inspect it. "Shit, I'm bleeding!"

Feighan got to his feet—slowly, cautiously, a little fearfully. InSecs had reflexes, not brains. "Ah—if you'd like, I could Fling you to the Infirmary."

"Shit, yes," said Washington, straightening. Crimson stained both his fingers and his pants leg. "He got poison in his fangs?"

"No." He bit down on a smile. *Trust an InSec to ask a question like that!* "And he's in perfect health, too. If you had to get bitten here, he's the one to get bitten by."

Bechett was muttering to Schintrino. Her narrow face was flushed; her eyes, slitted. "Gimme my gun back."

Feighan strolled over to her. "Listen, lady: that's my ward. His name is Sam. You touch one scale on his hide, and you know what I'll do to you? I'll set you down halfway across the galaxy, on the reef where the baby Delu grow up. They're little things—barely half Sam's size—so when they go to eat you, they'll only take little bites. I don't know how many rounds you've got in that gun of yours, but the reef'll have thousands of baby Delu. Hungry baby Delu. You'll live for ten or twenty minutes—until one of them chews through your eye into your brain. Now. You gonna keep your mouth shut? Or are you going to keep on making me mad?"

She paled. She did not meet his eye. "You wouldn't dare."

"Try me."

With a hand in the small of her back, Schintrino pushed her into the hallway. "Wait there." He closed the door, then turned around. "All right. You know why we're here. Has he Flung out?"

"Yeah."

"Okay—why don't you pop Jayeff over to the Building, then let me take a look around—for the report, you know? We'll lose our jobs if we don't eyeball the place."

"Sure."

"Hey!" said Washington. "Is this gonna hurt?"

"Not really—but don't worry, I do this for a living."

Washington bit his lip.

Feighan closed his eyes—concentrated on the other's tall gauntness—visualized the admissions desk in the emergency room of the Flinger Building Infirmary—felt how to place the first before the second—and—

Washington was gone.

"Thanks," said Schintrino. "Now, if you don't mind—?"

"Help yourself." Stepping back, he made a mock-bow and waved Schintrino into the living room.

The Internal Security agent gasped at the sight of H'nik, but quickly regained his composure. "Got enough aliens around here?" he said in a low voice.

"Sam's my ward; H'nik's visiting."

"You Flingers . . ." He opened the cupboard doors, walked through the kitchen and the bedrooms—though he disdained to look under the beds—pulled aside the sliding glass door of the shower so he could glance inside, and then said, "Okay. He's not here. Not that I expected him to be, but—" He shrugged. "Bureaucracy, you know?"

"I know."

"If he comes back, you will, of course, call us immediately."

"Of course."

"Of course. Let me find Officer Bechett and we'll get out of your hair." At the door, he dropped to his haunches and said to Sam, "Hey, you."

"What?" said Sam with a snarl.

"What you did—biting Washington's leg 'cause he knocked your boss on his can—it was dumb. I was a little slower, you'd be dead now, and you wouldn't have helped Feighan at all. But your heart's in the right place, and that's good. Next time: wait to see if the guy's really going to hurt Feighan—and if he is, tear out his throat. Got that?"

"Yeah. Why are you telling me this?"

Schintrino extended a hand—carefully—to rub Sam on the head. "Because my job is to protect Flingers, too—and if you're going to be doing the same thing, you at least ought to know how to do it right. Okay?"

"Okay." Sam twisted his neck so Schintrino's fingers could scratch to better effect. "I'll remember that."

"You do that." He rose.

Feighan said, "You'll never catch him."

"You don't need to tell me that. But . . ." He shrugged, and started to turn.

Feighan grabbed his arm. "But what?"

"You're his friend; I hate to say this; but . . . but about five minutes after we report to Director Davis, we'll be ordered not even to try to catch Mr. Greystein. He goes Rogue, we don't have to. All we have to do is shoot straight."

Wincing, Feighan released him. "Yeah," he said. "Yeah."

Schintrino left.

Half an hour later, the phone rang. It was Walking Mule; he sounded tired and dispirited. Without preamble, he said, "The Hunt's on."

"Rogue Hunt?" The words clogged his throat.

"Yup. It's official. Davis just held a press conference. Shoot on sight. One million dollars cash, no questions asked, to whoever brings in the body. And—" He stopped.

"What?"

"The detective—"

"Who is this Avis Louder, anyway?"

"I don't know. Honest. I don't. Davis is handling all that on a confidential basis. But she forwarded a holo; took it with a tele-setup, she said. It showed Greystein eating lunch on Rehma with a man named Milford Hommroummy. Ring a bell?"

"I don't believe it," he said. "No. Not—not Greystein. He—he—"

"The computers have the ID cold, McGill. There is no chance whatsoever of any kind of mistaken identity. It's Milford Hommroummy. The man The Organization assigned to get you."

· Chapter V ·

"Well, thank you." He settled back in his swivel chair. "Considering that my own people have done nothing but object, it's most kind of you to support my decision. Did you catch my press conference?"

"Yes," said the voice on the phone. "You were marvelous."

"'One bad apple...'" He shook his head mournfully. "I had to do it; I really did, even if it does impact our productivity negatively. Really, the unchecked influence of someone like Greystein can be devastating."

"I respect your ability to make the hard decisions," said the anonymous caller. "In this day and age, you are all too rare."

"Well..." He knew it was flattery, but relished it nonetheless. "It is my job, to keep Earth linked to the interstellar community."

"And a fine job you do. Especially considering your comparatively low remuneration—your salary *is* less than half of McGill Feighan's, is it not?"

Touched on a sore point, he mumbled an affirmative.

"Public sector officials as competent as yourself should be compensated appropriately. When you return home, do lift the paté tin in your refrigerator. We left a little something for you. A token of our appreciation, as it were."

"Well, thank you." Perhaps he could visit that restaurant, after all.

"You're quite welcome. Oh, and by the way—do investigate Feighan. Carefully."

· Chapter VI ·

"It's a lie!" He squeezed the telephone receiver. A tendon in his wrist went *pop*, then cramped. Groping behind himself for the forcechair, he lowered himself into its soft resilience. On the other side of the room, Sam broke off his conversation with H'nik and turned to stare. "Walking Mule, Greystein would never—"

"The holo says different, McGill."

"Then the holo says wrong. I know him. He's my friend."

Silence ensued, broken only by the clicks and crackles of a patient line. Then Walking Mule sighed. "Decide for yourself."

A hologram appeared on the Flop Table in the corner. "Wait a minute." He went over and picked it up.

Fifteen centimeters on a side, in full color with good detail, it held two miniature Terrans who sat at a wicker table in a treetop restaurant. One was Greystein. The other, with the tonsure of dark hair and caterpillar eyebrows and machine-smooth planes of his cheeks, was Milford Hommroummy.

Feighan scowled at the two, who smiled at each other. Hommroummy was handing Greystein something small and green; it sparkled where light hit its facets full on: an emerald. "Walking Mule, this doesn't mean a thing."

"One of the top men in The Organization is paying off your roommate and it doesn't mean anything?"

Extending the receiver to arm's length, he gave it a glare

that should have melted its plastic, then returned it to his ear.
"No."

Sam waddled over. "What's wrong?"

"Later," said Feighan abruptly.

"What?" said Walking Mule.

"Not you, I was talking to Sam."

"So answer my question."

"What—about the meaning of this—this frame?" He eased
himself into the chair again, settling a centimeter as its contours
adjusted to his.

"Come on, McGill."

"No, you come on! Let's put you in the scenario. You're
sight-seeing on Rehma. You can afford a posh restaurant so
you go to one. It's crowded. Somebody says, 'Are you alone?'
and you say, 'Yes.' He says, 'Mind if I share your table?' and
you say, 'No.' Over dinner you talk. He says he's a jewelry
salesrep. He digs into his valise and says, 'Here, this is what
I peddle,' and you say, 'Migod, is it real?' and he laughs. A
real, deep, straight-from-the-belly laugh. And he says, 'Hell,
no! We grow them in a lab at L-5.' You go 'Whew!' and wipe
the sweat off your forehead. And you don't know—you don't
ever know—that somebody's in the next tree taking your holo
with a tele-setup. And even if you did know, you wouldn't
care, because you don't know the guy across from you is the
guy who's spent twenty years trying to kidnap your best friend.
You see what I mean, Walking Mule? This picture isn't evidence or proof or anything but a hologram of one lousy
moment in time that could have been accidental or could have
been staged or could have been any goddam thing—"

"McGill," said the Senior Flinger firmly, "calm down."

"My best friend's got a million bucks on his head and you
tell me to calm down?"

Sam tugged his sleeve. "I thought I was your best friend."

He looked down into his ward's unhappiness. "You are.
Greystein's my other best friend."

Walking Mule said, "What?"

"I'm talking to Sam again."

"Oh . . . look, McGill, it could be your scenario's the
truth—it strikes me as one hell of a lot more likely than Davis'
theory that Greystein's done himself a dirty deal—but there
is no way anybody in NAC-HQ will believe it until Greystein
comes back and defends himself in person."

"Hah!"

"What?"

"First off, I mean just for starters, who is he going to defend himself against, huh? An anonymous accuser? A holo?"

"Well, now—"

"And second, just how much defending could he do with scrambled eggs for brains?"

"It ain't that bad!"

"Yeah? Somebody's gone to a lot of trouble to smear him. If you think about it, you'll realize somebody hired a Flinger to shadow him. So you tell me this: what guarantee is there that the 'behavior modification' *isn't* going to turn him into a carrot, accidentally on purpose, if you know what I mean?"

"Hold your horses, son—are you saying somebody *here* is out to get him?"

"It sure looks that way, doesn't it?"

"McGill..." Walking Mule sounded old and frail; it was clear the strain was telling on him. "I see what you're saying, but there is only one way for that boy to clear his name. This is his only chance."

"Ah, Jesus Christ!"

"If he turns up, talk him into it, will you? You got my word on this, McGill: if he turns himself in to the PsychSection, nobody—but nobody—is going to hurt him. I will watch them all like a hawk."

"Yeah, I...if he turns up." Sickness rose in the pit of his stomach. Even a moment's more debate with the old Indian would bring on despair. "I'll talk to you later." He hung up.

H'nik still stood—squatted? sat?—in the shadows of the far corner; motionless, it could have been dormant or eavesdropping. Sam lay sprawled beside Feighan's forcechair; his tail thumped a melancholy beat. His snout rubbed circles on the carpet. A half-full stein was going flat on the bar. And Greystein's bedroom was empty.

"Dammit!"

H'nik rippled its spines; Sam sat up with a jerk.

"I'm sorry," said Feighan. "I didn't mean to disturb you two."

"It is no disturbance," said H'nik. "I understand the agony of soul which you are experiencing. Two centuries ago my favorite teacher stood accused of civic disobedience and would not reform; we its pupils were forced to assist in the ceremonial root-and spine-stripping. It lived less than a month before it was forced to tap down—now its bud is my pupil. It is genetically identical to its forebear, yet it is not the same. I miss my teacher greatly."

"Ah . . ." His thoughts spun in spirals then flew off on tangents. He appreciated the Actuni's attempts to soothe him, but not its timing. The world had turned topsy-turvy: his closest friend, his roommate for over eight years, an Organization pawn? True or false, it needed to age, to soften with time, before its edge dulled.

If only everyone else did not believe it to be true!

Wait. "Sam."

The Rhanghan lifted his head. "What?"

"You've spent a lot of time around Greystein—did you ever notice, did you ever feel, any, ah, malice on his part toward me?"

"What's malice?"

"Did you ever feel him wanting to hurt me?"

Sam crinkled his forehead. "If he'd wanted to, he would have, wouldn't he?"

"No. I mean . . . do you know what a plot is?"

"Part of a story?"

"No . . . it's a secret thing, where people get together and decide they're going to hurt somebody else at some time in the future, but until that time they pretend they like the person and—"

"Oh, yeah, I know what you mean, McGill. No. Greystein never felt that way about you."

"Dammit!"

H'nik rubbed the spines below its left "eye." "Should that not please you?"

"Well, yes, but . . . I mean . . . it's good to hear that Greystein wasn't plotting against me—not that I thought he was— but I said dammit because what Sam says is proof that he wasn't working for The Organization. If he wasn't, he was being framed. And . . ."

"And he is in mortal danger, yes?"

"Yeah, he is." The chair helped him up. He began to pace, then snapped his fingers angrily. There was only one thing he could do: find Greystein himself. If he could do that, he could convince him to return to New York and straighten the whole mess out. Somehow.

It was the only way.

"Sam."

"What now, McGill?"

"How about helping me look for Greystein?"

"I'm pretty sleepy. It's twelve-thirty in the morning, you know."

"You want somebody else to find him first?"

"But why? I thought he was your other best friend."

"He is!" He clenched his fists. He needed Sam's skills at their most acute, so it frustrated him when the child acted, well . . . childish. "Listen . . . anybody else will kill Greystein for the reward. If we can find him first, and talk to him, then maybe—maybe—"

"Can I have some candy?"

"If you have it quickly; then we'll take off."

"Where?"

"Canopus Eighteen—Hideaway—I have a hunch he's basking in the sun right now."

While Sam slithered into the kitchen for his bonus snack, Feighan went to his own bedroom. In the doorway he paused, and bit his lip. Then he crossed to the chest of drawers that stood against the wall. Opening the bottom drawer, pawing aside the mismatched socks and torn shirts he had never gotten around to repairing, he retrieved the bag of fifty-millimeter ball bearings.

He hefted it thoughtfully. Once upon a time, in a hotel room on the Moon, he had defended himself against Milford Hommroummy and company by using his Talent to impart high momentum to pebbles. At two kilometers per second, a pebble acts like a bullet. And the Talent permits more accurate aiming than do lands and grooves.

He wanted to put the bag back—he wanted to believe that he, of all people, would be safe with Greystein—but . . . the holo. The plague. The "rape". They scared him. Wittingly or no, Greystein had done them all—and if he could do that, he could threaten Feighan, as well. Shaking his head in true sorrow, he tucked the bag into his pocket.

Then he went to find Sam, who was slamming cupboard doors in the kitchen. "You ready?"

"Not yet." The Rhanghan chinned himself on the counter

edge, planted his front feet on its top, and, balancing on his tail, dragged the rest of his body up. He opened a cupboard. "You want some fried grasshoppers?"

"You kidding?"

"They're dipped in honey."

Feighan made a face. "They're all yours, kid."

"Gee, thanks, McGill!" Clutching the box, he swung his tail over the edge and began to clamber down.

"Save a few, huh?"

"I thought you said you didn't want any."

"I don't, but somehow I don't think it's good for you to eat a whole box of—of those things. Not all at once. Take a few, put the rest back."

"Oh, all right." He poured himself a double handful, and replaced the box. "Can I ride on your shoulder?"

"Now I know you're kidding."

"Aw, come on, McGill—I'm tired."

"You're too big."

"I don't feel big."

"That's 'cause you're more horizontal than vertical—but there is no way I'm going to lug your forty-five kilos around, kid. You've got feet. Twice as many as I do, in fact. Use 'em."

It was Sam's turn to make a face. "Okay." He dropped to the floor and pressed up against Feighan's right leg. "I'm ready."

"Let's go, then." He concentrated on the black sand beach in the quiet cove, concentrated—visualized—felt—knew—

PING

The gale pelted them with rain like ice; it sucked the breath from their lungs and bent Feighan backward with its force. Forearm over his eyes, he peered into the storm. He could see less than five meters. To his right thudded the surf, its spray salting the rain. Squinting, he tried to spot the glow of Greystein's energy tunic. All was a haze.

Sam tugged at Feighan's jacket. "He's about fifty meters away, McGill." He had to shout it. "Behind that big rock."

Leaning into the wind, they slogged through the wet sand. Sam had to lead them; Feighan could not see the boulder until they were almost upon it. He doubted he could have found it on his own.

Greystein huddled in the outcropping's lee. Though wet and bedraggled, he retained his insouciance. "Welcome to Hideaway!" He cupped his hands around his mouth to make a megaphone of them. "You come to drag me home?"

Feighan squatted and brought his face close to his roommate's. "No! I want to *talk* you home."

"What?"

He leaned closer yet. Their noses almost bumped, but the wind still whisked away one word in three. "I want to talk you home."

"No way! I'm not having my brain molded."

"Come on, Greystein, don't make it any rougher on yourself."

"I'm NOT going back." His tunic flared a reflection of his defiance.

"Jesus! You planning on spending the rest of your life on the run?"

"If I have to."

He stared into Greystein's pallor. The rain streamed down his neck; it soaked through his underwear. Every time he wiggled his toes they squished. He shivered with cold—and with fear. "Come on."

"No!"

"But they've Rogued you! Anybody can shoot you and get paid for it."

"So what?"

"For Christ's sakes, Greystein—"

"No!"

He wanted to grab his friend by the shoulders and shake him till he came to his senses. He had crossed half the galaxy to help Greystein save his own life, but Greystein seemed intent on throwing it away. It angered him. And it goaded him into saying, "What are you going to do, run to your buddy Milford Hommroummy?"

"What?"

"I said, you going to hide behind Hommroummy's skirts?"

"What the hell is that supposed to mean?" He wiped the water out of his eyebrows.

Feighan patted his pocket. *Damn, left it at home.* "Wait here with Sam."

PING

He trailed wet sand from the Flop Table to the end table by his chair, where he had left the holocube. After pressing the button to test the batteries, he—

PING

—returned to the beach. "Look at this." He pushed the cube close to Greystein's face and turned it on. "The detective brought this to Davis. The NAC is saying you work for The Organization."

Greystein's dark eyes widened. "Tha —that's Milford Hommroummy?"

"Yeah."

He took the cube from Feighan and scowled into its leafy spaciousness. "The same guy who's been trying to snatch you?"

"You recognize him, huh?"

"Holy shit." He sagged back against the boulder, apparently oblivious to the water coursing down its face. "Jesus, McGill, I didn't know."

He had defended Greystein to Walking Mule, but now he had to know the truth. "What happened? Why were you together?"

Greystein's tired head move might have been a shrug. "I went out to Rehma between shifts one day—I was supposed to meet a friend in that restaurant there—she never showed up. The guy you say is Hommroummy did; he came over with a message for her. He introduced himself as her uncle." His eyes unfocused slightly; he seemed to be watching something over Feighan's right shoulder.

It was enough to make Feighan want to look in that direction, too—but he could let Sam worry about that.

"Anyway," said Greystein, "he says his niece feels bad about standing me up, and he's supposed to buy me lunch to make up for it. Okay, fine. I never argue with people who want to buy me lunch." A flash of the old Greystein emerged with the words: "There aren't enough folks around like that; it doesn't pay to discourage them."

"So what's he doing giving you an emerald?"

"It was a bribe."

Feighan swallowed hard. "For what?"

Greystein tilted his head back and let the rain splash his eyelids. "For the obvious—a bit of unauthorized Flinging."

"Why?"

"He had two or three tonnes of artwork to go from Rehma to, uh . . . Edbarg, I think. There was a six-month waiting list at the local Flinger Building; he said he couldn't wait because he'd already paid to rent an exhibition hall on Edbarg, and if he didn't have the paintings by the time the exhibit was supposed to open, he'd be indicted for some kind of fraud or something..." Greystein leaned forward, set the cube down, and spread his hands. "I didn't know, McGill. The Network's crazy; I believed the guy. So when he offered me the emerald for an hour's work—" This time he shrugged with his shoulders.

"Let's go back, Greystein. Tell all this to—"

"No."

"Jesus, man! Would you—"

"No!" He scrambled to his feet. "I'm not going back."

Feighan stood, too. Squatting had stiffened his knees; they wobbled. "Please."

"No."

"For me and Sam."

"No."

"Listen, what have you got to lose?"

"My soul!"

He made a mistake: he reached for Greystein's arm.

Greystein backed up against the boulder. "I thought you were my friend."

Feighan opened his mind, his Talent—and grabbed Sam's hand.

Greystein vanished.

But Feighan was ready. When the other's Talent tugged at him, he unleashed his own. Promptly unmooring him from that point in space, it hooked onto Greystein's for a tow across the light years.

The darkness hurt, as always, but it frightened Feighan, too, because he no longer knew who Greystein was. A fugitive, yes, but with what destination: life, or death? If he had collapsed as completely as his behavior suggested, he could be trying to commit suicide—and would take Feighan and Sam with him.

A mechanism he could not describe sensed Greystein's change of momentum. It was like knowing without seeing whether it is light or dark. He altered his own inertia to match Greystein's.

They materialized. The room held a bed and a chest of drawers which Greystein was already jerking open. Feighan looked around, frowned, then smiled as he oriented himself: they were home.

"Thank God you changed your mind."

Greystein stiffened. He spun. "You! You—" He disappeared.

Feighan had almost but not quite relaxed his guard. He followed, hand in scaled hand with Sam.

Again the darkness and the tearing and the infinity that was no time at all. Again the shift in momentum, slighter this time, a banked curve on a high-speed track.

But now he sensed something in his way, something standing where he and Sam would materialize. For a moment he panicked. If he were to appear in a place that was already occupied, the explosion would waste a metropolis.

Then he relaxed. If Greystein fled, he wanted to live, not die. He would not risk such a blast.

A burst of light blinded him: sunlight. He drew a breath of hot, humid air. With a blink and a gasp, he recognized the harbor and the Peak on the other side of it. Hong Kong. Or that part of it called Tsimtsatsui, the most densely populated neighborhood in the world.

The crowds had already swallowed Greystein.

"Dammit."

Swarms of brightly colored sports shirts pushed past without a glance.

"That way, McGill." Sam pointed up Nathan Road. "Around the corner."

He was tired. Two Flings in less than five minutes, even with Greystein doing most of the work, had sapped his strength. But he caught his breath because he had to, and fought his way through the crowds.

Around the corner, a panting Greystein leaned against a fruit vendor's stall. His eyes were closed. The sun made his cheeks look ghostly pale.

Feighan approached him. "Greystein—"

PING

In the interstitial darkness Feighan bellowed out his anger and frustration. Flinging exhausted one when done properly; repeatedly to teleport without enough rest between each move invited collapse.

But he had to do it; and he had good reasons.

If he let Greystein escape, anybody with a gun and greed could collect one million dollars simply by pulling a trigger.

And no matter what Greystein said, he was not acting normally. He needed therapy—fast.

And sooner or later, the bureaucrats of the North American Consortium would begin to wonder about Greystein's immunity to the behavior modification fields emitted by the computer that had monitored the room he and Greystein had shared back at the Academy.

And he, McGill Feighan, feared brainwashing every bit as much as Greystein did.

So he bellowed, and adjusted his angular momentum as soon as his roommate did, and materialized simultaneously with him on the shoulder of a road.

The forest beyond the gravel was yellow.

The sun in the sky was red.

The sky, at least, was blue.

Where the hell are we? he thought in desperation, afraid even to breathe lest the atmosphere be poisonous. He clamped his hand over Sam's muzzle; the Rhanghan raked him with his claws.

Greystein turned. "You bastard!" Spinning, he ran.

Feighan ached to lie down and sleep. Three Flings in six minutes. Not fair. He could not keep it up. But he forced his legs to pump, because Greystein was clearly trying to open such a distance between them that when he teleported out, Feighan would not be able to follow.

Gasping, he ran; the air burned his lungs but seemed to have no other effect on him. *Silly—he wouldn't take us someplace he* couldn't *survive.*

The pavement hurt his feet, his shins. Strange sounds chittered out of the forest. Overhead wheeled something with a wingspan much too large. He hoped it was a scavenger, rather than a carnivore.

Greystein looked over his shoulder. "Damn"—*breath*—"you"—*breath*—"Feighan."

"Come"—*breath*—"home!"

"No!" His arms churned as if they could give him extra speed. His leather soles slapped the roadbed. He kept looking back, looking to see if Feighan had fallen far enough behind.

But Feighan was in better shape. If he had not exercised during the past several years, neither had he dissipated himself. Whereas Greystein drank too much, slept too little, and partied too hard.

His breath came short and sharp, but he was gaining. A few

meters more. A flying tackle. Bring the other down and—

It was then that he realized that he would take Greystein back. No matter what.

Greystein, just out of arm's reach, glanced back, and—
PING

Feighan twisted frantically as he materialized in midair, nose to snout with a boggled Rii—edsch. He was in an elevator shaft, falling. Panic raced his heart—

Sam vomited on his pants, then said miserably, "I'm sorry, McGill. When I saw how far up we were, I just couldn't help it."

"That's okay, kid."

"Where are we?"

"The Hub." The world-city of Flinger Network Control Headquarters was New York cubed. Buildings shot three klicks up and five down; more people lived in one of them than in all of Iowa. "Where's Greystein?"

Sam pointed below their feet. "He's moving faster than we are, though."

The anti-grav gripped them so firmly that Feighan could not understand how the other could fall more rapidly—then it came to him. Greystein was giving himself little bursts of momentum—inertia that the anti-grav field quickly canceled, but which did widen the gap between himself and his pursuers.

Feighan smiled grimly. Pulling Sam closer, he unslung his Talent and had it add a few meters per second to their velocity. They jumped ahead.

Greystein, floating upside down so he could watch them, widened his eyes. He porpoised, then spurted for/downward into an unoccupied stretch of shaft.

Feighan teleported to within half a meter of him.

He promptly disappeared.

Feighan and Sam followed: to a spot a kilometer above New York Harbor, where the winds whistled crisp and the running lights of tramp schooners flickered on aluminized sails far below. Gulls scattered as the three appeared with a slight upward velocity that carried them fractionally higher, then wilted under gravity's demand. They fell. And fell. And—

Sam shrieked. Feighan hugged him. The water rushed up at them; to hit it would be like smashing into a brick wall. Two meters ahead of him, Greystein tucked in his arms and legs and sped up.

Feighan did the same. A four-meter gap, now. And the harbor's choppy waters clear and swelling in the moonlight.

He could put them into their penthouse easily, or would be able to if he were awake, but even with the updraft forcing his eyelids apart they kept sliding closed, and he yawned massively, and—

PING

The stars chilled him with their clarity, their numbers, their unblinkingness. He screamed at once because Greystein had taken them to vacuum. He squeezed Sam's ribcage so hard that bones cracked, but the kid had to scream, too, to empty his lungs so he would not explode like an overblown balloon. His eyeballs were drying. Steam rose from his skin and vanished at once. Greystein hung a meter away, watching them steadily while the small veins of his face and nose ruptured. Feighan thought, *I ought to go now but if I do—*

PING

And the rain whipped them with cold fury.

Whimpering, Sam fell to the black sand.

Feighan breathed, raised his eyes to the clouds, and thanked God.

Greystein looked a wreck, but he slogged through the clinging sand to the strip of rocks that ran from the water to the dunes behind the beach.

Feighan followed. He almost dropped from exhaustion, but he had come too far to give up the chase.

Sam cried, "McGill!"

He kept going.

The Rhanghan dragged himself after them.

Falling to his knees when he reached the rocks, Greystein scrabbled among them. He raised his head. Triumph gleamed in his eyes. "Get back!"

"What?"

The wind softened. Greystein held out his hands. They were full of pebbles. "You remember you taught me this?"

A pebble disappeared from his hand, and thudded gently against Feighan's chest. He jumped back in alarm—then understood what Greystein had done. He slipped his own hand into his pocket. "Careful."

"Go home, McGill."

"Only with you."

"I won't go." Another pebble winked out of existence on his palm, and reappeared a centimeter in front of Feighan. This had more momentum. It jabbed at his flesh, almost breaking the skin.

"Hey!"

"Go home."

"No. Not unless you come, too."

Sam tugged his left hand. "McGill, he's going to hurt you."

"Listen to the lizard, Feighan. Get out of here before— before I do something I don't want to do."

"Give it up, Greystein. Come on home."

This pebble knocked him on his ass. When he moved, rib bones grated.

"The next one comes fast enough to kill, Feighan. Get out of here!"

Sam grabbed Feighan with his six-fingered hands. "Stop it! He *will* kill you! What's wrong with him? Why are you doing it? Stop it! Stop it!"

"Please, Greystein, don't make me—" He shrieked. The pebble had burned right through his upper arm.

He had never felt so close to death. He looked up. The maddened, vacuum-reddened eyes of his closest friend focused on the pebbles, then shifted to him. Blood ran down his own arm. His body ached and he was angrier than he had been in years. Scooping a ball bearing out of his pocket, he said, "Don't."

A pebble smacked through his upper left arm. He groaned, but got to his feet, still holding the shiny ball bearing. And staggered forward.

Greystein's tears mingled with the rain. "I don't want to! I don't want to but I will!"

Between them, Sam ran from one to the other, his tail whipping, his hands clutching desperately at theirs. "Don't! Stop! Oh, please you two, why, please! Stop!"

Feighan's teeth chattered. "Put it down." He stood alone on an alien beach with a child he had sworn to guard, and a crazed stranger who had been his friend. He stood there alone. If he did not act, he would die.

Greystein bent his head to study the pebbles. He had two left.

"McGill!" screamed Sam.

Feighan moved. The pebble seared his neck. He choked. Pain filled his mouth and nose and eyes and ears with red metal fog—

"McGill! McGill!"

Greystein held the last pebble between the index finger and thumb of both hands. He lifted his arms above his head, a warped priest raising the sacrament of death—

"No," whispered Feighan, but—

Greystein triggered his Talent. And grinned.

Time slowed. Feighan's Talent felt the other ready his. Ignoring Feighan's conscious mind, it spoke directly to his subconscious—which did not even think before saying, "Survive! Kill!"

It did.

Bearings burst out of their bag, charring Feighan's pants. A swarm of angry silver bees, they sped for Greystein at ten kilometers/second. Gone in a flash, they left a hole through his chest where his heart had been. The pebble rolled out of his fingers.

Feighan limped over to kneel in the sand. Wind tore at his hair. He eased the corpse onto its back and let the rain and his own tears wash its face. Head bowed, he groped for words he had not spoken in years: "Our Father..."

Then he lifted his friend, though the sand shifted beneath his feet, and he cradled him in his arms. "Come here, Sam."

The Rhanghan said, "Why—"

"I had to."

"I know that—and so did he. Why didn't he just come back? Why did he make you do it?"

Feighan bit his lip. "I don't know." Greystein dead was heavier than he had looked alive; Feighan's arms hurt. "We've got to go."

"Okay." Sam came over to him.

PING

NAC Director Nathaniel Davis sat behind a desk spun of glass and steel; it reflected the underside of his jowls and the front of his powder-blue suit. He was talking to Gina Maccari. They both looked up in surprise.

"McGill!" said Maccari. "Wha—" She saw Greystein, and sat down heavily.

Feighan's feet sank into thick grey carpet as he crossed the room. It pleased him to drip water and sand and blood all over that rug. He lay the corpse across Davis' desk. "There. You wanted him dead? You've got him dead. Bastard."

Davis leaned back, his eyes unreadable.

Maccari said, "You're bleeding."

"Tell the Director that his quarry is dead."

She leaned forward, head cocked. Eyes closed, she touched Greystein's cheek. Then she straightened. "There's no brain activity at all, Mr. Davis." She did not look at him.

The Director nodded. "We'll credit the reward to your account, Feighan."

A reflex Fling of anger gave the Director one meter/second's momentum; it sent him sprawling across the carpet. "You're a pig, Davis." Again he called on the Talent. Shutting his eyes, he concentrated on the corpse—visualized intolerable radiance torn like taffy by fields of magnetism—felt—knew—

PING

Davis said, "Where'd he go?" and gestured to the empty desk.

"The sun," said Maccari in a murmur. "The Flinger's Burial."

"Come on, Sam."

PING

The doctor on duty at the Emergency Room in the Building's Infirmary was chatty and curious, but when Sam showed his teeth, he patched Feighan up quickly, efficiently—and silently.

PING

They got down from the Flop Table slowly. Sam avoided Feighan's eye. He said, "I'm going to take a shower and go to bed, okay?"

He understood. "Sure. I'll see you in the morning, huh?"

"Uh-huh." He waddled away, tail dragging.

As Feighan made his way to the bar, H'nik scuttled forward. *Oh my God!* he thought. *The last thing I need is*—

"You grieve deeply for him."

"Yeah."

"Your friend Walking Mule visited earlier, and left with me a message for transmission to you: 'There was no detective. Maccari provided the facts. Davis provided the holo himself.' He told me to tell you that when you were alone."

Drink in hand, he stood as if frozen. *Maccari provided the facts? Gina helped destroy Greystein?*

Just then Oscar chimed. The printout chattered. Torn off,

the hardcopy bore the return address of the Office of the Director, North American Consortium. It read: "McGill Feighan must report for behavior modification tomorrow morning at 9:00 a.m."

▪ **Chapter VII** ▪

Davis was still simmering—*outright assault!*—when the phone rang. His hand trembled as he picked up the receiver. "Yes?"

"Congratulations again! I never thought you would dare to challenge Feighan—since your Board is so pleased with his ratings."

"He attacked me!" In his voice ran an undercurrent of fear that he would not admit even to himself: Feighan had just *looked* at him.

"I had mentioned that he would bear investigation."

"I'm still on shaky ground, though."

"Then you might consider this: Greystein was an electronic genius. It is most probable that he interfered with the behavior modification field generated by the room computer at the Flinger Academy dormitory. It goes without saying that Feighan could thus have escaped indoctrination, as well."

He slapped his desktop. "That would clinch it! But how do I prove it?"

"Come, now. As you did with Greystein—only this time, do not use the Maccari woman. She is too deeply involved with Feighan. Your Board of Directors might not be enthusiastic, but I am certain that they will not stand in your way. In fact, I can almost guarantee it."

He nodded. Elegant, effective. "Thank you." He smiled slightly.

"You're entirely welcome. One down; one to go. Oh, and do look under that paté tin—again."

▪ **Chapter VIII** ▪

He stayed on the terrace till the dull pink of dawn seeped into the sky. The plastic lawn chair bit his thighs and cramped his elbows; the drinks numbed him, but no more. The cold wind ricocheted from his skin, never penetrating. Feet on the railing and cheeks wet, he tried very hard to understand why Davis had signed Greystein's death warrant—and why Maccari had drawn it up.

H'nik kept vigil with him. Roots sunk into the redwood tub, the monk offered the solace of an anchor through the long dark night. It broke silence only when Feighan did, and then only if Feighan asked it to.

By daybreak he had regained his composure, if not his strength. He stood, blew his nose, and stretched the stiffness from his body. "I have to go."

"Do you visit your Director?"

He shook his head.

"You are still full of rage."

He snorted.

"The sound signifies agreement?"

"It means, 'Yeah, so what else is new?'"

"You will control your anger?"

"If you mean will I do something stupid, I won't. I don't plan to hurt anybody, just get some answers."

"Be aware that even the most innocuous of questions can branch time in a different direction."

He raised his eyebrows. "Does that mean something, or does it just sound good?"

"We live in presents nourished by the roots of the past—be careful of where you spread your roots today, because of what they might nourish in the future."

"Yeah, right. Listen, I've got to go. I'll be back."

PING

The office was small, more a cubbyhole than a real room. Gold speckled its floor of synthetic tiles; years of careless heels stippled it. Three fluorescents almost compensated for the lack of windows. The holocube built into the rear wall showed a desert scene in which a burro grazed on a patch of prickly pears, its shadow cut sharply by the burning sun halfway up the sky. Maccari slumped over her desk, head pillowed on her crossed arms.

Feighan jogged her elbow. "Wake up."

She sniffed, and lifted her head. Her eyes were red. She sniffed again. "I—"

"You fingered Greystein."

"No, I—have a seat, okay?" She pointed to a tubular plastal chair.

Sitting would be the wrong move for too many reasons. "Why'd you do it?"

"Look, I was just doing my job."

"You used to say you wouldn't probe somebody without his permission. You said anything else was immoral."

"I didn't probe Greystein! And it wasn't my idea, anyway."

"You were just an innocent eavesdropper, huh?"

"Yes—no—I don't know, I had to. Davis ordered me to. But Greystein didn't know. I was in the next room, listening through a headset. Davis asked the questions; all I did was Mind the answers."

"So how did you get the truth without probing?"

An expression half-pained, half-embarrassed, flitted across her broad face. "He was in a bad way—all the true answers were at the top of his mind—I didn't *have* to probe! Davis'd ask a question, Greystein would lie but think the truth, and he'd think it so loudly, so clearly, that it was like he was talking to me. I never had to go inside, not once. I just wrote down the real answers and gave them to Davis."

He looked down at her. The strands of her black hair, limp

and greasy, told how many times she had run her fingers through it during the preceding hours. Coffee stained the right sleeve of her wrinkled white blouse; the splotch of pale brown reached nearly to her elbow. Puffiness cupped her bloodshot eyes. He wanted to believe her. "You know Davis is saying that Greystein worked for The Organization?"

"What?" She sat up straight and startled.

"Yeah, he's got a holo of Greystein and Hommroummy. Before—before, Greystein told me about it—said it was a phony. Did Davis *ask* him about The Organization, or Hommroummy, or—"

"Yes!" She leaned forward, dismay displacing her fatigue. "I forget the exact wording of the question—it was something like 'Are you now or have you ever been in the pay of The Organization or any other crime syndicate?'—but Greystein said no, and damn him anyway, McGill, that was the only true thing he said all day."

"You told Davis that?"

"Of course!" Her hands curled into fists; her jaw jutted forward. "You think I *liked* it? Greystein needed therapy, not—" She swept her arm at the holo's desert sun. "I *told* Davis that whatever else Greystein was doing, he wasn't taking any money from The Organization."

He sucked in his breath, stunned by necessity. "Then Davis must have framed him! But why?"

"He couldn't have! Everything else was true...maybe he just got carried away?" Her head sagged. "I don't know. I didn't know he said that. All I knew was that he'd declared him Rogue."

"Were you there when he signed the declaration?"

"No. No. If I had been, I'd have...I don't *know*, McGill, I would have said something! I'd have tried to stop him, but...but I didn't know until it was too late."

"Ah, Jesus!" Davis had lied all around, and, in the lying, had soiled the North American Consortium. *But why?* he thought, while his anger built to a seething boil. *Why did he want Greystein dead?* He was furious at Davis, and she, Davis' aide, was close to hand. He wanted to turn his rage on her as Davis' surrogate, vent it like a building cleaner screeches steam on dirty bricks, but he clamped his jaws tight. Yes, she had played a part in Greystein's flight, and yes, that flight had led Greystein to his death, but she was too obviously innocent.

Blasting her would hardly wash away Davis' sin—or his own guilt. He scowled. "When you were Minding Greystein, were you listening to Davis, too?"

"Well, of cour— oh. I see. No. Not directly, I mean. In a situation like that, you always hear a little off to the side of your head, you can't ignore it, but I was concentrating on Greystein. He was coming through very loud and Davis..." She shrugged. "Davis is quiet all the time, anyway. Like he's not even there."

"I sort of wonder if he is." He reached into his pocket for Oscar's printout. "Here."

"What is it?"

He smoothed it out for her. "Read it."

She did. Her eyes widened. "McGill! He—you—"

"Did you know about this?"

"Of course not!" Dropping it, she looked at her hands as if it might have contaminated them.

"I've talked to Davis a few times—have you been Minding me for him, too?"

"McGill!" She pushed back and away, her eyes round and moist and red. "How could you think—"

"Well, you did it to my best friend without telling either of us, didn't you? 'Just following orders,' you said, didn't you?"

"But that—"

"Aah." He waved a hand. "I know it's not your fault. I'm just...I'm not in good shape, okay? And getting that—" He pointed to the printout. "—getting that made everything worse. Look, you know Davis—"

"Not really."

"Well, you've worked with him often enough, you—"

"That's what I tried to tell you before. He's practically inaudible."

"But you—" Her meaning finally penetrated his confusion of emotions and suspicions. He cocked his head to stare at her. "Isn't that rare?"

"Not really." With a sigh, she brushed a strand of hair over her ear. "I mean, it's not something you expect to find, so it's not common, but a lot of people are quiet upstairs."

Snakes usually are, he thought.

She raised an eyebrow. "I heard that, McGill."

"I wanted you to."

"Well, you're wrong. There's no creepy-crawliness to it at

all! Usually, you brush up against it, you feel like somebody's just popped you a shot of serenity. The people you can hear a mile away are the people in turmoil, grinding like gears a klick high." She made a sound of sadness, of sympathy. "There's an awful lot of them—a society this complex just churns them out—and my God, they're so noisy they drown out the ones like Davis. You just don't hear somebody who's at peace with himself."

"I don't know how the hell he can be."

"I imagine," she said mildly, a remembering look on her face, "that he thinks what he's doing is right."

He wanted to deny her balanced evaluation, but only hours earlier would have agreed with it himself. Davis had never shown anything to suggest that he was doing other than his best—by his own lights. Yet it disappointed—even hurt—Feighan that she did not see the man's crime as clearly as he did. "I've got to go." ·

Her glance dropped to the printout. "Are you—"

"No way."

She winced at his intensity. "But—"

"I'll call you later." He paused. "Look, I don't blame you. Really." He bent down swiftly and kissed her cheek. "I'll let you know what happens."

"You do that." Her arms enveloped his neck in a warm, strong hug. "You matter to me, McGill Feighan."

"That makes it mutual, then." He stepped back, closed his eyes, and—

PING

—and the Director's soft grey carpet gave way beneath his feet. Davis sat behind the steel-and-glass desk, eyes closed, hands folded across his belly. His face was pale and drawn; a pulse throbbed lightly in the folds of his neck. His grey suit bore the wrinkles of an anxious night. A star of mustard burst across its left lapel.

Feighan stalked up the desk, and rapped on its glass top.

Davis jumped; his chair squeaked. Then he relaxed. "Oh, McGill."

"Uh-huh."

Davis rubbed his eyes and yawned. "What can I do for you this morning?"

"Rescind this stupid order." He slid the printout across the expanse of glass.

Davis pulled it closer. His face fell. "I'm afraid that's impossible."

"What do you mean, impossible? You issued it, you cancel it."

Davis touched the knot of his tie. Then he leaned back, and measured Feighan with his eyes. They were grey, sympathetic, and a little bit hollow, almost haunted. "We have reviewed the records. The behavior modification unit in your dormitory room at the Flinger Academy was, shall we say, altered? We suspect it to have been the handiwork of your late roommate, of course; his propensity for electronic wizardry is well-known to the North American Consortium. Which is to say that we attach no blame for it to you, so of course disciplinary action is not even being considered." He smiled shyly.

"I came to get this order canceled," said Feighan, barely controlling his anger, "not to listen to a speech. Now—"

Davis held up a hand. "McGill, I *am* sorry, but I can't. You alone, of all living Terran Flingers, have never been satisfactorily indoctrinated. Until such time as you have been—"

"When hell freezes over!"

Davis shifted his weight forward, clasped his hands, and rested them on the desk. "McGill, you're distraught. Greystein's death has hit you too hard. I understand that; I've been there. I also understand that you are not thinking clearly. If you will allow me, I'll explain—"

"Hold on a minute. You want to brainwash me—"

"Indoctrinate, McGill. Orientate."

"Brainwash. And you want to do it because you claim it hasn't been done to me before. But tell me this: have you ever had a complaint about me? Have I ever screwed up on the job?"

Davis gave him a gentle but pained smile. "As a matter of fact, just the other day a Professor van der Voort filed a formal complaint against you."

"Who the hell is he?"

"She, and she—"

"Wait a minute. She smokes a pipe?"

"Now that you mention it, yes, she does."

Feighan relaxed. "All right. You've got tapes of it. Play 'em. See what happened and why. And then tell me I screwed up."

"I already have, McGill. You were within your authority

to act in the manner you did. Nonetheless, your language *was* intemperate, your behavior antagonistic, and the incident a bad reflection on the image of the North American Consortium. It was one of the factors leading to the conclusion that you had not been indoctrinated properly."

"Now, look—"

"No, McGill. You were ordered to report to the Psychiatric Section at 9:00 a.m." He touched the arm of his chair. Blue numerals appeared in the glass of the desktop. "You have ten minutes."

"No way."

"I am sorry, but I hereby order you to report—at once."

"You can order all you want, fat-face, but I'm not going, and that's final."

Dismay and hurt shook Davis' jowls. "Your attitude is distressing—and ultimately harmful to yourself, as I'm sure you would see with just a bit of reflection."

"Reflection?" Resting his knuckles on the desk, he stared into those call grey eyes. "When I look in the mirror I want to see myself, not a puppet with my face."

"McGill, you know you're exaggerating."

"No." He slapped the desktop. "No way I exaggerate." He pushed his face to within a centimeter of Davis'. The man's breath had no odor at all. "See, if I could trust you, it would be an exaggeration. But I can't trust you because you lie."

Now the eyes chilled, but the voice stayed calm and soft. "About what do I lie?"

"About Greystein and The Organization, for one."

"Oh?"

"You asked Greystein if he had any links to the Organization—he told you he didn't—and your own Staff Telepath told you he was telling the truth. But you went ahead and smeared him anyway."

"That's dangerously close to slander, McGill."

"Of whom? You? No, there's no danger of my slandering you. It's dangerous for you, fat-face, yes, because when the FNC finds out you lied to frame a Flinger, they won't like it. They'll come down on you and you'll lose this cushy job, maybe even have to trade your fancy office for a cinderblock cell in the pen."

"I had holographic evidence—"

"Did you, now? And where did it come from?"

Davis pushed himself to his feet. "I am a busy man. I do not have to suffer through your ravings. You will leave at once, and report to the Psychiatric Section."

"No."

A flush rose into the Director's cheeks. His nostrils flared. Fingering the pressure pad on the desk that would summon guards when pushed, he said, "It is required that all Flingers submit to behavior modification, and you—"

"I will not."

"To remain a Flinger you must!"

"Then I quit."

Blinking, Davis recoiled as though from a slap. "Pardon?"

"I quit. I hereby resign, effective immediately. I'm not a Flinger any more, so I don't have to put up with being brainwashed. Got that? Or do you need it in writing, in one-syllable words?"

"I—" He blinked again, and lowered himself into his chair. It creaked. "I, er . . . I'm afraid I don't know what to say. In all the history of the Consortium no one has ever resigned. Retired, yes, voluntarily or otherwise, but you—" His gaze ran up and down Feighan's body. "You're nowhere near retirement age."

"Well, I just hit it."

"McGill, you can't!"

"Watch me." With a smile, he straightened up. The directness of it exhilarated him; it was such a simple solution that he wondered why he had not come to it earlier. "And that's that, so—" He threw the Director a mock salute, and—

PING

—and stepped down from the Flop Table of his living room. Morning sun streamed through the windows; outside, still planted in the redwood tub, H'nik chatted with a basking Sam.

Feighan yawned. "Order, Oscar: Pour one cup coffee, cream three sugars; do it now."

"Yes, sir."

By the time he had crossed to the bar and lifted the panel of the dispenser, rich steam rose from the full cup. He took a sip, chuckled, then frowned as his Talent, barely called upon as yet, reminded him that it had to be used. *I forgot about the pressure—how am I going to bleed it off if I'm not Flinging? And come to that, what am I going to do with all this free time?*

Out on the terrace, Sam laughed all high and wheezy.

Feighan nodded. Setting the cup down to cool, he walked out to join his friends.

Sam said, "Hi, McGill."

"Hiya, Sam. Good morning, H'nik." He turned the plastic lawn chair so it faced the sun, and sat down with a grunt. "A beautiful morning, isn't it?"

"Yeah! And once H'nik's got enough energy up, I'm going to take it to Central Park. It says it's heard about it all over the place, and wants to test it."

The Actuni's lower bristles rustled. "Ah, did I mispronounce the word? I meant 'taste,' of course. It promises to be most interesting. And you, McGill Feighan, will you join us?"

"He's got to work," said Sam, before Feighan could speak for himself.

"Not any more, Sam. And yes, H'nik, I'll be honored to join you."

"What do you mean, not any more?" The Rhanghan twisted around to stare at his guardian; his tail swept the concrete of the terrace.

"I resigned."

H'nik scraped out: "Do you branch tropicly or has the tip bud been lost?"

Mouth open, he tried to decipher that. "Uh—"

"I do apologize, McGill Feighan. I spoke in my idiom, not yours. What I meant by it was that the course of your life has been altered. Has it changed direction because something draws you away from what you have been doing, or because something has made continuation impossible?"

"Oh. I see." The sun in its deep blue sky cheered him, but burned off none of his fatigue. He stroked his jaw; the stubble rasped. "It was either quit, or get my head scrubbed."

"You refer to the indoctrination?"

"Uh-huh. And I won't be brainwashed, either."

"I don't understand," said Sam. "You make me take baths all the time."

Extending a hand, he scratched his ward on the skullbone. Sam wriggled about. "A little to the left, that's it, that's it."

"Brainwashing's not quite the same as taking a bath, Sam."

"Why not? You make me wash behind my ears."

"Because brainwashing is when you do things to a person's mind to make that person believe something different—when you change that person's character, or personality."

"Ah," said H'nik, "now I begin to comprehend your reluctance."

"Oh?"

"The problem lay with a mistranslation of the word 'indoctrinate.' We had translated it as—forgive me, you do not speak our language. We had thought it synonymous with the concept of ensuring that one fulfills its social responsibilities; we had not realized it had to do with altering one's beliefs."

One hundred twenty-four stories below, Manhattan murmured to itself, raising its voice only to demand passage for an emergency vehicle. The sun's warmth soaked into his face and arms, lulling his body, dulling his mind. Too lethargic to explain that the Actuni had translated 'indoctrinate' properly but too narrowly, he said instead, "Were you serious about wanting to interview me eight hours a day for a year or so?"

The monk's long spine twitched. "Quite. Would you consent?"

"Now that I have some free time, yes. But . . . I'd like to make it conditional. You've been researching the Far Being Retzglaran for a long time, and you have to know a lot that I've never heard of, and if we could work something out—"

"It would be a privilege for me to share my knowledge with you."

"Then I would be delighted to tell you what I know." He yawned. "Once I wake up. But I warn you, I don't know all that much."

"A researcher does not look for all its facts in one location, McGill Feighan."

"That's good, because you won't find all of them here . . ." Sun on his face, he could barely keep his eyes open.

"Will you come to Actu?"

He groaned.

Sam said, "That'd be neat! You want to go, McGill?"

"Not really . . . no offense, H'nik, but I'd rather not spend a year on Actu. I seem to recall you have things like volcanoes and earthquakes and really foul air . . ."

"I understand completely," said the monk. "I have devoted most of my life to my quest; I can spend a year of it on your planet."

"Anything you need, just say so. Soil, water, fertilizer—

what was that kind you wanted? 8-10-20 or something?"

"5-10-5, McGill," said Sam. "Don't you remember anything?"

"Actually, Sam, I remember too much... anything you want, H'nik. And listen, if you'd like to make a few trips home while you're interviewing me, that's no problem, either—even if I have resigned from the North American Consortium, I still have my Talent..." The adrenalin that had kept him awake and aware was evaporating in the heat. He wondered if the NAC would call him in for removal of the device that generated his energy tunic... and decided, sleepily, that it would not, because... his eyes closed.

They scrunched themselves against the glare. It was hot enough to melt him into a greasy puddle, like butter left on a stove. That wind in his ears whistled straight from a blast furnace. The light increased in brilliance until it threatened to burn away his eyelids.

"Well, well, well," said a too-familiar voice. "If it isn't McGill, my young daffodil, finding out how much fun it is to be in the hot seat."

Moaning, he rolled his head so he would not have to look. "No."

"But yes! So tell us, how does it feel to kill your best friend just to cover your ass—and then get caught anyway?"

"Greystein, I—"

"You thought it would save you and it didn't. A terrible waste of time and effort, wasn't it? All that chasing, all that suffering you put me through—and it didn't fool Davis for a minute, now, did it? The heat's on, McGill, and now you'll know how I felt when you wouldn't let me be, when you wouldn't let me flee..."

The light pulsed brighter, whiter. Sunspots danced in his eyes; magnetic fields seized him. In the distance rang a chime and Greystein said, "Hah! There it is! 'Ask not for whom the bell tolls' and all that, 'cause it's tolling for thee, Feighan, for thee!"

A small, scaly hand woke him with its touch. "Huh?" He blinked. The dream faded, but not quickly enough. His heart still thudded; he still felt that awful guilt. He swallowed hard. His mouth tasted so dry and stale that he made a face. The gesture hurt his cheeks. "Dammit," he said, because the only alternative was to cry, "I'm sunburned."

"Is that why you're all red?" asked Sam.

"You know, you could have called me earlier." He had a headache, too. Sitting, up, he winced. The anesthetic had worn off and the wounds Greystein had inflicted ached. From the penthouse came a strident, metallic voice. "What's Oscar babbling about?"

"There's somebody at the door, a deputy sheriff, just like in the cowboy shows."

"Is that what Oscar said?" Stiffly, he got to his feet, put his hands in the small of his back, and arched his spine. He hurt all over.

"Oscar didn't say the part about the cowboy movies."

"You didn't let the guy in, did you?"

"McGill!"

"Yeah..." His vision finally cleared. "Oh, hi, H'nik— 'scuze me a minute, will you please?"

The monk rippled its spines. "Of course."

Feighan stepped into the welcome cool of the dimly lit living room. "Oscar, query: Who's at the door; answer it now."

"Deputy Sheriff Ralph T. Dogherty; computer check verifies ID."

He nodded to Sam. "Go ahead, let him in."

Sam scampered to the door and swung it open.

From outside came a gasp.

"May I help you?" said the saurian.

"Holy shit! What the hell are you?"

"A boy. Why?"

"No, I mean—"

Feighan hobbled over. Patting Sam on the headbone, he said to the rumpled, paunchy cop, "Sam's a Rhanghan, from Throngorn II. You looking for me?"

Dogherty fingered his mustache. "You McGill Feighan?"

"Uh-huh."

"Here." He thrust an envelope into the Flinger's hand. "It's a subpoena—you'll find all the details inside."

"Gee, thanks." Slapping the envelope against his left palm, he toed the door shut.

"What's a suh-peeny, McGill?"

"Suh-PEE-nah, Sam. It's an order to appear in court." His biceps throbbed as he tore the envelope open. "My God!"

"What's the matter?"

"I have to show cause why..." He moved his finger along

the line of tiny type, trying to read it and make sense of it at the same time. "... show cause why I should not be required to fulfill my contractual obligations, and all that they would entail. The bastards! They're trying to force me to keep on working for them. How can they—they're not going to get away with this!"

"Get away with what, McGill?"

He made a fist, and stifled a yelp of pain. When he winced, the side of his neck stung. He headed for the bathroom.

Sam's tail swooshed through the carpet as he followed. "What are they trying to get away with?"

"They're trying to make me go back to work for them. But they can't do that. That's slavery, indentured servanthood or something. And that's unconstitutional." He peered into the mirror. "Oh, God."

"What's the matter now?" Sam clambered onto the edge of the tub, his favorite perch. "Your sunburn hurt?"

"That, too." He was a mess. Tousled hair, reddened eyes, coarse-stubbled cheeks ... he reached for the ultrasonic shaver, but the thought of its tingle made him shudder. Maybe that was why Greystein had—"To hell with it."

"What?"

"Huh? Oh, nothing ..." From the medicine chest he took first-aid cream; smoothed over his cheeks, it soothed them quickly. He gulped two paintabs, then wielded the shampcomb so that at least his hair would be clean. "I've got to go out for a few minutes."

"Where?"

"Take care of H'nik; I'll be back soon. Don't let anybody in, okay?"

"I won't," said Sam. "But can we go to the park?"

"Ah ... yeah, sure, why not? You got money in your account?"

"Uh-huh."

"Well, don't forget your charge card."

"It's no fair that I have to use a card when everybody else gets to use a thumb."

"Well, bankplates don't read Rhanghan fingerprints too well. Look. I've got to go. I'll see you later." With a last gloomy look at his mirror image, he closed his eyes, and—

PING

—and appeared in the anteroom of Goodthorpe, Goodthorpe, & Mongallo, P.C., the firm that handled all his legal work. Ignoring the receptionsim—a computer-generated shimmer of light and color—he walked for the door with the brass plate reading Jason Goodthorpe. Behind him, the simulacrum said, "But Mr. Goodthorpe is in conference! If you will take a seat—"

Shutting the door from the other side cut the receptionsim's protest in half. "Hiya, Jase. Nice conference."

The tall, angular man on the force-couch blew a smoke ring at the ceiling. "Jesus, Feighan, didn't anybody ever teach you to knock?"

"That only gives you time to lock your door." He spun one of the three black leather chairs around and eased himself into it. "Got a problem, Jase."

"You got a problem? I've got a problem. I've got a client who doesn't know he's supposed to deal with his attorney over the telephone." He held his fat brown cigarette before his eyes and focused on its ember. A wisp of grey spiraled upward. "I'm beginning to regret I ever showed you where my office was."

"Hey, I call you, you don't answer, you're always in conference. Which means you're lying around in your underwear again, drinking good beer and smoking bad tobacco. God, that stuff stinks." He waved a hand in front of his face.

"Call me on the phone, you don't have to smell it." He puffed another cloud at Feighan.

"The last time I tried, it took a week before we talked to each other, 'cause neither of us was ever in when the other was. I don't have time to do that merry-go-round again."

"Yeah?"

"Yeah."

"Oh, all right." Swinging his legs over the edge of the couch, he sat up. He had knobbly knees, and polka-dotted shorts. "So what's your problem?"

"This." He passed over the subpoena, and waited for Goodthorpe to scan it. "See, they ordered me to submit to behavior modification. From what I understand, they can do that—they have a right to scrub my head—*if* I work for them. So I quit. And now this."

"You quit, huh?" Goodthorpe's blue eyes were clear and piercing.

"Uh-huh. But now they want to force me back to work, and

then brainwash me, and Jase, I don't want that. Strange things are going on down there. I have a feeling I wouldn't come out of it in too good a shape."

"I told you not to sign that contract."

"But I did. I had to, if I wanted to work for them—and dammit, Jase. I'm a Flinger. I couldn't *not* Fling; I'd explode if I tried that."

"I know, I know—and they'd screw you if you tried to Fling for anybody else, too, because only employees of the Consortia are allowed to teleport cargo or passengers." He frowned. "Aw, hell, McGill, they have you over a barrel. I mean, you signed that contract. When's the hearing?" He squinted at the subpoena.

"Tomorrow at nine." He slumped in the chair, and stroked the slick black leather. "Which seems awful quick to me. I mean—"

"I could maybe get you a continuance till the afternoon, but frankly, we don't need one."

"You're not going to present a defense?"

"Of course I am." Goodthorpe's eyebrows shot up. "What do you think, I plan to throw you on the mercy of the court?" *Your Honor, have mercy on Feighan; he just killed his best friend and hasn't been the same since.* "But is one day enough time?" He rolled another smoke ring past his lips. "The only reason I'd need more time is if my computer crashed—and I'd have to swear to that to get the time."

"Well, you know what you're doing, I guess."

"Since that's what you're paying me for, you'd better hope I do."

Feighan pushed himself to his feet. "Okay. I suppose I'd better leave you to it. What time should I meet you in the morning?"

"Nine a.m., in Courtroom—" He glanced at the subpoena. "—C."

It all seemed wrong. Feighan had come to have his anxieties quelled, but Goodthorpe had increased them. "You don't want to get together ahead of time?"

The attorney stubbed out his cigarette. "McGill, when you send somebody to the other side of the Galaxy, do you get together with him half an hour ahead of time and work things out?"

"Well, no—there's no need."

"Exactly. You just be there, neatly dressed, *clean-shaven*, and for God's sakes, do something about that permanent blush of yours."

"It's sunburn. I fell asleep on the terrace."

"A likely story . . . oh, before you go. One last point to clear up: your objection is *not* to working for the NAC, but to being indoctrinated. Correct?"

"Right."

"And avoiding that indoctrination is your highest priority?"

"Right." He scratched the welt on his neck. Goodthorpe's questions seemed no more than a bald restatement of the obvious. "Why?"

"And everything else is subordinate to avoiding that indoctrination?"

"Yes. That's what I said. Why?"

Goodthrope shook out another cigarette, lit it, then waved it at Feighan. "Just checking, McGill. I'll see you in the morning. Sleep well tonight."

"Oh, sure." He meant it to be sarcastic.

As it turned out, he did sleep well, or at least well enough so that, when he strode into Courtroom C, Sam in tow, he felt as mentally alert as Oscar must. It took him a minute to spot Goodthrope—bright-eyed old men and women filled the twelve rows of seats and blocked his view of the defense table. Then he nodded, and worked his way down the aisle. The attorney was hunched over a computer printout. "Hi, Jase. You know Sam?"

"Sure, we met a few years ago, when I drew up the guardianship papers. How you doing, Sam? You sure have grown." He held out his hand; nicotine stained his fingers.

"Good morning, Mr. Goodthorpe." They shook.

"Call me Jase, everybody does." He folded up the printout and pushed it to one side. "You can sit here."

As Feighan reached for the chair, Goodthorpe said, "No—*Sam* can sit here—you sit over in the booth." He pointed to a glass-walled cubicle opposite the jury box.

"There?" The prospect of lexan isolation made Feighan squeamish—he would feel like a monkey in a cage. "I thought that was for criminal trials."

"Not any more. But look, at least you'll know nobody's going to take a potshot at you." His expression was sympathetic. "Go, now—the bailiff's coming."

Every step across the expanse of bare floor below the bench made him conscious of the curious eyes on his back. The time-killers who watched trials instead of holo-shows rarely saw a Flinger as a defendant. Whispers skittered back and forth across the courtroom.

At the booth, the uniformed policewoman asked his name, then motioned him inside as the bailiff called, "All rise!"

The chair filled most of the booth, leaving him barely enough room to turn around. The ventilator puffed hot air in his face. The speaker picked up the shuffling feet and thudding seats, and amplified them painfully. He tried to catch the attendant's eye, to have her turn the volume down, but she had her back to him. Short of rapping on the transparent wall, nothing could get her attention. He decided to put up with the noise. The heat, though . . . sweat ran down his back.

Judge Coznowski entered the room. She had to be eighty, but she walked with the brisk, erect carriage of a woman half her age. Taking her place, she touched her bun of white hair and looked from Goodthorpe to the attorney for the NAC. "Gentlemen, I have reviewed your arguments. Frankly, Mr. Goodthorpe, I am disappointed. Barring a sudden burst of inspiration on your part, I would have to rule for the plaintiffs."

Goodthorpe rose. "If Your Honor would be so indulgent, I would appreciate hearing Your Honor's reasoning before I emit such a sudden burst of inspiration."

An appreciative smile crossed Coznowski's thin lips. "Your client stands in breach of a properly executed contract, Counselor."

"But performance of that contract would endanger Mr. Feighan's sanity."

"Not proven, Counselor, and irrelevant in any event. The possibility of behavior modification was a condition of the contract, one upon which Mr. Feighan knew the plaintiffs could insist, at their discretion."

"Very well, Your Honor."

What do you mean, "Very well"? Feighan gripped the arms of his chair. He wanted to shout "Jase, what are you doing to me?" But the mike was off, and the lexan, soundproof. Had Greystein felt this trapped at the end?

Goodthorpe continued. "In that event, Your Honor, my client insists that he must breach the contract to preserve the integrity of his personality, but is willing to pay reasonable damages to the plaintiffs."

Fingers uncurling, Feighan exhaled. *That's better, Jase.*

The judge inclined her head. "What damages would the plaintiffs suffer, Mr. Scheriner?"

The attorney for the NAC, a wrinkled old man with a shock of implanted red hair, stood. "Your Honor, this contract has eleven months before it expires. During that time, Mr. Feighan would normally work nine days out of ten, making ninety-six 'Flings,' or acts of teleportation, each day. The NAC charges fifty Flinger Network Credits per Fling."

Goodthorpe bounded to his feet. "Your Honor, I would point out that the North American Consortium pays Mr. Feighan one-half a Fancy per Fling, which should by rights be deducted from Mr. Scheriner's estimate of the revenues the NAC would collect should Mr. Feighan agree to full performance of this contract."

Coznowski nodded. "Point taken, Counselor. If you will grant me a moment for calculation." She bent her head to study the benchtop; her fingers worked a keypad invisible to the spectators. "Twenty-one million, one hundred seventy thousand, one hundred sixty dollars," she said after a few minutes. She raised her plucked eyebrows, then cleared her throat. "Mr. Goodthorpe, those are the damages the plaintiff is likely to suffer should your client breach his contract. I presume he is willing to make such restitution?"

Scheriner's tone trembled with outrage. "Your Honor! The North American Consortium desires Mr. Feighan's services, not his money."

She turned her ice-blue gaze on him until he paled and sat back down. "I am quite aware of the plaintiff's desires, Counselor. I am also aware of Mr. Feighan's desires. By the terms of his contract with you—a contract, I suspect, which you drew up—Mr. Feighan had pledged to indemnify you against all damages you suffer as a result of his failure to fulfill the terms of that contract. Mr. Goodthorpe?"

Feighan did not like the way the hearing was going. Biting his lip, he leaned forward, hoping that Goodthorpe would find a way out for him.

"Your Honor," said Goodthorpe, "my client would ask you to release him from the terms of the contract, on the grounds that—"

"Out of the question, Counselor. The contract is legal and binding. What are the extent of Mr. Feighan's assets?"

"To the best of my knowledge, Your Honor, my client's assets consist of a trust fund with a principal of ten million dollars, stocks and bonds with a market value of approximately one million dollars, and a credit balance in his thumb account of—" He consulted a slip of paper. "—two hundred thirty-nine thousand, seventeen dollars and eighty-eight cents. More or less."

Frowning in concentration, she worked the keypad again.

Feighan's sweat ran cold, now, and his stomach fluttered.

"Fifty-three point-oh-nine percent," Coznowski said at last. "Very well, then. Mr. Feighan?"

A wave of nausea passed through him. He picked up the microphone, and fumbled with the on switch. "Yes, Your Honor?"

"Are you willing to return to work until the expiration of your present contract?"

"Your Honor, they want to brainwash me!"

The NAC lawyer popped up. "Objection, Your Honor."

She waved a hand at him. "Mr. Feighan, please answer the question I asked: are you willing to fulfill the terms of your contract?"

He could see where things were heading, but could not stop them. The nausea intensified; he had to clench his teeth to keep his breakfast down. "No, Your Honor."

"Very well, then. I hereby direct the defendant to surrender his assets to this court, for transmission to the plaintiff, before he leaves the building. I further declare the defendant bankrupt. In accord with the procedures established by NYPL 2060-2089, the defendant will have garnished—" She tapped the keypad. "—forty-six-point-nine-one percent of all his future earnings, until such time as he has repaid—"

"McGill!" Sam bounced onto the defense table. Goodthorpe reached for him, but the Rhanghan slapped the attorney's hand with his tail. "Get out! Get out! Quick!"

For one-tenth of a second it embarrassed him that his ward could behave so badly in a court of law—even one that had just impoverished him. He winced—then understood.

PING

He touched the blinking Goodthorpe's shoulder and whispered, "Here I am," just as the judge's gavel began its downswing. Goodthorpe twisted around.

The gavel struck.

A muffled roar shook Courtroom C. The booth rocked; grey smoke filled it.

Coznowski stared at the gavel in horror.

The bailiff disappeared through a side door.

And Feighan said, "That's it. I've had it. Jase, the judge wants my money, she can have it. All of it. Everything. Come on, Sam." Taking the saurian's hand, he closed his eyes and—

PING

—and Flopped them on the table in his living room. "Pack your things, Sam, and tell H'nik to uproot itself—we're leaving."

"But where?"

"Actu. Right now." He threw his clothes into a suitcase, looked around at the furniture, and bit his lip. The penthouse had been home for four years; he would miss it tremendously. Sniffing, he went into the other bedroom for a holo of Greystein, and carefully packed it among his shaving gear. Then he marched out to the terrace, where H'nik wiggled its spines in the gentle spring rain. Sam waited, too, a small bundle slung over his back. "Are you two ready?"

The monk said, "Yes."

PING

The air, dry and acrid, reeked of sulphur. Cracks ran up and down the walls of the Flop Booth. The floor radiated heat: and one minute after they materialized, it snapped up and down like a carpet being shaken by a giant. A freight train rumble boomed through the Booth, dislodging plaster from the ceiling and puffing dust up from the floor.

"My God!" said Feighan. Sam huddled against the side of his leg. "What the hell was that?"

"Only the volcano," said H'nik. "It is nothing to worry about . . . yet."

▪ Chapter IX ▪

It had gone so smoothly! The bailiff had taken mere minutes to suborn, and for only a third of the paté tin, had agreed to stick the plastique to the booth chair's bottom. He had even wired in a micro-transceiver so that Davis could be sure he got Feighan when he detonated the charge.

But then that damnable lizard had warned the Flinger.

And now his enemy had fled.

The phone rang. He glared at it, but picked it up anyway. "What?"

"Are you a fool, a madman, or both?"

"What are you saying? Who *are* you?"

"You know who I am, if not what I am named. Spare me your lies. The bailiff you bribed is also in my employ—and owes his first loyalty to me, always. What lunacy moved you to attempt an assassination?"

He had never heard the voice so hard. "But I thought you wanted—"

"I wanted him penniless, friendless, and unemployed—not dead. Had I wanted that, I would have arranged it myself. I do not leave matters of importance to bumblers like yourself. Where is he?"

The insults stung. Who did the voice think he was? "How should I know?"

"Find out. Quickly. And remember: I record *all* my calls. Even this."

The trap snapped shut on his life, never to open. He whispered, "Yes, sir."

▪ **Chapter X** ▪

"Volcano?" The floor bucked again. He wanted to run, but where? Sam hissed and whimpered; Feighan tried to reassure him with a hand on his shoulder. The problem was, he needed reassurance himself.

What had he gotten into? He could die here! What was he— *Stop* it, he told himself. No matter how bad the situation was, panic would be worse. He tried to keep calm as he asked, "Your Flinger Building is next door to a live volcano?"

"Oh, hardly next door," said H'nik. Slowly it moved toward the door. "Come. As I understand it, this room should be vacated as soon as possible after arrival."

He balked. "You're not going outside, are you?"

"Well, of course."

"But the volcano—"

"Ahhh. It is no cause for alarm, McGill Feighan. Although it seems to be erupting again, it is many of your kilometers distant. Only during the mightiest of its upheavals does this vicinity suffer more than ashfall."

Does that mean ashfall is common? *Maybe I should have stayed in New York . . .* He listened for screams; hearing none, he was not sure if he should feel more secure—or less. "Are you *positive* it's safe?"

"At this distance, yes. Closer up, of course, it can be uncomfortable."

"Lethal, you mean." His voice shook. The last few hours, coming so soon after Greystein's death, had destroyed his nerves. First the trial, and the verdict, and the bomb, and the abrupt flight . . . He wanted to curl up in a corner and twitch for a while.

"Lethal? Ah, lethal . . . oh, no. Tap-triggering, perhaps." It swayed forward to touch a spine to a pressure-sensitive panel; the door zipped into the ceiling, shedding dust as it disappeared. "Ah," it said again. "I must apologize. For you the volcano might be lethal. I forgot what can kill a Terran."

As it trundled into the corridor, Feighan gulped. "P-pardon?"

"Your people do die permanently, do they not?"

"Uh—yes. Frequently. And always permanently."

"So many races," said the monk. "One forgets precisely what each does. This is especially so of those entitled to the blessings denied us."

"H'nik—" Feighan cast a wary eye at the corridor ceiling, which bellied down almost to the point where it would have to collapse. "—you have me totally confused. What are you talking about?"

The monk stopped, jiggled up and down as it turned around, and said, "We find it most difficult to die once and for all. Very nearly impossible, in fact. And so we forget how kindly the deity regards other races in the galaxy."

"Kindly?"

"I sense, McGill Feighan, that we have stumbled upon a conversational topic that could occupy us for hours, to no end of mutual profit. But let us postpone that delight to a more propitious moment. I must report to my superiors as soon as possible, and since I know at least one of the questions they will ask, I would put it to you right now, if that would be convenient."

"Uh—sure. What's the question?"

"You have, most abruptly, changed your mind about visiting Actu—to our great pleasure, I hasten to add—and I would inquire as to your motivation, if that would not strike you as offensive."

"No. It's not at all offensive." He paused for a breath that he hoped would maintain his self-control. On the ragged edge of hysteria, he would lose himself completely if he stepped a centimeter too far in the wrong direction. "I said I'd let you interview me because quitting the NAC gave me a lot of free time, but in the beginning I didn't want to come here because—" He cut himself off before he stated his opinion of the planet. "I had a lot of ties to New York City. I didn't want to break them, but Davis did it for me. I lost my money. I lost my house. My best friend is—" He bit down hard to hold in the sob. Sam shot him a sharp glance. He winced. "Dammit! I changed my mind because I wanted to get out of there, because I hate, it, the people, everything. Okay?"

"I understand." The monk dragged one spine across another in a long slow hum of sympathy. "Perhaps now is not the best time to broach such a subject, but you stated that you have had your money taken from you. Does that not mean you will require employment?"

"Oh, Jesus." *How could I forget* that? He sagged against the dusty wall, his shoulders slumping. "That's right. I will need a job."

"I can offer you employment for an indefinite period of time."

"Oh?"

"One of the greatest problems the monastery faces is placing missionaries where they are needed—we have no shortage of eager spirits, but as you have noticed, we walk very slowly. We are also so susceptible to the whimsies of Nature that we must either mat out or tap down with distressing frequency— especially in hostile areas. Thus, to make certain that one monk reaches the far side of the world, we must send out a dozen, fifteen years before the one will be required. Could we hire you, our problem would be solved."

At least it will keep the pressure down. And take my mind off what I did to poor Greystein . . . He shrugged. "Sure. But don't you have Flingers of your own?"

"Of course, but they must devote most of their strength to their Network tasks—Actu owes the FNC just as much money as Terra does, McGill Feighan, and we buckle under the same burden to repay it that Terra does. Come." With a hop and a shuffle it turned itself around. "Let me show you where you live."

"Isn't this the Flinger Building?"

"Yes, but you will live at a site adjacent to the monastery. I should mention that 'monastery' is an approximate translation of our word and concept; it is not the same as, let us say, a

Franciscan monastery or even a Tibetan lamasery. Come. It is no more than a four-hour walk."

Feighan did not want to sound rude, but he was still on edge, and had not eaten since that morning. "Ah, H'nik, do you think Sam and I could postpone that a bit, while we rest and freshen up?"

"Freshen up?"

"Yes—change clothes, get something to eat, unpack our suitcases, wash our hands—that sort of thing. Freshen up."

"But the dew does not fall till dawn."

"Pardon?"

"Something has just occurred to me." H'nik's spines rustled in apparent agitation. "You will require housing of some sort, will you not?"

"Yes." The entire building shuddered, almost jarring him off his feet. Remembering that the ceiling had looked ready to fall, he glanced up—and a cinder dropped into his eye. "Ouch!" He tried to ease it out with the tip of his little finger. He had no luck. "Sam—can you give me a hand?"

"Sure, McGill. What is it?"

"Something in my eye." He squatted so the Rhanghan would not have to balance on his hind legs and tail. Grasping his eyelids and spreading them apart, he said, "Do you see anything?"

"A bloodshot eyeball?"

"That's not funny!" It was a Gina Maccari sort of line, and he would have to speak to her about warping Sam's sense of humor—on second thought, there would be no need. Sam would not be seeing her for a long, long time—if ever.

"I see it." He looked dubiously at his clawed finger. "You sure you want me to—I've got it!" He moved closer. His dark, double-lidded eyes stared directly into the Flinger's. "Now, don't move—" His tongue flicked out, barely touching Feighan's eyeball, and retracting just as the human blinked. "Got it. Geez, that tastes rotten."

"My eye?"

"No, the thing." He spat it out. "Tastes like rotten eggs."

Feighan stood. Tears blurred the vision of his right eye, but he could see well enough to walk. And H'nik waited for them, half-in and half-out of the doorway. "Let's go." Together, he and Sam crossed over to the monk. "I apologize for the delay."

"That is quite all right. Your organs of vision were not

designed for Actu's atmosphere. Now, ours—" It moved around until its left ocular aureole faced Feighan. "Ours depend on infrared radiation, and are extremely sensitive. Any one of our 'eyes' can sense a degree's worth of temperature difference at fifty of your meters; moreover, trinocular perception establishes for us the pattern in a being's infrared radiation. Did you know that no two beings have exactly the same emission pattern?"

"Uh—"

"That is how we distinguish one alien from another, with virtually one hundred percent accuracy." It pirouetted, then froze. "Ah, me. I forgot again. About the housing—"

"Yes?"

"You will desire some, will you not?"

Taken aback, he cleared his throat. "Uh . . . I think so, yes."

"This is quite embarrassing. "I—all of us, really—we get so few alien visitors that even after decades of membership in the Network we are rooted in our ethnocentrism. I quite forgot that most intelligent races live inside structures they build themselves."

The floor shimmied like a flat of jello. Feighan refused to look up. If the ceiling wanted to fall, it would have to do so unobserved. Eventually, things steadied themselves. "So?"

"We . . . this way, please." It led them through a doorway into a hot, bright world. The sun shone through a yellow haze that obscured the distant mountains. Jagged fissures ran through the parched ground, which fell away beneath their feet into a dry-bottomed valley. "You see, McGill Feighan, we Actuni have no hands."

"I, uh, I had noticed that."

"Because of that we can not build."

With a frown, he jerked his thumb at the low stone building behind them. "But—"

"Oh, no. That was constructed by the Network when it found us. Believe me, we had nothing to do with it."

He had an unhappy premonition. "So what you're saying is—"

"We have no place for you to live indoors. A gentle southern slope with moisture only eight meters down, yes—but no walls, no roof. This would dismay you, would it not?"

He sighed. "Yes, it would."

H'nik tilted its body a degree or two away from him. "Is there not something called a 'tent'?"

Feighan nodded.

"These can be purchased?"

"Yes, but—"

"Excellent! If you would be so kind as to buy—"

"Uh, there's a slight problem with that—"

"Of course." It crept a few paces onward, then shook its spines. "Ah, the solution: our account with the FNC shows, to my understanding, a small surplus—in fact, it is out of that with which we had planned to pay you. We will simply advance you the requisite sum."

He looked at the sky—at the ground—then tried to remember, from the few experiences in the outdoors he had had as a child, what it was like to live in a tent. He could not recall much beyond the fact that, on the first morning, one awoke stiff; that once, when camping with his father and Jose Schwedeker, the man who had discovered his Talent, he had fallen from a tree and fractured his skull; and that— "I don't suppose you get a lot of rain here."

H'nik's spines rasped with a sound akin to laughter. "Very little."

"I guess a tent will do it, then . . ."

"Fine. Let me take you to the monastery, now."

"Uh, H'nik?"

"Yes?"

"You did say it was a four-hour walk?"

"Why, yes, I did."

"If you'll point the way, I think I can get us there a little faster."

"Ahh . . . but will it not tire you?"

Feighan chuckled. "I'm used to doing ninety-six a day, H'nik—ninety-six across the entire Network. I think I can Fling us a couple of kilometers without dropping." Once, Greystein had taught him how to travel quickly through a series of line-of-sight hops. It hurt that Greystein would never teach him anything again.

"Excellent! It lies just beyond the far ridge of the valley below us. I must confess, I had not looked forward to making the trek on foot."

Sam said, "I thought those were roots."

The monk leaned forward so it could look downwards. "They are roots, but I have a feeling that the English idiom would not work half so well if I substituted 'root' for 'foot.'"

Feighan stood between the Actuni and the Rhanghan, and

focused his gaze on the haze-shrouded ridge. "Is everybody ready?"

"Uh-huh," said Sam.

"Need I be ready," said H'nik, "if you are?"

PING

The ground shivered as they materialized. Dust boiled up around them. Feighan coughed and blinked; Sam, who had yet to part his inner, transparent eyelids, told H'nik, "He'll be okay in a minute."

When Feighan had wiped his eyes with a handkerchief, he took a few steps forward for his first sight of the valley of the monastery. Expecting more of the cracked, baked soil and the scraggly vegetation that had surrounded the Flinger Building, he let his jaw drop. "A lake?"

"A what?" said H'nik.

By then his vision had adjusted. A thousand meters below, a rich blue-green carpeted the valley floor: plants. Millions of them. Vibrant, healthy, rain-forest dense—"My God, it's beautiful!"

"We are proud of our handiwork. Perhaps too proud—you have a word 'hubris'?"

"Are you really afraid of that?" Feighan could not stop staring at the sea of vegetation. It was such a contrast to the baked-dust beige of the encircling slopes, terraced neatly though they were.

"The Actuni were created to suffer, McGill Feighan."

His eyes kept swimming in and out of focus; he shook his head. "Is there an underground river, or what?"

"A very high water table—you will note the depth of the valley?"

"Uh-huh. Nice set-up."

"Until the next eruption."

He looked up instinctively, but smoke plumed from so many peaks that he decided he had better not worry—it would take too much time. "Frankly, H'nik, I don't see how hubris enters into it. I mean, is just living in an oasis a challenge to the gods?"

"God. We, too, are monotheistic. And in answer to your question: no. But that does not describe our situation. We were not content to accept our lot. We came upon this valley several hundred years ago and found, the instant we dropped our roots, that the soil was moist, and rich in minerals. That was, truly, a gift. But we were not content to accept our lot. We have made the valley our garden. We have loosened the soil, and leveled it, and made it fertile. We have terraced the hillsides, and made gentle walks of torturous slopes. We have become proud."

Feighan shifted his weight uncomfortably. "Uh... well, I don't know much about theology. Where should I Fling us to, next?"

"Near the head of the valley is a field of Actuni—do you see it?"

He squinted into the haze. "Not really."

"Up there, McGill," said Sam, pointing north-northeast. "Right in front of those white pillars."

"You mean those hedges?"

"Boy, you have terrible eyesight."

"And you have a tail that can be stepped on, kid." He concentrated on the neat green rows and—

PING

—the three of them materialized two meters away from the first: a line of closely spaced Actuni that stretched nearly to the slope on either side.

"This is our library," said H'nik. As it began to make its way through the line, distant music died away.

"But where are the books?" said Sam, looking over his shoulder in bewilderment.

"You will recall, my young friend, that we are not blessed with hands. We do not write. We remember. That—" The monk jiggled about and trained its long spine at a towering Actuni. Easily five meters tall and another meter in diameter, its barrel was nearly spineless; great patches of brown discolored its epidermis. "—is the book of Creation. Later, perhaps, you will have opportunity to study it, and to discover that it contains interesting parallels to your book of Genesis."

"Really?" said Feighan politely.

"Do you see that hollow beyond the, ah, 'white pillars'?"

Feighan stepped sideways to sight between the columns of Actuni. "Yes."

"Could you convey us there, it would be appreciated."

PING

The bowl-shaped depression dipped some ten meters down and yawned forty wide; a number of Actuni clustered in its gravelly middle. H'nik said, "Wait here, if you would be so kind." Scuttling down the sloping side, it went directly to the Actuni in the center. Their conversation sounded like hacksaws attacking sheet metal . . .

When the one—*monk,* Feighan presumed—backed off a pace, it left a vinyl pouch on the ground. H'nik moved atop the gold sack like a hen settling onto an egg, wiggled about, then came back to Feighan and Sam. It dropped the pouch at their feet.

"You will find a Network Credit card within. Take what you need."

Feighan picked it up gingerly—sticky to the touch, it smelled like methane—opened it, and removed the plastic card with the memory molecules embedded in its core. "Are you sure you want me to take this? I mean, it says, 'Treasury Account of Actu,' and if this is your government's—"

"We are a theocracy, McGill Feighan; we have no government, *per se.* You have been given the card to enable you to make purchases necessary to the success of the task you have undertaken for us. Naturally we will request an accurate accounting. Go now. Purchase your tent; darkness comes soon. Sam and I will locate an appropriate place for the two of you to sleep."

"All right." Shrugging, he stepped back, He closed his eyes—

PING

—and materialized in a quiet back alley off Nathan Road in Kowloon, Hong Kong. Around the corner was the People's Liberation Army Surplus Store; he stopped on the money-changer's window on his way in and picked up a wad of both Hong Kong and U.S. dollars. The turbaned Sikh who debited the Actuni account did not even raise an eyebrow.

Upstairs, in the camping section, he piled up binoculars, mess kits, lamps, a chip player for music, a stove and bottles of gas . . . The clerk said, "The next Everest expedition?"

"Mountains, yes; Himalayas, no. Is this stuff fireproof?"

She turned her head a little, as if she could not have heard him right. "You mean waterproof, sir?"

"No, that I don't have to worry about. I mean fireproof."

She blinked. "I don't believe anything is, sir. It has, however, been treated with a flame retardant."

"I guess that will have to do." Ignoring her headshake, he

peeled off the right number of bills, gathered the equipment into a neat pile, and—

PING

—returned to the monastery.

Sam was waiting, a glum look on his face. Before him lay a mound of bluish-green berries.

"What's the matter?"

The Rhanghan raised his head. "While you were gone, I checked out their food—we can't eat it, McGill."

"Is that more of your instinct?"

"No, I talked to some of the people here—H'nik translated—and they said, I dunno, the chemicals are lined up wrong? Something like that. And there's a lot of metal in it, too, and I guess you can't pick it out."

"They don't mean pieces of metal, Sam. They mean . . ." Frowning, he scratched his head, and gave it up as a bad cause. Greystein had always made the scientific explanations around the house. "What they mean is that it's poisonous. Where's the campsite?"

"On the side of the hill—" He pointed to the west. "—where H'nik is. See it?"

"Uh-huh." He—

PING

—flung Sam, himself, and the gear over to the waiting monk. The ground quivered; a sleeping bag rolled off the pile. He picked it up and started to lay it out before he realized that, no matter how tired he was, he had more to do before he could rest. He yawned. "I'll be back in a while."

PING

Returning to America was risky, but Houston was not the kind of town to treat a moneyed stranger unkindly. Still, he looked over his shoulder before entering the plumbing fixtures store.

"Yes?" said the middle-aged man leaning on the counter watching the cube.

"I'd like to buy a water tank—say, about—" He did rough calculations in his head. "About five hundred liters?"

"We got a couple in stock."

"That'd do fine—wait. What's it weigh?"

The clerk straighted up abruptly. "Weigh?"

"Yeah, weigh."

He shrugged. "I'll be damned if anybody ever asked that before . . . couple hundred kilos, I suppose."

"All right." He reached into his pocket. "You do take cash money?"

"Long as you didn't print it yourself."

"What's it cost?"

"Depends on where you want it delivered."

"I'll take it myself."

"Suit yourself . . ." He touched the keyboard of the cash register, and read from the display screen: "That'll be $1497.11, tax included."

Feighan counted out fifteen one-hundred dollar bills. "You charge for water?"

"There's a glass in the men's room; help yourself." He peered past the Flinger to the street. "Don't see your truck— you already parked out back?"

"Uh—I don't think I'll need one—"

"I wondered about that." He gestured to Feighan's energy tunic. "Don't like to pry, though. People have a tendency to take offense. So you're just going to teleport it away, huh?"

"That's right. Now, what about the water?"

"Oh." He pointed to a battered metal door at the rear of the display room. "Men's room's over there."

"No, for the tank."

"You want it *filled?*" His eyes widened till their whites showed.

Feighan nodded.

"Suit yourself . . ." He stared at the ceiling for a moment, lips moving. "Water costs down here, though . . . you've given me fifteen hundred?"

"That's right."

"Well, I'll fill the tank for you and we'll call it even. Take me a while, though—I'm alone in the store today."

"How long will it be?"

"Call it half an hour?"

"Okay. I'll be back."

Feighan went from the store to the telephone booth on the busy corner. While vehicles hissed past, he checked the commercial listings for a dried food supplier. Hurrying over, he bought five hundred kilos of freeze-dried foods. The manager looked at him dubiously, but took the cash and had two sweating stockboys stack the cartons up. When Feighan—

PING

—Flung it all to Actu, the manager immediately crossed back to the register to make certain that the money was still there. Then he forced a smile. "Have a real nice one, you hear?"

Feighan said, "Thanks," and—

PING

—teleported back to the plumbing store, where the clerk jumped up from the telephone, alarm on his tanned face. "Something wrong?"

"Sorta took me by surprise, boy." He wiped his forehead with a pink Kleenex. "Your tank's just about full—"

"Where is it?"

"In the back room, but—"

Feighan pushed through the swinging door, the clerk at his heels. A cylinder of porcelain and metal gleamed in the far corner; up its side snaked a garden hose that disappeared through its top. "I'm in sort of a hurry, so—"

Grit crunched under a shoe. Something hissed.

PING

At the tank, he spun. A nightstick clattered onto the floor. The cop who had tried to club him unconscious was drawing his service automatic. "You bastard," said Feighan to the clerk.

The clerk shrugged—and smiled. "Seen you on the news, boy."

The cop drew a bead on Feighan's chest. "Hold it right there."

"Are you really that dumb?"

PING

The tank wobbled as it sank into the uneven surface of the campsite. Feighan was still shaking his head: *Did he really expect a Flinger to freeze?*

The sun was setting behind the ridge above them. Bands of red and purple streaked the sky. He wished he could Fling to the opposite crest, from which the view had to be magnificent, but pitching tents in darkness is a good way to smash a thumb or two. "Hey, Sam, give me a hand. We'll eat later."

The Rhanghan set down the aluminum foil bag he had opened. "That stuff is awful chewy, McGill."

"You have to add water. Here. Hold this pole."

The ring of mallet on metal peg echoed back and forth across the valley. "A most appealing sound," said H'nik. "In the morning you will meet K'rach'a, who will introduce you to one of our own Flingers, who will teach you the locations to which you will be Flinging our missionaries. I hope you and Sam sleep well. Until then—"

The sun dipped below the ridgetop and surrendered the valley to shadow.

H'nik began to scream.

· Chapter XI ·

Numb in body and soul, he sat at his desk, doodling on its glass with the oils of his fingertips. He had been told to await a phone call.

It terrified him to be owned. It sickened him. If he had been proud of anything in his life, it had been his independence. He had always been his own man, deciding for himself what was right and what he would do. Now he belonged to someone else. To a criminal.

It was all Feighan's fault for disobeying orders. Greystein's fault, too, of course, but Greystein had paid the price. Feighan had not. Feighan still owed him.

The phone rang. He shuddered, then steeled himself. "Yes?"

"Where is he?"

"We have reports of sightings in Hong Kong and Houston."

"But where is he now?"

"I—" He swallowed. "I don't know."

"Find out. Quickly."

"Yes, s—" But the connection had already been broken. Fear lay in his gut like lead. He wondered which other of his strings the puppeteer would be pulling.

It was Feighan's fault. Feighan would have to pay. For all of it.

▪ Chapter XII ▪

Feighan leaped to his feet. "What's wrong?"

The monk did not reply. It continued frantically to saw its spines, producing a noise both anguished and agonizing, like the sound of a violin being tortured by a small, resentful boy.

"H'nik! Jesus, what is it?"

Shivering, Sam pressed against the back of Feighan's legs, curling his tail around the Flinger's left ankle. He twisted his torso so he could slip his snout and neck under his guardian's right arm. "It's spooky, McGill—H'nik's not mad or afraid or anything—it's just . . . it's like it's crying but happy at the same time."

"Huh?"

"Yeah, H'nik's really happy about something—and I don't know what it is—but at the same time it's ancitipa-anpiti—" He hissed frustration.

"Anticipating?"

"Yeah, anticipating something else, something really awful, yecchy—but I don't know what that is, either."

Feighan hugged the child's shoulders. "At least it's not in trouble. How about giving me some room? My arms're hurting again." When Sam had untangled himself, he sank back into his cross-legged position. The night breeze riffled his hair, and the hazy air whipped the stars into dark cream. From the valley below—but not from higher up the ridge—came the hoarse wailing of a mournful, off-key chorus.

Sam lowered himself to the ground by Feighan's side. He breathed easier, and the muscles of his flanks had stopped trembling, but his tail still twitched spasmodically. "This is scary, McGill."

Feighan snorted. "It's irritating, is what it is—and I have the feeling it's just getting started."

As if in answer, new voices from the valley west of the ridge joined the dirge. Feighan sighed. Sam hissed, spat, and covered his ears with his hands.

He stroked his ward's skullbone. To the east, a line of pink showed behind the ragged hills. *It can't be morning already,* he thought.

Sam said, "How come the moon is red here, McGill?"

He winced, embarrassed that the young Rhanghan had understood what he had not. "It must be the dust in the air. I'm not all that sure how it works, but it does something to the light."

"Oh." Sam yawned. "When are they gonna shut up?"

"When they're done, I guess."

"But when will that be?"

"If I knew the answer to that, I'd be a lot happier than I am."

"You don't like it either, huh?"

"To put it mildly." It rasped on him like sandpaper on a bare belly. He tried to re-direct his thoughts, to ignore the caterwauling, but it was just too loud.

So he started listening to it, instead. Before too long he found in it a pattern, a rhythm almost. The husky cries rose and fell with a long slow beat that surged forward in gladness only to draw back in slow and deep dismay. He heard in the music a lamentation, a bewilderment held in check by a deep-rooted sureness, a constant reaffirmation that that for which the singer longed would surely come, would surely offer ease and surcease, even if it meant the long and terrible passage through the . . .

And now that he was listening, hearing—understanding!—his mind with its customary perverseness drifted away. It towed his thoughts from the harshness of Actu to all that he had left behind, and all that lay before. Greystein's still, pallid face floated before his eyes, and whispered accusations through cold, dead lips. Gina Maccari rolled over in bed, mumbled a sleepy endearment, and wrapped her strong right arm around him. Oscar called, "Wake up! Wake up!" The night brushed his cheek with dry, clean air, but it had the metallic tang of New York's on a late summer evening, with a hundred stories muting the machines on the street below, and—

H'nik fell silent.

Sam said, "Boy, it's about time," and crawled into the tent.

"H'nik," said Feighan, "what was that all about?"

The monk said nothing.

"H'nik?"

It loomed bristly and still, its spines cocked and apparently frozen.

"To hell with it. I'm going to bed myself."

But he had to lie on his back because his arm wounds ached, and that made him sleep poorly. He tossed and turned in the sleeping bag, snarling it around his legs until he had to get up and untwist it. Sharp pebbles jutted from the soil like broken glass from the top of a cement wall. No matter how many times he swept them away, a new one would break the soil to stab his shoulderblade. Stiffness set in before sleep did. In the morning, even breathing would hurt.

And all night long, H'nik's wails reverberated through his dreams. Dreams of exile. Of wandering. Of quake-torn lands and lava seas and scaly hands patting his cheek—

"Wake up, McGill!"

He blinked open his eyes. Dust immediately flew in, and his vision blurred. "Oh, God." He groaned as he lifted his head. "What do you want?"

"It's almost morning," said Sam with evident indignation. "And you have to go to work, remember?"

"With you around, I don't need to remember things like that—you do just fine without any help at all." Painfully, he pushed himself into a sitting position.

"Is that an insult?" The Rhanghan lowered his hindquarters to the ground and studied Feighan through the gloom of the tent.

"Not really . . ." Blinking and blinking again, he scraped at the corner of his eye and finally hooked the dust-mote under a fingernail. "I just had a bad night and I'm sort of grouchy. How'd you sleep?"

"Me, too! First all that noise, and then the ground was hard and it got chilly and there was a funny kind of bug I had to keep chasing out of the tent and then the noise again..." He shook his head mournfully.

"What noise?"

"That noise?"

Feighan tried to cup a hand around his ear, but his arm would not go that far that early. "I don't hear anything."

"It's real high, like the whistle Mrs. Estwund uses to call her dog."

"Oh." He yawned. "Ultrasonic, huh? No wonder I can't hear it."

"You really can't?"

"Really."

"You're lucky." Glancing at the tent flaps, he hissed. "There's that bug again."

An antennaed head about the size of Feighan's big toe slipped backwards through the flaps.

He shuddered. "Did you see the pincers on that thing?"

"Uh-huh. Didn't scare me, though."

"Only 'cause you've got thicker skin." Suddenly his arms felt good enough to pull his boots on. "Remind me to zip the flap shut tonight."

"But then it gets stuffy!"

"You want that thing back in here?"

"Uh...no, I guess not," said Sam resignedly. "But I can't sleep when it's stuffy."

"I have the funniest feeling that you're going to sleep real well—tonight, at least."

Sam's magenta tongue flickered out. "Maybe."

Feighan covered another yawn with his hand. "Let's go outside."

He pushed through the tent flaps, stepping carefully. A pebble clinked a few meters away, but it was too dark for him to see anything. The sky was paling, though. Overhead the stars were beginning to fade, and to the east swirled pre-dawn's milky-grey.

He stretched. His joints, tendons, and ligaments cracked and popped, sounding surprisingly loud in the quiet. Then Sam hissed.

"What is it?"

"You still can't hear it?"

"What?"

A wail wafted over from the eastern ridge. A rusty, grating noise, it filled the air and echoed off the hillside. After a moment, it doubled in volume. Then tripled.

"Oh, no!" Feighan had awakened to a number of unpleasantnesses in the past, but this . . . this ranked high on the list.

A nearby boulder offered itself as a stool. After first making sure that nothing had already claimed squatter's rights, he sat, drew up his leg, planted his elbow, and rested his chin on his hand.

"You look like that statue," said Sam. "Can I come up?"

"I suppose." He reached down, grabbed the Rhanghan's right hand, and pulled. His arm protested sharply. "Go on, get your front legs up, there's toeholds in the rock."

"Yeah, but they make my claws hurt."

"Well, I'm not going to lift you, so you'd better find 'em."

"You're no fun." With the scrape of ivory on basalt, Sam scrambled to his side. Tail scales made a soft susurrus against the rock. "Can you see better from up here?"

"It's only a meter higher."

"Hey, look, the sun! Oh wow! Look at H'nik!"

He lifted his head. Light as red as blood lanced through a notch in the distant mountains. It would have shone in his eyes, but H'nik stood in the way. He blinked—and smiled in surprised delight.

Dew beaded the spines of the Actuni, and the droplets broke each ray of light into a million tiny rainbows. They shimmered and glittered as the sun inched higher.

He held his breath, afraid that the slightest motion would shatter the scene. The screeching from the crest above seemed to soften as he focused on the jewel-hung figure before him. The wind stirred; he prayed it would not blow the magic away. Beside him, Sam gave a long, low hiss of rapture.

H'nik awoke. Its spines rippled like meadowgrass teased by a zephyr. The million tiny rainbows spun and shivered and—and died, as the monk twitched its spines to flick the dew onto his skin. It was like a dog shaking off water in reverse.

Feighan let his breath out wistfully.

Sam spat at the ground. "Aw, nuts."

"Well, you couldn't expect it to last forever."

"No, but—there's that bug again!" His tail flashed in the sun as he leaped off the boulder and bounded toward the insect. It was nearly the size of Feighan's hand, and its carapace glinted a dull blue-green. Its antennae drooped for an instant, then came to full attention. It skittered to its left.

Sam threw a pebble in its path.

Its dozens of armored legs milled as it spun, and scurried into the nearest shade: between H'nik's roots.

The monk dropped down.

Something crunched. Something else slurped. And H'nik wriggled its spines. "Thank you," it said. "A delightful way to begin the day. I am indebted to you for your thoughtfulness, young Sam. Brx'gn are rare delicacies to us, given their exasperating mobility. Good morning, McGill Feighan."

"Good morning. I take it your inner half is omnivorous?"

"Very." It rose. The ground beneath it was bare. "Are you ready to begin the day?"

Sliding off the boulder, Feighan brushed the dust from his hands. "Once we've had a little breakfast ourselves."

Two of H'nik's lower spines snapped together once, twice. "Something has just occurred to me, McGill Feighan."

"Yes?"

"If you will forgive a root in your bed—"

"Huh?"

"I do apologize; I transliterated one of our idioms. If you will forgive me, I meant to say, for intruding on what might be a private matter—?"

Feighan wanted to be cautious, but fatigue made his tongue clumsy. "It's hard to say in advance." *Damn, I didn't mean to sound rude.*

"Well, I—" The monk seemed flustered, but only momentarily. "I am aware that some of your Terran cultures have taboos about the subject I am about to mention, and I wish to assure you in advance that I have no intention of giving offense." It twisted 40° right, then 40° left, back and forth and back, so that one flankeye after the other could get a look at Feighan.

"Assurance taken," he said.

"We have very different metabolisms, McGill Feighan, and as I understand it, you need to eliminate your waste products rather more frequently than I do—and in rather greater bulk, as well."

He cleared his throat. "Ah . . . I really couldn't say."

"In many respects, Actu is a very poor world—we suffer the travails of too much sun and too little water—in consequence, our soil, though rich in minerals, magnificently aerated, and beautifully drained, is barely sufficient to permit life."

He gestured to the lush, clipped fields below. "But—"

"*That* soil results from centuries of close attention."

"Oh." Again he wished he could still call on Greystein's scientific expertise—his roommate had known something about almost everything, and could explain it well.

"You see, it needs organic matter between the particles of sand and silt and clay—organic matter to provide a home for our smallest cousins which, in dying, provide us with our nutrients. Organic matter to retain the infrequent rainfall. Organic matter to lighten it so that our roots might work through it more easily. We need this, McGill Feighan."

He made a face, and hoped at once that H'nik could not interpret it. "I, ah, I think I know where you're heading—at least I think I know what you're talking about—but what is it exactly you want me to do?"

"We would consider it a deep courtesy if you were to donate your waste products to the monastery."

He visualized himself and Sam, in suit and scale polish, solemnly proffering their "donation" to the monks. Though his nose twitched, he kept a straight face. But when a determinedly literal portion of his mind decided that such a donation had to be tax deductible, he giggled aloud.

Sam looked at him strangely.

Tilting its barrel a bit to one side, H'nik twiddled a dozen of its lower spines.

He nipped his tongue to sober himself up. "I'm sorry, H'nik—a private joke. Forgive me, and please, go on."

"I assure you that your gift would be put to good use—"

Pressing the bandage on his left biceps helped—some.

"—for the general public, and not for the private benefit of the clergy, as I understand was once the case in your Christian religion, and which, I understand, has left a lingering suspicion as to the actual altruism of the religious orders."

"I—" A cough into his hand concealed well enough his helpless grin. "I see no reason why we couldn't, ah, endow the monastery in the manner you have described—" Only the formal, stilted language kept him from total collapse. "—but I would appreciate your taking the time to explain a few of the details: for example, where you would like it delivered, how you would prefer it to be packaged, and how often we should, ah, ah—"

"Defecate?"

"Deliver," he said firmly.

"What's defecate mean?" said Sam.

"To make a BM."

"Why are you talking about *that?*" The Rhanghan looked from one to the other, and his expression accused them both of idiocy.

"The Actuni use it as a fertilizer."

"Can't they buy the chemical stuff we have at home?"

H'nik rustled its spines. "It is not the mineral enrichment which we require, young Sam; rather, we need the fibrous bulk as a soil conditioner."

Sam grimaced. "And you eat what grows in it?"

"We *are* what grows in it."

"Yecch."

Wincing, Feighan reacted as his training had taught him to. With a bow, he launched into the all-species speech every Flinger knew by rote: "From the depths of my heart I apologize. Sam has, unwittingly, given you offense. He did not intend to. Being alien to this world, he is ignorant of many of its customs. Pray forg—"

"It is quite all right, McGill Feighan. Even within a single species, the habits of one cultural grouping can profoundly disturb members of other groups; for example, it revolts the peakroots to see us eating lizards, bugs, and the like. The differences between species can be far more upsetting. I recall that when I visited Sam's mother many years ago, I found incomprehensible—even nauseating—her family's insistence on spending the winter sealed into a cave in a chalk cliff. Many weeks passed before I could consider that the act of an intelligent being."

Sam spoke up again. "She spends the whole winter indoors?"

"That is correct, young Sam."

"She doesn't go outside even once?"

"That is correct."

"Yecch." He flicked his tongue. "When we were there, it was summer."

H'nik shuffled around to face the valley. With the longest of its spines it pointed to the one patch of brown on the entire valley floor, some two klicks south of the monastery. "Do you see the line of faithful down there?"

The haze obscured all but the dominant colors. "No."

Sam hissed, and scurried into the tent.

H'nik said, "Were you to go there, you would find many hundreds of Actuni preparing to make their tithes. One simply gets in line—"

Sam returned with a pair of binoculars. "Here, McGill."

"Thanks." He pushed them against his eyes, then spun the knob. A long bristly line sprang into focus. One Actuni walked from the field to the head of the line, touched spines with the native there, then led it into the open ground. A hundred meters in, it stopped at a spot just beyond one that looked freshly tilled. *How do they plow?* thought Feighan. The second Actuni sank its roots deep. The spines banding its middle twirled aimlessly for a minute, then stopped. It rocked back and forth, and its roots reappeared, bringing subsoil with them, It rose, and departed in the general direction of the monastery.

Feighan scanned the line. It stretched for perhaps a kilometer. "Are they all, ah, waiting to make a donation?"

"To tithe," said H'nik, "though of course we do not use that word, nor is the percentage the same, but the concept is similar enough. They are—again I must use one of your words that only approximates our concept—they are communicants, adherents. The faithful do not donate, for the faithful know what they owe."

"So we're supposed to go down and get in line and wait our turn?" The thought made him queasy for a number of reasons. Not the least of which was that the second being in line was only now moving into the field.

"If you would be so kind."

"H'nik, I have a feeling you don't understand our metabolism quite as well as you might think you do. Those, ah, people at the head of the line must have been waiting a day or so—"

"Perhaps a bit longer."

He spread his arms. "We can't, ah, see, we need to ah, relieve ourselves several times a day, and ah—"

"You seem uncomfortable discussing this topic. Is it taboo after all? For if it is, I do not wish to cause you embarrassment or unpleasantness—"

"Well, it's just not something we usually talk about in public, if you know what I mean...I'll tell you what. What if we, ah, collect it all in say a paper bag—"

"McGill!" All four pair of Sam's eyelids popped as wide as they could open.

"—and I just Fling it down? The bags, of course, are bio-degradable also...it would probably make things easier all around, wouldn't you say?"

One of H'nik's forward roots curled around a stone, and with that scratched the rocky soil of the terrace. Then it said, "Yes, that would be agreeable, if you are willing to sacrifice the grace."

"The grace?"

"Again an approximation, deeply though I regret the necessity of resorting to words that fail to communicate fully the concepts they are intended to express. You see, to tithe—to donate—before every eye is to prove to the world at large that you are accepting God's will, that you are suffering as you were intended to suffer. Theologically speaking, one acquires more grace by announcing one's willing acceptance of suffering than one acquires merely by accepting suffering willingly...but I digress. The stones already speak back to the sun. There is work to be done. If you would be so kind as to take us to the monastery—"

PING

They stood on the lip of the gravel-lined hollow; down below, a clump of six monks listened to a seventh address them in ear-aching tones. Quietly, H'nik said, "When the Abbot has finished, I will introduce you to—" It gargled, clicked glottally, and hummed. Then it clacked two dorsal spines, which sounded remarkably like "tsk-tsk." "It would probably be easier for you to call it K'rach'a."

The native pronunciation felt like a regurgitated fishhook to his throat, and even he could hear that his accent was atrocious. For this language he needed the synthesizer Greystein had built into Oscar.

Sam, however, who had cocked his head and listened sharply, repeated the name guttural for guttural, up to and including the "tsk-tsk."

"That is very good, Sam," said H'nik, "but those two final sounds were an expression of exasperation, not part of K'rach'a's name."

"I was wondering about that, but I couldn't tell."

In the hollow below, the Abbot still spoke. In its upper torso, a flame-orange flower blossomed. Feighan took the opportunity to ask, "Last night, right after sundown—and again this morning, right before sunrise—you were all, ah—"

"Praying. You did not hear the warning call to prayer, perhaps because human hearing is not overly keen, but as the sun approaches the far horizon, a cry of joy springs from the faithful in the land newly dark. It warns the faithful in twilight that our moment to praise is almost upon us."

"Okay," said Feighan dubiously. "But what about this morning?"

H'nik stepped back a pace. "You will learn more as your stay lengthens." Its voice rasped more harshly than usual. "The Abbot is finished, so let me introduce you to K'rach'a."

Six monks came clambering out of the hollow, each headed in a different direction. One hobbled directly for the trio, calling, "Good sun, H'nik! And wasn't that a lovely dew today?"

"Good sun, K'rach'a. Allow me to introduce you to McGill Feighan and his ward Sam, the Terran-speakers to whom I have assigned you as interpreters."

"Feighan McGill, how nice to meet you!"

H'nik scraped something in their own tongue.

K'rach'a said, "I apologize; I had thought McGill to be a surname."

"Quite all right," said Feighan. "Apparently everyone does."

K'rach'a was a few centimeters taller than H'nik, but much thinner. Most of its gnarled roots were short, stout, and splintery on the ends; from one or two dripped glittering sap. Wrinkles radiated from its top, running so deep it looked shriveled. It seemed to be aware that Feighan was studying it, for it said, "It was that flipping earthquake last month that did this to me—"

H'nik sawed on its spines.

"Don't be rude," said K'rach'a. "Speak English."

H'nik clacked those two dorsal spines. "It sounds as though you are lamenting your suffering, rather than accepting it."

"That's moonwind, H'nik, and you know it. I was just explaining to Feighan here—"

"His given name is McGill."

"Of course his given name is McGill, but his surname is Feighan. By damn, I didn't spend twenty years in London and five in Los Angeles for nothing! Adult Terran males from

English-speaking cultures tend to call each other by their surnames—right?" It aimed its central ocular aureole straight at the Flinger.

He shrugged. "Either way; your choice."

"Thank you. I was just explaining to Feighan, here, H'nik, why I'm bald on bottom and flabby on top—sort of the reverse of the Terran aging process, eh Feighan?—because he was staring at my stumps." It rocked backward, raised one of its roots, and wriggled it. "I was sunk pretty deep when the quake hit—matted out, in fact—and I just couldn't get free in time."

Sam ambled over to inspect the mutilated roots. "Can you still walk?"

"Oh, sure, I manage to limp around just fine. The real problem is that I can't root right these days—no, H'nik, that's not a lamentation, just a statement of fact; I accept my suffering joyously because to be an Actuni is to suffer; it is our station in life—" It turned its attention back to Sam. "You probably won't believe this, but before the quake I was twice H'nik's size."

The other monk clacked its dorsal spines.

"Oh, all right. I'm exaggerating again—you'll have to watch for that in me, Feighan; I have a horrible tendency to hyperbolize everything—but I had at least a long spine on you in girth, and a short spine in height, yes?"

"What happened?" said Sam.

"With my roots torn up, I can't sink as deep as I used to, which means I sorta get by on dew. And let me tell you, it's tasty stuff, but there's just not enough of it. Even a good rain wouldn't help 'cause I can't spread far enough, either."

H'nik made a clucking sound. "The day brightens; I must leave you. K'rach'a—" It clattered into their own language for a few moments. "McGill Feighan, Sam, I will visit with you at the end of the day." Then it turned about, and trundled down the slopes of the hollow.

K'rach'a waited till H'nik was well out of earshot. "That monk is one hell of a theologian—did I get that idiom right?— but it is also the most touchy, peremptory, grouchy bastard in town. Well, let's get a move on before it comes back and chews me out again." It shifted awkwardly about until it faced the western mountains. "I'm supposed to escort you to the Flinger Building, so let's go."

The trail was bare and rocky. Once it left the valley floor, it wound up terrace after terrace—always fully exposed to the glare of the sun. Feighan looked at it with distaste. "Ah, K'rach'a, why don't I just Fling us there?"

"You know the way?" it asked with apparent surprise.

"It's where I arrived yesterday."

"Well, hot damn! I have to admit—"

PING

"—I wasn't looking forward to cooking this new growth of mine on that frying pan of a pathway." It did a small dance and spin. "Are we here already? That is such a fine skill you have, Feighan! It must make you just about the happiest guy in town, eh?"

He touched the welt Greystein's pebble had left on his neck, and he grimaced. "It has its drawbacks."

"Yeah? Well—come on, down this hall." Its roots made a broomlike noise on the tile floor. The fluorescents cast a purple-tinged light that sallowed the green of its skin. "Drawbacks, eh? I do seem to recall hearing that you're here because of something that went wrong back home—nothing serious, I hope?"

Sam caught Feighan's eye before the Flinger could open his mouth; the Rhanghan gave a small shake of his snout.

Feighan frowned. *What's up?* K'rach'a came on friendly enough—but Sam did have a track record. So he shrugged, and said lightly, "Oh, a small contretemps with, ah, the father of a young lady of my acquaintance."

"Huh?"

"I'm sorry." He hoped Sam never repeated that to Gina Maccari—she might not understand. "Contretemps means—"

"I know what it means," K'rach'a's tone sounded gruff. Feighan could not decide if that were a reflection of its feelings, or an effect of the echoes in the corridor. "What I don't get is—oh, ho! My mistake. I forgot that you Terrans breed, not bud."

It was Feighan's turn to be confused. "Don't you?"

"Us? Hell, no. No knocked-up women around here."

"Then, how do you, ah—"

"Well, we don't!" They rounded a corner; before them lay a row of doors leading to the Fling Booths. "Unless one of us taps down, in which case the death root buds a month or two later."

One of the doors opened. A short, very stout Actuni emerged. It wore an energy tunic similar to Feighan's; the bands of light wove in, around, and through its bristles. It said something to K'rach'a, who replied in their language.

Feighan glanced over at Sam, who was picking at a loose scale. Everything was okay, then.

K'rach'a said, "This here is Ghu'h'o, who's going to take us to all the points on the planet that you're supposed to learn. Later on, you'll be Flinging our missionaries to the points."

The Actuni Flinger spoke again.

K'rach'a said, "Whoops! Slight change in plans, folks—Ghu'h'o says it's pretty worn out today. Just came off its second shift, I guess. Anyway, you're only going to see three points today—"

With a quick rasping, the Flinger interrupted.

Again K'rach'a translated. "The thing is, Feighan, Ghu'h'o isn't going to go with us, so it'll be up to you to get us back from the places it Flings us to—is there going to be any problem with that?"

The building quivered slightly; dust puffed off the walls. Feighan held his breath till the tremor passed, then sighed. "I don't think I'll have any trouble remembering this place."

"Good, good! I guess we're supposed to get into the Booth here, so—" It shuffled backward, clearing a lane for Feighan and Sam to pass in front of it.

Feighan was uneasy about allowing another to Fling him— it was something he had not permitted since his high school days at the Flinger Academy. It was more than just pride or independence; it was, rather, that his Talent reacted to the use of another's Talent anywhere in his immediate vicinity. And the last time he had felt that reaction was when he had followed Greystein. It was too soon to be reminded of that.

K'rach'a said, "Our first stop will be at—"

PING

A roar filled the air, and a stink of sulphur gushed over them. They stood a hundred meters from an erupting geyser.

"—Yellow Springs. Oh, we're here already." Gingerly, it pivoted, seemingly oblivious to the clouds of reeking steam that billowed past.

Feighan coughed and rubbed his eyes. Sam had all his eyelids shut, and his nostrils were puckered, too. He had clamped his jaws so tightly that the muscles along his snout bulged; it was clear he did not want to whip his magenta tongue through that air.

K'rach'a loomed over them. "Are you two all right?"

The mist began to clear. Feighan took out his handkerchief to wipe his eyes. "I feel like I've been gassed."

"Really? I am sorry. This is one of our health spas, you see—we come here for the air—I didn't know it would bother you." It shuffled back and forth; the spines on its upper barrel made a lullaby sort of hum. "It won't blow again for another thirty or forty minutes, but if you need to get out—"

"No." The hot breeze was thinning the fumes. "No, we should be okay in a couple of minutes." His throat hurt. "So this is the monastery's health spa, huh?"

"No, it's the people's, not the monastery's—in fact, monks are expressly forbidden to come here except when they get lucky enough to get sent here as missionaries—or as guides for visiting dignitaries."

"Yeah? Well, why—"

"Do we send missionaries here? Believe it or not, there's a lot of ground water in this area, and there must be, oh, five hundred thousand of us—Actuni, not monks—living within a couple hundred of your kilometers from here. I know that's not much by your standards, I remember in London they had a hundred thousand people in a *building*, but you know, we don't get much rain here, so our population density's pretty low. And that's why we send missionaries here."

Eyes finally clear, Feighan looked around. They stood in the bottom of a depression ringed by rugged hills that rolled back into the haze; saucer shaped, the depression had to measure ten kilometers in diameter. "So the missionaries Flop here and spread out in all directions, right?"

"No, we're not allowed to sleep within three of your kilometers of Yellow Springs."

Feighan scratched his head, then understood. "When a Flinger says, 'Flop,' he means to arrive in a place after having been teleported. I didn't mean sleep."

"I am sorry. The idioms you English-speakers have come up with are enough to drive us aliens to total distraction . . . and you know, I've gotten half of them out of books—"

"I thought you couldn't read," said Sam.

"Oh, we can read perfectly well, if we let the page sit in

the sun for a while. It's sort of a strange skill, but we can learn it. What we just can't do is write—it's not easy to hold a pen with one of these spines. But like I was saying, I picked up my idiomatic English from books, and I'll be damned if I can figure out whether or not any of it's contemporary. I mean, do you guys still use 'flop' as a synonym for sleep?"

"Not really. Maybe some people do, but I've never heard it in conversation—the only reason I knew what you meant was that I've read some old books myself. So what I asked was, your missionaries arrive here, and—"

"Head for the hills."

Feighan winced.

K'rach'a drooped its spines. "Wrong again, huh?"

"Uh-huh."

"Damn it," it said crisply. "Very well, then. They arrive and disperse among the farmers in the outlying districts. Some take up residence along the highways—"

Feighan raised an eyebrow.

"To us, Feighan, a highway is a path five or ten meters wide, smoothly graded, and free of rocks with sharp edges."

"Now I'm sorry." He wished he had not given vent to even that little sarcasm. Aliens could be touchy when they detected sneers. "Please, go on."

"As I was saying, some take up residence along the—" It did a quick jig. "Along the caravan routes, all right? They proselytize among those coming to the spa: the vacationers, the ailing, the tradesmen. This is a place of overweening materialism, Feighan, and it is in such a place that one must remind the people of their debt to God. At least that's what the Abbot says."

Feighan looked around again, then bent one knee so he could scratch the soil surface and rub its grit between his fingers. He sniffed the air, still tainted with sulphur, and closed his eyes, slipping into a quasi-trance that held just long enough for his subconscious to memorize the location. Then he blinked. He "knew" Yellow Springs, now, knew it in a way only a fellow Flinger could—and when it came time to teleport a missionary to that spot, he would have no trouble. "Okay. I'm done. Shall we go back?"

K'rach'a's spines made a sound like a sigh. "I picked that up in London. Sound Terran enough?"

"Were you trying to suggest wistfulness?"

"Precisely."

"You got it, then. Let's go." He stood, and—

PING

—brought them back to the Flinger Building, where Ghu'h'o waited in the corridor. It snapped its spines loudly.

K'rach'a said, "It's a litle p-o'd at us for taking so long."

"Explain about the geyser and what it did to us."

"Ghu'h'o understands English—just can't speak it, that's all."

Feighan turned to his native colleague. "I'm very sorry about the delay. We arrived just as the geyser was erupting, and the sulphur, ah, sort of incapacitated Sam and me. It took us a few minutes to recover."

Ghu'h'o spoke at great length, pacing up and down with its bristles waving.

K'rach'a said, "It's really ticked that I didn't know the air at the springs would be hazardous to your health."

On the Actuni's far side, Sam nodded.

K'rach'a continued. "It says, even though I didn't know you guys didn't like to breathe that stuff, I shouldn't have taken any chances—I should have timed things so that we got there long after the geyser blew."

Sam nodded again.

"But honest, Feighan, I didn't know—and I didn't even stop to think that maybe the timing on that would have been better. I mean, if you took me to, say, Calcutta, you wouldn't stop to wonder if it were monsoon season and what effect that would have on me, now, would you?"

Sam hunched forward. Eyes slitted, he wagged his snout slowly, slightly, from side to side.

Feighan thought, *What's going on here? Sam thinks K'rach'a did do it maliciously, but why? Soon as I get a chance, I better find out . . .* "These things happen, and it didn't do any serious harm, so let's not worry about it. Ghu'h'o—"

The Actuni Flinger literally jumped up and down, rasping its spines so loudly that both Feighan and Sam stepped back. Feighan would have covered his ears, but to do so would give offense. So he tried to maintain an expression of polite interest until the other had finished. It was difficult.

K'rach'a said, "As I think you can see, Ghu'h'o's angry—it feels its reputation's been besmirched; that it has, uh, what's the phrase? Lost face?"

Feighan said, "No, Ghu'h'o, really—it was a perfect Fling,

and it's not your fault we Flopped just as the geyser was going off. We don't blame you in the least." As he finished, he wondered which represented the Actuni norm: imperturbable H'nik, or temperamental Ghu'h'o. He hoped the Flinger was atypical—he really did not want to spend all his time on the planet smoothing ruffled spines.

But Ghu'h'o had apparently been placated, for it turned and strode back to its room. Before it closed the door, it snapped something at K'rach'a.

"Time for the second locale, guys." It led the way into the Fling Booth. The door whispered shut behind them; Feighan's boots crunched gravel on the tiles. "This time we're going to the badlands—"

"Aren't we there already?" hissed Sam, a shade too loudly.

K'rach'a's spines stiffened; it seemed to swell before their eyes. It gave a hum, high and ominous—

PING

—then rocked its top as a Saharan landscape materialized around them. The hum quieted. Its spines relaxed. "I hadn't noticed the transition," it said to Sam. "I'm sorry I got mad."

Feighan shot his ward a single warning glance.

Sam, doing his best to look innocent, scratched the middle of his back with the tip of his tail.

A rock landed at their feet, kicking up dust.

Feighan spun, scanning the horizon for whatever had hurled the head-sized stone at them. *Catapult? Some kind of bi-i-ig shot-putter?* The sun burned grainy brown sand, boulders softened by years of abrasive wind, and nothing else. "K'rach'a, are we under attack, or what?"

"Naw. Tell me, Feighan, why do you Terrans think everybody's out to get you? Seems like anytime something happens around a Terran, the first thing he says is, who's got it in for me? A little paranoia's a healthy thing, but as a species, you people take it too far."

Thinking, *Even a paranoid can have enemies—look at poor Greystein,* he said, "Then what the hell is this?" He kicked the rock. It was warm. Fifty meters away, sand fountained as a small boulder thumped into the side of a dune. "And that? What is it, who did it?"

"These are the badlands, Feighan." It hobbled through a pivot until it faced in the opposite direction. "See that smudge on the horizon?"

"Clouds?"

"Mountains."

"That was my second guess."

"More accurately, volcanoes. There's a line of them, running north and south for a couple thousand of your kilometers. It's more a belt than a line, and the belt's about five hundred kilometers wide."

Feighan walked over to a basalt outcropping and sat on its smooth top. Sam stretched out in the sand like a sunbather. "Okay, fine, you've got a lot of volcanoes over there—what does that have to do with this bombardment?"

K'rach'a waddled up to him. "The volcanoes are doing it."

"What?" He squinted, but the dark line on the horizon would not resolve into separate peaks. The Rockies looked that way from Kansas... "Those have to be hundreds of kilometers away."

"They are—but they're tall. Very tall. And there's a what-doyoucallit, a jet stream, up above them. It goes from west to east. If one of those cones spits a rock in this direction, the wind carries it a little farther than it would have gone on its own. It's awful damn rare for two of 'em to hit so close together, but it's what the badlands are all about. Dig around here and you'll turn up rock after rock after rock, all of them from those cones."

"Then why in the world do you want to Fling missionaries here?" Even as he spoke, he kept an anxious eye on the sky. He wondered if, did he see a chunk of hot rock rainbowing toward him, he would have time to get out of its way. He rather thought not. He squirmed.

K'rach'a waggled its long spine in a westerly direction. "About a hundred kilometers that way is some of the finest farming land on this planet. It's another belt, parallel to the cone belt, and it's a hundred, two hundred kilometers wide itself. See, the cones leak ash all the time, and that gives the water vapor in the air something to condense around, and so it rains—not like London, of course; in fact, there isn't a place on this planet as wet as Los Angeles, even—but then, the stuff we grow doesn't need very much water. And the ash really enriches the soil."

Feighan shook his head. Actu was *insane*. "If that's the case, then why Fling missionaries *here* instead of a hundred kilometers to the west?"

"It's half politics, and half theology." It burrowed a root

into the sand to raise a ridge, down the sides of which slid the sparkling grains. "See, the farmers have this thing about strangers just sort of showing up and dropping root—they're pretty possessive about their land. In fact, after the FNC brought us into the Network, the farmers spread the word that any Flinger—any Actuni Flinger—who showed up on their land would have its roots chewed off. If you walk in, though, they're a little more hospitable."

That made as much sense as anything did. "So what's the theological part?"

It rasped a few spines in random noise. Then it said, "Mortification."

"Pardon?"

"A missionary can't go straight into the goodlands! It has to suffer, first. It has to understand our role in life. So it has to walk."

A pebble hit centimeters from Sam, splashing dust onto his snout. He opened one eye wearily, studied the pebble, then let his eyelid slide closed. "McGill—" His voice verged on a whine. "—can we go home now?"

"You really did sleep bad, huh kid? Hold on a minute." Squatting, he sifted a handful of dirt through his fingers. His eyes blurred out of focus. While the wind rushed past, he sniffed at its dark, smoky undercurrents. Then he stood. "Okay."

PING

Sand spilled off K'rach'a's roots onto the white tiles of the Flop Booth floor. Ghu'h'o was in its room, behind the plate glass window. It shook a spine at them.

"Feighan, you wouldn't believe what a rotten temper that Ghu'h'o has," said K'rach'a. "Do you know what it's threatening to do?"

"I don't speak Actuni." Holding open the door to the Fling Booth, he motioned Sam in, and waited for the monk.

"He said if we'd taken a minute longer, he would have Flung me into the middle of your Atlantic Ocean."

Sam's tail swished restlessly. "And I'll bet you can't swim, either, huh?"

"No."

"So you'd *drown!*" His eyes were very wide.

"No, I'd bob like a cork."

"Well, then, why—"

"And then I'd rot from too much water."

"Oh."

"Just between you and me, Sam, I'd rather drown—it hurts to rot. First thing goes is your spines; they just fall off. So you're all bald, and then you shrivel a little 'cause your veins have shut down, then you go soft and puffy—sorta squishy— when the rot sets in. No, I'd really rather be able to drown."

Behind the plate glass window, Ghu'h'o's spines quivered. Its energy tunic dimmed almost to invisibility, held steady for a second, then flared—"

PING

The breath torn from his mouth condensed into a puff of white that the wind promptly shredded. He stood knee-deep in snow; Sam, neck-deep. The sky above was purple, and the air was damn thin. Gasping, he hugged himself. "K'rach'a! What the hell is this?" To shout made him pant for oxygen.

"The Crown of Actu." The monk scraped harder to speak louder. "It is the highest mountain on the planet."

Already the cold had seeped into him; his teeth chattered and he bounced up and down. In this place he did not need to stoop, to scratch, to sniff—this place had already sunk into his bones.

PING

The Flinger Building was an oven, and he was glad to be in it. Beside him, Sam shivered. K'rach'a said, "You didn't want to look around?"

"No. Why ever do you send missionaries up there?"

"You have a saying, 'All roads lead to Rome.' On Actu, all roads lead to the Crown."

"To the peak?"

"Well, no. To the base, actually, which is something of a high plateau."

"Then why not Fling to the base—or is it more mortification?"

The monk seemed amused. "More politics. Or actually, self-preservation."

Sam looked from one to the other, nodding slightly.

Feighan said, "Self-preservation?"

"The mountain folk are a hostile, suspicious people, especially—well, never mind about that. To put it very simply, if you don't approach them by coming down from the Crown, the peakroots'll trigger your tap."

"But why?" said Sam.

The monk's roots ground slowly against the tiles, as if straining to push through them. "It's a very long story, Sam, and to understand it you have to know a lot more about our physiology, our theology, our agriculture, and a whole lot of other things. Okay? After you've been here a while, after you've gotten to know us better, then I'll try to explain."

"All right." The Rhanghan's tail rose, to swing from side to side in steady, measured beats.

That alarmed Feighan. "Sam!"

He did not take his eyes off the native. "What, McGill?"

"No."

"But—"

"No."

K'rach'a said, "Is something wrong?"

Sam hissed at the same instant Feighan said, "No."

The monk backed away, did a stutter step on its lumpy roots, and spun around to face the door. "Then let's go."

Feighan let it get into the corridor before he dropped to his knees. He rested his hand on Sam's lower back. "What's wrong, kid?"

"I don't know." He still stared out the doorway.

"You were ready to attack."

"I know," he said miserably, "and I don't know why."

"Is K'rach'a planning to hurt us?"

"No, but—" He snapped his jaws shut.

"But what?"

"It'll sound silly."

"That's okay."

"It wants to eat us." The words out, Sam hung his head in embarrassment.

Feighan rocked back on his haunches. "What?"

Sam glared. "If you laugh at me I'll hate you."

He spread his hands. "No. I promise. I won't laugh. But— I mean—K'rach'a wants to eat us?"

"No."

"But you just said—"

"*It* wants to eat us. Not K'rach'a. The other one. Inside." He made vague stuffing motions with his hands.

"You mean its symbiote?"

"Whatever you call it. K'rach'a's our friend—sort of. I mean, it's not, really, but it doesn't want to hurt us. The symbio, though—"

"Symbiote."

"Symbiote. It's hungry. For us."

He did not know what to make of a guide/translator whose inner half wanted to make a meal of its outer half's responsibility. "Are we in danger?"

"Sometimes," Sam said thoughtfully. "I can feel it. And then . . . we're not."

Feighan looked at him skeptically. He wondered how much of what Sam felt was the truth, and how much sprang from the child's undoubtedly fertile imagination.

"I told you it'd sound silly, but it's all true."

"Hey, I believe you, kid. It's just . . . it's just I wish I knew how you did it. I mean, you're not a Minder . . . you're not, are you?"

"Uh-uh. I can't hear thoughts like Gina can."

"But the instant anybody plans to hurt us—"

"Then I hear it. But not before. And I don't hear like words or anything—I just sort of know."

"Well—" He stroked his ward's skullbone, scratching the spot behind the ears that Sam preferred. "I'm glad you're with me, and if you hear—"

"Hey, Feighan!" The raspy voice came from the corridor. "You're late for work."

The Flinger rose. Physically he was exhausted and in pain, but his Talent had lain on the shelf for the past couple of days, and it wanted to be used. For a moment he felt as two-minded as K'rach'a: half of him yearned for a cool, shady place to nap in; the other half needed a seat in the booth of echoes and tiles, there to expend its energy with one sure Fling after another. He smoothed back his hair and shouted. "I'm coming." To Sam he said, "Let's go."

The Rhanghan followed obediently, but at the door said, "Later—not now, but in a while—ask K'rach'a about the long spine."

"Huh?" Ahead, the monk motioned for him to hurry up.

"Just ask him."

"All right." Five paces down the hallway, a door opened into an empty Flinger Room. Ghu'h'o had left already; the only being inside was K'rach'a. Feighan looked around for a chair.

"I took your pot—figured you wouldn't have much use for it—you mind?"

The terra cotta container, a meter high and wide, was filled to within five centimeters of the top. He could have perched on its rim, but that would have gotten very uncomfortable very quickly. "Uh-uh." He waved a hand. "It's all yours."

"Good soil in here. You Flingers do all right by yourselves." Its roots squirmed around in the rich black loam, stirring it as they spread, releasing its leaf-mold fragrance. "This stuff's imported all the way from Rii—edsch; nothing like it anywhere here."

"Is there a chair around?"

"Uh . . . no, no, can't say as there is." It riffled its bristles. "We don't sit much, you see."

"Uh-huh." He sighed, and made a mental note to pick up a chair the next time he went home for water. Or sooner, if standing by the observation window grew as tiring as he figured it would. He walked over to the glass.

Down below, in the Fling Booth, half a dozen Actuni stood spine to spine in the exact middle of the room. They did not move or speak.

"Where's this group going?"

"The Crown."

Feighan glanced at his console. It looked like the sort of machine Greystein used to build—only more so. "That should be displayed here somewhere."

"It is."

"Where?" He frowned at the panel. Most were standard issue, distributed by the Flinger Network Control, but he had never seen this model before. Of course, the standard issue was designed for use on worlds whose dominant species had hands . . . "I can't make heads or tails of this board."

"It's the fourth light from the right."

"This purple one?" He tapped it.

"Purple, huh? But yeah, that's the one. It's the infrared pattern we associate with the Crown."

"Right." As he scanned the board, his frown twisted into a scowl. "Where's the weight read-out?"

"Right next to it, the third from the right."

"But it's dark! Is it broken?"

"Dark! It's—I keep forgetting. You guys can't see into the infrared. Obviously, I'm going to have to hang around and read these for you. Tsk-tsk, poor me. It says, uh, wait a minute, let me work this out—" It fell silent for a long moment; one patch of spines twitched from its normal position to point at the ceiling, then twitched again to aim at the floor. "Okay, it's nine hundred four kilograms. I think."

"You mass about one fifty, huh?" Feighan turned back to the window.

"On average. Me, I'm down to about a hundred these days—"

"Can you tell them we're ready up here?"

"Sure." It scraped out a long, wavering note. Each member of the party repeated it. "They're ready, too."

A shudder ran down Sam's vertebral fins; he whispered, "Are they going to do that *every* time?"

He shrugged, then closed his eyes so he could concentrate on the group, and visualize that icy peak, and feel the first on the second, and then he knew how to put the one onto the other, and—

PING

—the missionaries vanished.

Feighan leaned forward. The glass of the window cooled his forehead. "Five minutes and we'll do the next."

K'rach'a sawed out a series of different notes. The door below opened; another batch of missionaries began to file in.

"Something I wanted to ask," said Feighan.

"Yes?"

"Your long spine—it looks different from the rest, and you don't seem to use it the way you use the others."

"We don't. We point with it, of course, but the only other thing we use it for is to trigger taps." The monk shifted around in the pot, spilling dirt over the rim. "That means to kill somebody."

Feighan's jaw dropped. "To kill?"

"Yeah, didn't you know? It's not permanent; they always bud up from the death root, but it's as close as we can get."

He studied it with new respect. "You use it like a lance?"

"Sort of. But it's got a high metal content—copper, mostly—and it's hooked to our brain case for the tap shot."

"Uh . . . what's a tap shot?"

"You didn't know about that, either, huh? See, our brain cases function a little like your—hell, they are like your storage batteries. We can deliver a pretty good jolt if we want to. But the tap shot is when you poke your long spine through the other guy's eye and brain till you make contact with the far side of its brain case—at which point you throw the switch and short the sucker out. Takes a good long time to line yourself up for it, but boy, it's over in a second."

"And you don't short yourself out?"

"Nah. Your spine fuses to the other guy's brain case, though, and you've got to rip it off before you can break away from the corpse. It takes forever for it to grow back, too, and even then it usually regenerates in a different place."

Six more monks had clumped in the middle of the Fling Booth floor. One stood at the center; five surrounded it. Their bristles interlocked: except for their long spines, which they swiveled up into the Actuni equivalent of "right shoulder arms."

Feighan said, "Where to this time?" The display panel glowed rust orange.

"The badlands."

"Are they ready?"

"Let me ask."

Sam covered his ears immediately. Feighan wished he could do the same.

"Squaw-wa-wa-wa-wriiiiiiik!"

The monks returned the cry.

Feighan was only too glad to send them on their way.

He made forty-six more Flings before K'rach'a called a halt.

"I can do more," he said. His body was ready to quit, but his Talent was just getting warmed up. Over the years, it had gotten used to ninety-six Flings a day. Fifty-one was nothing.

"Ah, but night's coming on. Why don't you take us back to your campsite?"

PING

The tent lay in shadow, though sunlight still bathed the top terrace on the eastern slope. Sam headed straight for the water tank, and Feighan said, "Pour me a glass, too."

"In a minute." The Rhanghan paused, and cocked an ear. "Oh, no!"

"What?"

"They're at it again!"

"Every night," said K'rach'a. Hobbling about, it faced the east. As the last band of gold slivered off the opposite peaks, it, too, began to screech.

"I think I brought some cotton," said Feighan. "In the first aid kit. You want to get it?"

"Will it help?"

"It's got to cut the racket some."

Wisps of cotton protruding from their ears, they cooked dinner over the camp stove and tried not to shudder as the litany wore on. "Jesus," said Feighan. "It's like gears with broken teeth."

"Claws on a bathtub," said Sam mournfully. "I don't like the sound when *I* make it, but when somebody else does—"

"Maybe tomorrow I'll Fling home. I need a chair, and I can pick up some ear plugs at the same time."

"I'll love you forever if you do, McGill."

At least K'rach'a did not fall asleep right afterwards. It explained to them that the litany actually went on all day. "In fact, our history roots eighteen thousand years back, to the Great Drought, and in all that time the liturgy has not stopped once."

"But everybody quieted down."

"You see, as Actu spins on its axis, two groups begin praying—those who enter night, and those who enter day." Its spines quivered, then, and its long spine snapped into the locked position. Then it relaxed. "The theologians argue about which time is better for prayer, but the important part is that we do pray. When the prayers stop, the world ends." It made the sinewave rasp that Feighan had begun to associate with thought. "Well, that's what the Holy says, at least, but Holy's eighteen thousand years old. Today, thanks to Network science, we know better."

Feighan smiled into the darkness. With a trace of condescension, he said, "I would hope so."

"Today," said K'rach'a, "we know that if we stop praying, the entire universe will end."

"Ah..." The Flinger closed his mouth before something regrettable slipped out.

"My— I guess you'd call it my 'faction,' but that has political connotations that don't really jibe with our situation— my faction believes you ought to pray at dusk, and at least three times during the day. The other faction says you pray at dawn, and at least three times during the night. But what do they know? They're all mountain trash."

Sam gave a small snore, and Feighan yawned. "K'rach'a,

it's getting late; we should sleep." He picked up Sam and walked to the tent.

"Of course, of course, go right ahead. And if you don't mind, I'll just stick around—it's sort of hard for me to walk, you know."

Feighan was about to mumble a sleepy, "Sure, go ahead," but Sam stiffened in his arms. The Flinger came wide awake. "Oh, hey, no need! I'll Fling you back to the monastery." And before the monk could protest, he had done just that.

Sam relaxed.

"Was it hungry again, kid?"

"It was thinking about it. You want to put me down? I can make it on my own four feet."

"Just so long as you get the flap." In minutes he was asleep, wounds, night-prayers, and all.

In the morning he picked up K'rach'a, and Flung all three of them to the Flinger Building. Once again he teleported squat squads of chanting Actuni to the various reference points K'rach'a read off the display for him.

After forty-eight Flings, they knocked off for lunch, and wandered out onto the Building's patio, which overlooked a short, narrow valley with farms in the bottomland. K'rach'a settled itself in the sun. Feighan and Sam poured metallic canteen water into packs of freeze-dried stew. Sam said, "Yecch."

"Would you rather go hungry?"

Sam eyed the aluminized pouch with disfavor. "I don't *think* so."

Secretly, Feighan agreed . . . but they had a case of the stuff left, and would just have to put up with it for at least that much longer.

After lunch, Sam prowled the patio, peering over the cliff edge down into the valley. "Hey, K'rach'a. How come those guys over there haven't moved in a long time?" He pointed to a line of closely spaced Actuni which looped around a field of berry bushes.

"'Cause they're guarding the field."

"How come they're not moving, though?"

"Because they rooted themselves."

"I thought you all did," said Feighan, "all the time."

"Ah, but you've got two ways to do it: you can send out these—" It rocked backward to lift a root. "—quite a ways. They spread quick, and ingather quicker. But you can also mat out—that means you sprout fibrous hairs from these main roots, and the hairs grow and grow until they get so interwoven that you can't tell another guy's root from its bed. Fences and library monks mat out." It gave a long, low scrape: the sound of sadness. "And that's dangerous—you can't escape the soil so easily."

"Weren't you a library monk?" asked Sam.

"Until the earthquake. It's a great life—you think slowly, but oh so deeply . . ."

"But what do you do all day?"

"Oh, we sing the Holy—both as a focus for our own meditation, and to help out those who pass by."

Feighan said, "Would it be rude of me to ask about your God?"

The monk shuffled around in the sun. "Nah, it's never rude to ask that. But really, you don't need to."

"Why?"

"Because you know our God, although under a different name."

That surprised him. Greystein had been an accomplished amateur exologist, once, but had never mentioned that Terra and Actu "shared" a divinity. "Who—Jehovah?" He pictured Him in His long white beard.

"No. No, no, no."

"Who, then—Allah?"

"The Far Being Retzglaran, of course."

▪ Chapter XIII ▪

He wished he had a number to call. It frustrated him immensely to sit at his desk till midnight, waiting for the phone to ring, when he had finally obtained the information.

At long last, the instrument jangled. He snatched it up. "I've got him!"

"In your possession?"

"What? No, no. I mean, I know where he is!"

"It is about time. Give me the address."

That flustered him. "Well, uh, it's not an address, exactly— it's a planet. I mean, Feighan's on the planet Actu."

The sigh came clearly through the wire. "Inadequate. I trust you are aware that the surface area of Actu is rather larger than that of Earth?"

"Uh . . . well, I hadn't thought of it in those terms, but now that you—"

"We have a small base there. Devise a means of locating Feighan—without delay!—and put a Flinger on standby to transport us there. Be ready to depart on a moment's notice. Is that understood?"

"Yes." His palms were sweating again, and he hated it. "Yes, it is."

The dead line hummed to itself.

A Flinger on standby . . . He took a deep breath. *Harry Lipsiento. He'll do what he's told—he, at least, is programmed correctly.*

▪ Chapter XIV ▪

"The Far Being Retzglaran is God?" He had heard that suggested before, but never by anyone who believed it. His shadow spilled out as he leaned forward in excitement. "Listen, could you tell me—"

"Not right now, Feighan, because you have to get back to work."

"But—" A million questions bubbled up.

"Sorry—later, all right?"

He had to let it lie. Frustrated and vaguely resentful, he went back into the hot, dead air of the Building, and took up his prowl before the plate glass window. He could not concentrate. The questions that remained unanswered kept percolating through his consciousness for the rest of the afternoon.

At long last, he Flung the ninety-sixth batch of missionaries of the day, and turned eagerly to K'rach'a. "About the Far Being—"

"No." The monk clambered out of the pot, waddled down the ramp, and went outdoors.

"What do you mean, no?" As he stepped outside, the hot breeze dried his sweat.

"Feighan, I'm no theologian—"

"But you spent all those years as a library monk!"

"Centuries, actually, but that doesn't make me a know-it-all on God. It means I know the Holy, that's all—backwards, forwards, and upside down, you bet, but that's all. You want to ask about the Far Being, you ask H'nik. Besides, you're supposed to be meeting with it at eight arcs—that's three of your hours before sundown—so *it* can ask *you* about the Far Being. And that—" It tilted its barrel so its central eyespine pointed to the sun. "—oh boy, that's right now! Let's go."

"But—"

"No. Take us to the monastery."

"McGill—" Sam grabbed his wrist. "—do I have to go, too?"

The plaintive note in his ward's voice silenced his instinctive affirmative. He looked down. Sam's shoulders slumped, his arms hung loose, and his tail lay flat on the patio. Feighan felt for the kid. "Not if you don't want to go—but what are you going to do?"

"I don't know. There's nothing to do here. I'll just go back to the tent and lie in the sun or something."

Feighan squatted, bringing himself down to the Rhanghan's eye-level. "You sure? You're welcome to come with us, if you want."

"Yeah, I know, but it's no fun to sit around listening to you talk about the Far Being Retzglaran." He pronounced the name with a sharp swift twist of dislike. Then he brightened in a child's optimism. "Hey, K'rach'a! Are there any kids around here I can play with?"

"Afraid not, Sam. We don't have kids—only stump buds. By the time they can move around, they're thirty or forty years old—that's pretty grown-up, even for us. And as soon as they tear free of the death root, they go to work. They don't have time to play or anything."

"Aw, nuts." He bent over to pick disconsolately at a loose scale on his right front foot.

"What about your picture books?" said Feighan.

"I colored them in already." Straightening, he folded his arms across his chest. "This is no fun, McGill. When can we go home?"

He shook his head sadly. "I wish I knew, Sam. Not any time soon, though." As he stood, he muffled a yawn. "I'll set you down at the tent, and I'll be up later, okay?"

"Yeah, okay."

"And remember to use the paper bag."

"I hate that, too!" His tongue flickered out while his tail

arched up and over his back. "I hate everything here. I'm just going to go to sleep, that's what I'm going to do. Maybe I'll wake up in New York."

"Hey—"

"Just leave me alone, okay McGill? And Fling me back to the tent."

"All right. I'll see you later." He closed his eyes, and—

PING

—and Sam was gone.

It hurt that he could not cheer the kid up. "Aah . . . you ready, K'rach'a?"

"You bet."

PING

They stood on the lip of the monastery bowl. Late afternoon sun fell warm on the Flinger's face. "I meant to ask, why is the monastery down in a hollow?"

"Self-abnegation."

"Pardon?"

"The Actuni role in life is to suffer; the monks' role is to suffer more. That's what the Abbot says, and the Abbot's boss. So, over the years, we built this place by carrying off all the soil particles smaller than, uh . . . what is that thing you Terrans eat? Round and green and pretty small?"

He stretched and yawned. The heat was sapping his strength and replacing it with lethargy; his wounds still hurt. "A pea?"

"That's it! Nothing down there is smaller than a pea. If you spent your whole life rooted in the monastery, you'd starve to death."

"How's that?"

"There's no nutrition in gravel—wonderful aeration, you bet, but no food. No organic matter for the microbiota to live on, no clay particles to hold the nutrients for you . . . if we didn't get out and around, we'd shrivel to nothing in no time."

A monk trudged up the slope toward them, calling, "McGill Feighan! I am glad you were able to spare me the time."

"It's part of my job, isn't it?"

"In a way, yes. Rather, it will be, once you have acclimated yourself to what must surely be a difficult planet for a Terran to adapt himself to. At the moment, though, it is most certainly not a condition of employment. As I said, later on, yes, certainly. But for now, we really must consider your willingness to subject yourself to my inquisitiveness as an act of charity, so to speak."

H'nik's spines were twitching in preparation for further elucidation, but K'rach'a interrupted. "Feighan, I'm going to take off now. This guy here is just too wordy for me. I'll see you in the morning, okay?"

"I'll pick you up."

Shifting position to face the other monk, H'nik rasped at it in their own language for a good minute.

K'rach'a answered with a curt guttural.

H'nik sawed again, longer this time.

K'rach'a seemed to wilt. It dipped forward, hummed briefly, then backed away, dipping at three-meter intervals.

Feighan said, "What was that all about?"

"Oh, nothing for you to worry about, McGill Feighan, just a small matter between K'rach'a and myself. You know how these things go."

He did not, but was tired enough to let it pass. "K'rach'a said today that we know your God by the name of the Far Being Retzglaran?"

"Ah? Interesting . . . before we continue, perhaps it might be wiser if you were to transfer us to another location—say, perhaps, that small sandy knoll over by the, ah, the eastern slope? Somewhat to the south of the library?"

He peered at it, blinking against the dazzle of sunlight it reflected. "You sure you wouldn't rather find a shady spot?"

"You have a marvelous sense of humor, McGill Feighan. Please, take us there at once—life at the bottom of the soup bowl is perilously close to dormancy."

PING

"Soup bowl?"

H'nik sank its roots with audible pleasure. "I must confess I am of mountain stock, and was raised on brighter light than is available in the monastery hollow. About the Far Being . . . I do rather wish K'rach'a had not said that, for such knowledge might well prejudice your answers to my questions. But yes, the Far Being Retzglaran is God."

Feighan felt betrayed by the answer, and immediately astonished by his reaction. *Why?* But then he realized that he had been hoping the scholarly H'nik would ridicule the idea as the belief of a bumpkin, and go on to describe God in the vague, almost abstract and aloof terms favored by Terran theologians.

It was comforting to think that there was a God, a Shaper and a Creator now retired, working part-time as the universal security guard Who enforced the basic laws of nature. That was comforting precisely because it kept God at a distance, ever unlikely to affect the affairs of a twenty-two-year-old Terran named Feighan.

But to hear that the God of omni/ubi attributes was not only still in Its prime, but was still watching the sparrows fall in a trillion fields on a million worlds—to suspect that the gastropod which kidnaped you at birth was not an alien but an angel— to know that you are the focus of the interest of God Itself— this is scary. Even to approach those thoughts had always frightened Feighan, and so he had always shied away instinctively, like a horse pulling up at a rattle in the dry grass. Now H'nik was saying it was all true—and though it excited him, it terrified him as well. He shook his head.

"What is it?" asked the monk.

He let his breath out with a soft hiss. "So many things have happened to me because of the Far Being. The Organization got after me because of It, and they've cost me my family, friends, a lover. . . . I lost my money, my house, my job, a second woman whom I've come to love . . . if the Far Being is God, then I'm Its Job. And maybe . . . maybe that's okay, if it's part of God's plan . . . but I keep remembering that God's enemy is the Devil, and I don't want to—I *can't*—fight the powers of Hell. It scares the shit out of me."

"Tell me what you remember of the Far Being Retzglaran."

"Nothing."

"Oh, come now, one isn't impaled on a divine needle without its leaving a mark. Surely there must be something—"

The marks were there, all right: a scar for every death, a perpetual wariness, a life in exile . . . but they had been left by Its enemies. It frustrated him immensely. How could he talk about Something the nature of which he could only deduce from the reactions of its opponents?

"Well?"

"I told you, I've never met the Far Being! Right after I was born, I was seized by one of Its, ah, employees? A giant gastropod. It held me for three days, then released me. It offered no explanation, and I don't remember a thing about it."

He paused. It always daunted him to discuss intensely personal matters with anyone whose body language was different from his own, but to open up to an animated cactus—!

"I sense something," said H'nik. "A hesitation on your part; perhaps a reticence that branches from your new apprehension of the Far Being Retzglaran's true nature. K'rach'a should have known better."

Feighan's shadow, fuzzy around the edges, reached across the sand for the retaining wall of the first terrace. He studied it as he spoke. "I have these dreams—not often; once, twice a year tops—and in these dreams I'm someplace strange. I'm waiting. An alien landscape. I can't move. Brown, flat, a desert of the spirit . . . and this gastropod comes charging over the horizon and I *know* it has a message for me, an assignment, a . . . but this is a big world and the horizon's a billion klicks away. Before the gastropod ever gets to me, I wake up."

"You have spoken to the gastropod, have you not?"

Suddenly suspicious, he chose his words with care. "I don't remember telling you that."

"The telepath—Gina Maccari—mentioned it to me."

"Oh." From back among the distance-blurred peaks, dirty grey smoke plumed into the sky. Feighan waited for the temblor, for the lava, but nothing came. So he said, "Last year, on Delurc, I . . . it was very strange. Have you ever been there?"

"Yes. I visited there a good many years ago, when I was much younger, and when humidity bothered me less. It is an unnerving planet to visit . . . unhealthful, as well. The lights in the domes on the reefs do not emit enough of the radiation we Actuni need to thrive; as I recall, I spent much effort staving off dormancy. But what of your time there?"

"I'll skip the details," said Feighan. "Do you remember how the Delu trade you time and access to their minds in exchange for equal time and access to your mind?"

"Memory-swapping? But of course! It was exhilarating to move so smoothly, so sleekly, through so much water."

"Well, I swapped memories with an old female fish who had spoken to the gastropod—but when I was reliving the experience in her memory, the gastropod spoke to *me*. The memory was twenty years old, but the gastropod clearly expected me to be there, exchanging memories with the old female, twenty years after it had gone." He scratched his head.

The wind that ran over him dried his sweat instantly; its encrusting salts itched like mad. "I still don't understand the whole thing."

"But what did it say?" H'nik jiggled up and down by flexing its roots.

"It said I was supposed to lead a normal life—that the Far Being had not called me or anything like that—that I should just go home and pretend nothing had happened."

"And?"

"Well, up until all this—" He waved a hand in the direction of the last few days. "I mean, until Greystein and the trial and all, I was following orders—being normal, the works. And then . . ." He made a tired, disgusted rattle in his throat. "Then the bottom fell out of my life, and here I am."

"I see, I see," said the monk. "Well, that should be enough for today, do you not agree?"

The abrupt adjournment startled him. He straightened up, raising his eyebrows and tucking in his chin. "I thought you wanted to question me for hours at a time—not that I'm complaining, but that's what you said you wanted, back in New York."

"Though that is exactly what I want, McGill Feighan, my other duties intrude. Besides, it does strike me that you are suffering from considerable stress. Being new to this arid planet as you are, you must surely be experiencing enough cultural shock to distort the thematic accuracy of your answers. So . . . we will go slowly in the beginning, and every day we will spend a slightly larger wedge of time on the problem. Is that agreeable?"

"Fine by me." He lied. The less time he spent answering H'nik's questions, the less time it would spend replying to his. And he wanted a lot of answers from the monk.

A pea-sized clod of dirt splatted against his thigh as H'nik pulled up its roots and began to pivot. "I must go; we have received reports that a grove of . . . of . . . heretics is marching toward the monastery. They will reach it shortly before sundown, and I should be there."

"Is there going to be trouble?"

"Oh, I would rather expect not. We have eschewed mass violence since before the Day of Burning Water; it is far more likely that the confrontation will involve only haranguing—perhaps some name-calling—although it might go so far as to include insults to the ancestral roots." It began to toddle toward the monastery.

"Hey, wait!"

"I do regret my inability to linger, McGill Feighan, but really, I must go at once. You are, of course, more than welcome to walk alongside of me, at least until we reach the slope of the sacred precincts."

With one long stride he came abreast of the monk; another took him past it and he paused to wait. "You said if I let you interrogate me about the Far Being, you'd tell me what you know about it."

"Yes, I did say that, did I not? Ah, me, one would have thought that after all these years I should have learned not to make promises that circumstances might prevent me from keeping . . . but then, one could say with equal justice that you have failed to keep your promises, couldn't one?"

"What do you mean? I—"

"You remember nothing about the Far Being Retzglaran, and since you do not, you can not answer my questions, can you?" It struggled onward. Thirty meters from its right flank, a lean greyish-green shape slipped out of the shrubbery at the foot of the first terrace.

"But—but—"

"More importantly, the Abbot has instructed me to refer all your questions directly to it." A trace of rue seemed to infuse its voice, but Feighan was skeptical. Anthropomorphism was something he had been trained to reject. "Apparently my researches have aroused suspicions in higher quarters. There is talk that the truths I have begun, in part, to reveal—as an archeologist brushes dust from the corner of a building he is excavating—there is talk that these truths be heretical."

"Are they?" Feighan was more interested in the terrier-sized animal loping silently toward the fields of ripe berries, but he hoped that a sympathetic interest would embolden the suddenly evasive H'nik.

"To tell you the truth, McGill Feighan, I have not the slightest idea, because I have only begun to expose these truths. To return to my simile of the archeologist, he can not tell whether the flat surface he has uncovered belonged to a palace or to a castle or to a . . . a wine cellar, not when he first uncovers it. He must reveal far more than that single carved face; he must find the foundations and trace the walls and estimate their original height, width, and depth . . . then, perhaps, after years of careful work and far more careful thought, he can say, 'Ah, this was an outhouse.' Do you understand?"

"I think so." Feighan took another step. Walking with an Actuni involved more waiting than walking, and it was beginning to irritate him. "So you can't tell me anything unless your Abbot approves it, huh?"

"I regret to say that you have described the situation exactly as it is—you must remember, McGill Feighan, that I am under our equivalent of your monastic orders. I have taken a vow of obedience to my superior, and when my superior limits my freedom of speech, as it has done—"

"Then you have to shut up, yeah, I understand." Hands folded behind his back, he took another step. Sunlight iridesced on the scales of the animal up ahead. It was approaching a line of Actuni who stood with their backs to the field. To Feighan's astonishment, the entire line interlocked spines and flexed their roots to raise their barrels twenty or thirty centimeters off the ground. They made not a sound. Their roots bulged into gnarled arches and held firm. "So tell me, how can I convince your Abbot to let me hear what you've learned?"

"I warn you now that you will not like the answer."

"What is it?"

"I have been forbidden to discuss the content of my researches with any but the members of our order. Before I could tell you my findings, you would have to become one of us— a monk, I mean, of course."

"You'd let me in?"

"Of course! We are ethnocentric only by accident."

Something in the notion appealed to him. Perhaps it was H'nik itself, or, rather, the serenity that the monk seemed to embody. It would be very nice to be that much at peace with oneself. Then he pulled back and shook his head violently. *What am I thinking? Walking Mule has that kind of inner peace; it comes from letting somebody else program you. You're always placid 'cause you're always following orders! Uh-uh. No brainwashing for me.* Aloud, he said, "Hmph."

"I expected no other response—and to speak frankly, McGill Feighan, I disagree with my superior's ruling. However, given the political realities of our order's hierarchy, I could not appeal that ruling with any hope of success. Even to attempt such an appeal would jeopardize my freedom of investigation. And while, as an academic, I value the ability to announce the results of my research, as a scholar I assign the greater imperative to having the freedom to *do* the research, if you see what I mean."

"Yeah." *Neat, H'nik. You just told me you won't even talk off the record, dammit. I wonder how they indoctrinated you?* Ahead, the lizard-like animal lowered itself to its belly to wriggle under a root-propped Actuni farmer. "Yeah, I see . . ."

"Scccrrreeeeeeee!"

Feighan said, "Wha—?"

"That? It is regrettable, but given half a chance the *ghu'ghu'ru'ru*—ah, the grazing lizard? It would strip our fields bare. And, of course, lowlanders have large appetites . . ."

They passed along the line, which had dropped down to normal posture. The grazing lizard still screeched, while its tail drummed the soil. The farmer squatted astride its back, making squishy, crunching noises only barely audible beneath the lizard's frantic shrieks. Suddenly the squeals cut off. The tail still thrashed, but it was disappearing from view, as though the lizard had broken free and was squirming out the other side. But on that other side protruded its snout which, jaws snapping, was retreating under the bulk of the farmer. Feighan felt queasy. "Ah—"

"I would prefer to ignore this scene, if you please. Let us speak of you and the Far Being Retzglaran."

"Ah . . . all right." Just before he turned his head, the scaly green tail vanished with a slurp. He could not help thinking of Sam. *Remember to warn the kid never to crawl under one of these guys* . . . he shuddered.

"McGill Feighan, I understand your desire to learn about the focal point of your life. I would suggest to you that you give serious consideration to the notion of joining our order, at least temporarily."

"Ah . . ." Distracted as he was, he did not immediately understand what H'nik meant. Then he blinked in surprise. Though he had never practiced his Catholicism devoutly, he had been raised to believe that once a priest, always a priest. "You can leave your order? Stop being a monk?"

"Of course." H'nik waddled a shade faster because the edge of the monastery hollow had just come into view. "We are, in that respect at least, somewhat closer to your Terran Buddhists than we are to any of your other religions—although I do not wish you to interpret that to mean that we hold the same beliefs as your Terran Buddhists do."

Scratching his right temple, he outlined a scheme: he would sign on as a monk for a while—just long enough to learn what H'nik and the rest knew about the Far Being, but not long enough to get indoctrinated. Then he would drop out and go back to . . . He winced. There was the sticking point. What did he have to go back to? Nothing. To the best of his knowledge, only the Actuni monks would hire a Flinger in trouble with the consortia of the Flinger's native world—well, so would crime syndicates like The Organization, but he would burn in hell before he worked for those who had killed his parents and helped frame his very best friend . . .

"I sense your turmoil," said H'nik softly.

Still, it might be nice: *A quiet, peaceful life; I'd learn about the Far Being; maybe I'd even stop dreaming about Greystein . . . ah, Jesus, they'd be in my head, though . . .* "What can I say? I am confused. I want to learn about the Far Being, but not by making a phony commitment—I mean, I was just thinking, I could pretend to sign up, but . . ."

"It is as well that you have put that possibility out of your mind," said H'nik, "for any knowledge that you gained by deception would be so gnarled by your sin as to lack meaning and value. I really must leave you here. May I suggest that you stroll over to the library and wander through it? I believe you would find it to be the sort of experience from which you would benefit."

Feighan raised his eyebrows. Was H'nik hinting at something which monastic discipline forbade it to reveal openly? He decided it could not be; H'nik was probably revealing no more than scholarly enthusiasm for a remarkably old and complete collection of documents . . . *If you can call a matted-out Actuni a document,* he thought. "Aah, I don't know, Sam's alone back at the tent, and—"

The monk scuffled its roots in the sand. "The choice is yours, McGill Feighan, and no one but yourself can make it for you; I would, however, take the liberty of suggesting that when one is confused, one is unlikely to find the serenity necessary for meditation in the vicinity of a young child."

At that he had to laugh. Sam was not giving him much peace for anything, what with his questions, complaints, and general restlessness. But still, would rows of aged, semi-senile

Actuni—all broiling in the late afternoon sun—provide him with what he needed? *So you got anything better to do?* "All right, H'nik, I'll go wander through the library."

"I believe you will find that you have made a wise decision; at least I hope you will. Go. Inspect. Meditate. And afterwards, should you have the time, please let me know about the quality of your experience."

"I certainly will." He looked around. "Ah . . . which way is it from here?"

It swiveled its long spine to point to the south. In the sunlight, it glinted with a coppery sheen. "Two hundred some meters that way, just beyond what Sam calls the 'white pillars'. Oh. Feel free to Fling yourself there; there is no taboo of that sort connected with the monastery library."

"Thank you." It was so close he really should have walked, if only for the exercise, but his Talent was jumpy with untapped energy. He aimed for the white obelisks, and—

PING

—stood on loose, stone-free soil of the type he had come to associate with Actuni pathways.

Before him, in two columns of three, towered six strange plants. The smallest rose at least eight meters, and had to be two meters thick at its base. They were clearly cacti, but they had no spikes; instead, from a skin as green as a late summer oak leaf grew long white hairs that reached almost to the ground. He bent over to roll a hair between his fingers. It had a stiff, wiry texture; its ends were split and frayed because the wind rubbed them against the rocks piled against the plant's base. Rising, he put his hands on his hips and tilted back his head to see the plant's top. He was not sure if he liked leafless plants as tall as small houses. They always reminded him of a certain giant saguaro . . . *And now Greystein* . . . He let go of the hair and went inside.

Music welled up to greet him. A soft violin spoke of spring breezes; a drum away far off tapped the pitter-pat of rain. It entranced him because it was so totally unexpected. He stopped to listen.

A harpsicord plucked the passage of a being lost in desolation: hesitant, frustrated, back-tracking again and again as it sought the way to salvation. The rocks blocked the trail, though; the cliffs soared up to stymy it. It struggled: a step, another, a halt . . .

The violin wailed anguish.

A fiddle danced down the path, sure and light on its feet, twisting up the escarpment and never missing a beat or a turn or a climb or a foothold on the craggy, sun-washed cliff that had stopped the harpsicord stiff. The fiddle reached the top, and jigged to meet the sun in its dew-filtered dawn.

But a big bass doom came screaming across the sky, trailing flames a thousand klicks wide and ten thousand high. It hammered at the cliff with its deep persistent voice and the fiddle quaked, terrified—

"Ter-r-r-r-ran?" The hoarse rumble came from his right.

Startled out of his reverie, he jerked his head around. A monk matted out some ten meters away twitched six of its sparse spines. "What?"

"You Ter-r-ran?" It stood at least four meters tall; age browned its skin.

"Yes."

"Hot."

He assumed it meant the weather. "Yes."

Its long spine flashed.

Suddenly alarmed, he backpedaled until instinct succumbed to reason. Big and matted-out, this Actuni was far less mobile than average. Its lance-like spine deserved respect, but not fear.

The spine pointed to the shade the monk cast. "Sit. Co-oo-ool."

"Aah . . ."

"Sit."

"Okay." He shrugged. The heat had not bothered him till the monk had mentioned it, but once reminded of the sun, his cheeks burned. He moved into the being's shadow. Hot though it was, the steady wind dried his sweat almost immediately. He sat cross-legged a careful three meters from the monk's roots—just in case—and looked up. "So you speak English, huh?"

"Noooo—"

"But, ah, you—"

Few worrrrds know. No speak 'k'k'k'k.

"Oh." He did not know what to say to that.

"R-r-r-est."

He gave a half-smile. "Thanks."

It did not reply.

In the background, a viola waltzed on the village green.

Alone at first, it found a partner within a turn, and lost it to another within another. Soon it found a second partner, and the two moved about through the mist and the gentle rain. The green filled up with waltzing couples and triples and quadruples. Music played and dancers danced in ever-smaller squares. Soft balmy air so soothed their skins that more and more festivants crowded onto what had really been a very small area to begin with. It became impossibly small. One could not take a step without jabbing or being jabbed. The rich moist soil practically begged for the penetration of thirsty roots, but the law was the law. Even though there was no room to drop root anywhere else, all one could do on the green was dance, dance, around and around. With the newcomers. The goddam weedy sprouts who thought they had as much right to the space as did those who had lived in the fields nearby for generation upon generation. Not only could one not sashay without getting jabbed by one of them, one ran the risk of being burned out by a long spine with every step. Tempers were flaring. Harsh words scraped back and forth. One thing led to another. *Sizzle* it went. *Sizzle* as the long spines snapped down. And in. Brains shorted out.

A light burst in the sky.

A vast huge light, brighter even than the sun itself, it whizzed from east to west, leaving heat streaks on every eyepatch. It disappeared. And one moment later the entire western horizon burned red, then white, then brilliant enough to blind forever the eyespikes aimed in its direction.

The dancers stumbled about, dazed. The ground shook violently. Fully half of them lost their rooting and toppled over. A huge dark cloud spouted into the western sky. It reached toward them, closer, closer . . . It extended over their heads till the sunlight, the blessed loving brightness that with the moist and the rich made the feet so fleet and the trunks so thick so green, the sunlight faded.

The squabble went on, *sizzle* and *sizzle* and *sizzle*.

One had room to waltz, now, though one had to be careful not to dance across the decaying husk of a less fortunate partner.

But the cloud deepened. It became increasingly difficult to muster the energy for the sharp precise circles, dips, and bows.

sizzle

Darker.

sizzle

Darkest.
sizzle
The remaining dancers slowed.
And stopped.
And tapped down.

"Hey, Feighan!"

His eyes snapped open. Before him stood two Actuni—K'rach'a and a companion. Uncomfortably aware that he might have violated a law or a taboo or a regulation by dozing in the shade of a library monk—*but I wasn't!* he thought. *I was listening, and the music took over!*—he scrambled to his feet, hoping they would put it down to his alienness. "Ah, I'm sorry if I—"

"Not to worry, Feighan, not to worry one little bit. Want you to meet the Abbot here. It's been watching you, and I don't mind telling you, it likes what it sees."

He made a bow to the other Actuni. The Abbot's flower had begun to fruit. "I am very pleased to meet you, Your . . . Your Holiness." He turned back to K'rach'a. "Is that the right title? Or is there a better one?"

"That doesn't matter at all. It doesn't speak a word of English; when I translate, I put it right for you. Don't worry so much. With me as your interpreter, you come across as the most diplomatic being to visit this planet since the FNC Contact Team made us think we were getting a real bargain by taking on a four-billion fancy debt." It rasped a series of spines and waited for the Abbot to reply. "It says you were lost in the music."

He nodded. "I thought this was a library, but it's more like a symphony orchestra hall." *Someday I'm going to have to show this to Gina—she'll love it.*

"No, just the old guys reciting the Holy—it's all they do all day long, so they've gotten pretty good at it. You liked it, huh?"

"I couldn't understand it, of course—"

"Crap."

He blinked. "Pardon?"

K'rach'a swayed on its roots. "Doesn't 'crap,' used in that context, mean 'don't be so modest'?"

"Ah . . . no, not really." He was woozy from the music, the

sun, and his own fatigue. It made everything unreal. It split him down the middle so that half of him watched his other half stand in the slanting desert light giving a language lesson to a two-meter-tall plant with long sharp bristles. The observing half wanted to laugh—or to weep, it could not be sure. So it stayed silent while the teaching half said, "No, in that context, 'crap' means 'I know you're lying to me, so cut it out.'"

"Isn't that what 'don't be so modest' means?"

Now he had to laugh. "Literally translated, maybe. But the connotations are vastly different. One's an insult; the other's a compliment."

"Oh." It shifted on its roots for a moment. "And 'crap' is the—?"

"The insult."

"Ouch. I'm sorry, I didn't mean to hurt your feelings. What I meant to say—although to tell you the truth, Feighan, it's the Abbot who said it first, I'm just repeating it in English— is that anybody could see how the Holy affected you."

"It did." He wondered how. It was scary that something as alien as the library had reached right into his head like that.

"The Abbot says you understood the meaning even though the words slipped by you."

Why did it matter to them? Was it proof of his respect—or of his susceptibility? "I don't know. I sure got something out of it, but whether or not it's what you're supposed to get from it . . ."

"Doesn't really matter. It says a sensitivity like yours belongs in the monastery, and it invites you to join us. No entrance exam, nothing. Just say 'yes' and you're in. Wait a minute." It swiveled on its roots to speak to the Abbot.

Feighan took a deep breath and let it out slowly. He still did not know if he wanted to join the order. He wanted, most definitely, to hear what the Actuni knew of the Far Being, but to become a monk solely for the purpose . . . At the north end of the library, the violin spoke once more of the gentle rain that would cleanse the dust from the skin of a thirsty being, and the harpsicord reminded all its listeners that the way was long and crooked and easy to lose.

He inhaled again. He had not known such peace in a very long time. He liked it, no matter what evoked it. He wanted to wallow in it for the rest of his life. And all the monks— with the possible exception of K'rach'a—seemed to possess it. Did it come with the territory?

He opened his mouth.

K'rach'a spoke first: "The Abbot says you shouldn't decide today. Wait till tomorrow. Sleep on it; think it over during work tomorrow. Then, after work, let us know."

"Okay, but—"

"Fine. We'll see you tomorrow." It rocked through a 180° turn, then began to limp back toward the monastery. The Abbot followed.

Feighan watched them struggle across the sandy soil. He felt flattered by their attentions, but puzzled, too, and a little wary. He shrugged. And—

PING

Thirty meters from the tent, Sam lay sprawled on a rock, bright eyes fixed on the wings that fluttered over the eastern crest. He did not look over as Feighan walked up to him.

"Hiya, Sam."

Now he looked. "I ate dinner, and I used the paper bag, and just leave me alone, all right?" He turned his snout and studied the flying creatures again.

Feighan raised both his hands. "Hey! What's the matter?"

"You wouldn't understand."

"Try me."

"McGill, please?"

"I'm only trying—"

"You're just being nosy again, that's all, and I don't feel like having somebody be nosy all over me, so will you leave me alone?"

He sighed. It hurt him to be held at such a distance when his ward was so troubled. "Okay, kid. Whatever you want. Anytime you're ready to talk about it, you know I'll listen."

"Yeah, sure."

Exhausted, he lacked the energy to press the matter further. "See you later." He turned and walked back to their tent, where he fixed himself a quick, cold meal—used the paper bag—and went promptly to sleep.

Twilight prayers did not penetrate his dreams at all.

He knelt in the last row of pews in a small Catholic church. Sunlight slanted through the stained-glass windows. Day-old incense peppered the air. Decades of worshipping hands had smoothed the seat back beneath his fingers—and dozens of bored young parishioners had left toothmarks in the soft pine.

His eyes adjusted to the dimness. In the front row knelt a boulder of a man, with bookshelf shoulders and a muscled back that stretched the fabric of his shirt. Next to him hunched a small, black-haired woman.

The hairs on the back of Feighan's neck rose.

The priest at the altar chanted the Latin Mass, and had his back to the congregation. His voice rang high and tripping—glib, even.

Ice began to crystallize in the Flinger's stomach.

An altarboy holding a burning taper glided across the sanctuary to light the candles stuck on the spines of the giant saguaros that served here as candelabra. They grew in huge terracotta pots, and one of them shared its pot with a lump that could not be distinguished in the shadows.

Feighan prayed that the lights would not brighten.

But they did, first illuminating the crucifix mounted on the wall behind the altar. Furry arms pulled taut and torment twisting his face, a Timili hung from the cross. It was Rothono, once Feighan's best friend, whose life Sam's mother had spared; whose life The Organization had claimed.

Feighan's heart raced; he clenched his jaws against the nausea of fear.

The candles' glow grew impossibly bright. It reached down into the saguaro's pot to glint off an ivory cheek and reddish-brown hair. A bumblebee buzzed.

Frozen in terror, he could not move.

With a rustle of his silk chasuble, Greystein turned to raise the Host high and proclaim *"Resurrexit sicut dixit!* Alleluia! He has risen as he said!"

Feighan woke up screaming.

The tent pressed in on him, swallowing his labored breathing in its darkness. His heart still beat a hundred forty times a minute. *Oh, Jesus, please, no more, I can't take them*... gradually it dawned on him that the tent was empty.

"Sam?"

"I'm out here."

Still trembling slightly, he went to the flaps and stuck his head into the night air. It was cooler, with a hint of moisture and a tang of sulphur. "How come you're out here?"

The Rhanghan swung his snout about to stare Feighan full on. His eyes did not blink. " 'Cause it's hot and stuffy in there, and you make too much noise anyway."

"I'm sorry," he said, meaning it. "I . . . nightmare, you know?"

"I'll sleep out here."

"But—"

"Go to sleep, McGill." His tongue flickered in the ruddy moonlight. "I won't let the bugs get you."

He could not think of a thing to say except, "Okay . . . thanks. I'll see you in the morning."

"Yeah."

He stumbled back into the tent's stale air. He stretched out on his sleeping bag. Then closed his eyes. *God, I don't know Who or What you are, but the Actuni say they know, and I want to investigate. I want to find You. I need to find You. I hope I'm doing the right thing—but I don't know. Please. Help me?*

He slept.

He woke up so late that he had to skip breakfast and report directly to the Flinger Building. As he was pulling on his boots, he marveled at the fact that this was only his fourth day on Actu. So much had happened; it seemed he had been there much longer. He grunted as his heel slipped into place, then stood. "Hey, Sam, you want to come along?"

"Uh-uh."

"Well . . . okay. And say, thanks for keeping the bugs out."

The Rhanghan slowly nictitated his inner eyelids. "You're welcome."

"You sure you don't want to come?"

"You're late."

"All right. Have a good day." He—

PING

—stepped into the Building. Prickly rows of monks lined the long corridors; he counted three hundred twenty-one of them before he reached the Flinger Room. There he took his seat, just as K'rach'a finished settling itself into the pot of Rii—edsch topsoil. "You ready?"

"Feighan, I've been ready for ten minutes."

"Sorry, I overslept."

"That's the advantage to being a plant. It has to be awful cloudy for that to happen. We've got a full day ahead of us. This first group goes to the Crown."

The day went quickly, though he got progressively more

hungry as it wore on. After forty-eight Flings he went back to the tent for a break and a bite to eat. Sam, still basking in the sun, ignored Feighan's arrival.

"Hiya."

"Done for the day?"

"Uh-uh. I have go to back."

"Hmph." His tongue darted out and glistened in the sun.

"Hey, it's my job."

"I know . . . later on, you want to help me with that picture book?"

"I thought you colored it in already."

"I did—I mean help *reading* it."

"Okay." He smiled. "Later on, we'll go through it."

"Thanks." He turned his snout the other way, but his tail swept back and forth in the rhythm of contentment.

If you'd stop snapping at the kid, he'd be that happy all the time. Just relax, stop fretting—but again he saw the angry silver bees swarm, and Greystein fall. He shook himself, like an Actuni drinking the dew, and came to his decision. For a moment his choice surprised him. All his instincts screamed against it, but dammit, it was the wisest course! Safest, too, even if it might mean depriving himself of various things. He licked his fingers, crumpled the foil pouch, and tossed it into the garbage box. From within came a cranky snapping. A second later a multipedal red insect with serrated pincers half the length of its body scampered up and over the side.

Feighan returned to the Building, then, no longer eager to spend his four hours off sitting on a boulder, fearing a bug bite. Besides, he wanted to get his work over with, so he could go to the library and announce his decision to the Abbot.

Naturally, since something momentuous would happen when the shift ended, the shift refused to end. "K'rach'a," he said wearily, "where are they all coming from? You only have, what, two thousand people in the whole valley? By the end of the day I'll have Flung five hundred of them!"

"Something like about a hundred people a week join the monastery, Feighan. They come from all over the planet to spend a few weeks in the, uh . . . I guess you'd call it a cemetery?"

"Seminary?"

"Oh, yeah, seminary. And then they get shipped back out again. It's just for the last month or so we've been waiting for a Flinger to come, so we held them over. The workload will taper off in a day or two."

"Oh, for joy," he said softly. Minutes dragged. Seconds crawled. He drummed his fingers on the console and muttered "Hurry up!" under his breath.

"Feighan, they're moving as fast as they can."

"Sorry." He glared at the monks creeping into the Booth. "I'm just impatient today."

"It shows, believe me, it shows."

Scowling down through the window, he did not reply. Nor did he wait for the monks to complete the ritual of lining up and raising their long spines; rather, as soon as they were close enough together, he—

PING

—Flung them to the Badlands.

"Feighan, let them finish praying! The farewell liturgy means a lot to a bunch of green missionaries heading out to God knows where."

He squelched a pulse of anger. "Sorry." Then gritted his teeth when the next batch took forever to say its prayers . . .

But eventually the day came to an end. After Flinging K'rach'a to the monastery, he teleported back to the tent. The SolaRefridge had chilled the gallon jug of water nicely; there was even a thin film of ice on its surface. Uncapping it, he lifted the wide-mouthed jar to his lips, and drank deep. He made a small sound of satisfaction before replacing the jug. Then he closed his eyes—

"Hey, McGill!" said Sam. "Where you going? I thought you were done."

"Yeah, I am."

"Well, where—"

"To the library. Where else can you go on this planet?"

"But you were going to help me with my alphabets!"

He had forgotten his promise of that afternoon, and it embarrassed him—it irritated him—that Sam had remembered. He frowned. "That's alphabet, singular. And some other time, huh? I'm not in the mood, for one thing, and for another, I've got an important appointment."

"All right," said Sam unhappily. "I guess that tells me what your promises are worth." With a flick of his tail, he disappeared into the tent.

Feighan raised his right arm and opened his mouth—then

shut it, and let the arm drop. Really, he could say nothing to improve the situation. So he closed his eyes and—

PING

—materialized by the six tall plants with the long white hair. But something felt wrong, something in the surroundings . . .

Just inside the library entrance, H'nik and the Abbot conversed; they sounded like a congress of cicadas whose voices were changing. They hurt Feighan's ears, but had not caused his uneasiness.

"Good afternoon." As he approached, he looked around anxiously. What was different?

"Good day, McGill Feighan."

Ah, that's it! Beyond the north border of the library massed row upon row of bristly Actuni. Almost all of them displayed signs of gauntness. Not emaciation; just general skinniness. Surprisingly, their skins glowed more brightly green than did H'nik's, which seemed sallow in comparison. "What are they doing?"

"Ah, them? They are the dawn prayers, and for reasons known only to themselves they gathered here during the night, their caterwauling to commence as the sky began to lighten this morning. Did you not hear the cacophony?"

After the nightmare, he had slept like the dea—like a log. "But why are they here? I mean, this is dusk-prayer territory, isn't it?"

H'nik heaved itself out of the ground, and began to lead the way into the library. "They are attempting, through the good example they set and the prayers they utter, to help us find the true path to salvation."

"Missionaries, huh?"

"Precisely," it said glumly.

"Ah . . . huh. How's your own campaign going?"

"One wishes that one could say, 'Far better than theirs,' but alas, were one to make such a statement, one would be guilty of hubris—ah, perhaps not hubris itself, you understand, but a particular sin of pride which cannot be translated into English in any other way."

"About the same, huh?"

"Yes." Its long spine drooped.

"Are they converting your people, then?"

"Not in the least! Our communicants would hardly be misled

by such—" H'nik flattened its prickles for a moment. "—such peakroot Holy hailers!"

"But if you're no more successful than they are—"

"Ah, here we are." It stopped before a towering, time-ravaged monk. Years of dust-storms had sanded off its bristles; insects had gnawed tunnels through its three-meter-thick barrel. "This is Brother I'ghra, the oldest of all Actuni."

"Really?" He offered the monk a slight, polite bow; it made no response.

"Yes. Brother I'ghra tapped down on the Day of Burning Water, and has not had to tap down since. Allowing for the somewhat, ah, confused chronology of the years afterward, it still must be at least eighteen thousand of your years old. Even by our standards, that is ancient. But Brother I'ghra is privileged in another way: it is the only one among us who remembers hearing the Far Being Retzglaran."

"It *met* the Far Being?" Now he did not have to feign interest. "The Far Being was *here?*"

"Of course! I'm certain I must have told you—it was, in fact, the Far Being Retzglaran which set fire to the rain. To proceed: Brother I'ghra would question you, but before it does, the Abbot would ask your intentions concerning its invitation to you to become a member of our beloved order."

He caught his breath. He had changed his mind at least fourteen times since lunch. But facing someone which had met the Far Being—"Yes."

"Yes, what?"

"Yes, I would like to join your order."

H'nik interpreted; the Abbot spoke; H'nik translated again. "Excellent, McGill Feighan, excellent!—ah, I am quoting the Abbot here—I am pleased with your decision, and proud of you for having had the courage to make such a testimony to your faith. As has been foretold, you will make a monk of surpassing quality, I am convinced."

"Foretold?" said Feighan blankly.

While the Abbot addressed I'ghra, H'nik leaned closer to Feighan. Softly it scraped out: "Really, Acolyte McGill Feighan. I am certain that I mentioned that we have been waiting for you for eighteen thousand years."

▪ **Chapter XV** ▪

It surprised him to feel so good, considering that he had just invented a way to locate any Flinger, anywhere, with off-the-shelf technology. But then, although the NAC still paid him, his real employer now was—

The phone rang. Jauntily, he picked it up. "Got it!"

"Really?"

He shuffled the specifications into a neat stack. "Guaranteed. With one electronics technician and two long-duration aircraft, I can do it easily."

"You sound confident."

"A few days ago you called me a bumbler. I'm not. I'm really very, very competent. As I believe I've just proven."

"Until I see it work, you have proven nothing."

"You'll see it. My Flinger's ready, by the way. Are you?"

"Yes. We shall leave from your office. Tell the guard to admit me."

"And what name should I give?"

"Mil—no, 'John Smith' would be better. Oh, Davis—let me make one thing absolutely clear. Do not, repeat do not kill McGill Feighan—"

"All right." It disappointed him. But he had to jerk as the strings pulled. "I won't."

"—until I tell you to."

· Chapter XVI ·

Feighan stood stunned in the sun. "What—?"

H'nik kept its voice low. "According to I'ghra—who is, after all, the only one of us who can remember it directly—the Far Being Retzglaran promised that some day someone, ah, answering your general description would arrive to provide us with the answers we have desired for millennia. As a scholar, I find it particularly interesting that at the time the promise was made, we desired water, not answers to questions which we hadn't the wit to formulate anyway. Apparently the promise also foretold the rise of our curiosity..."

He shook his head. It was disturbing to be the object of an eighteen thousand-year-old prophecy. What disturbed him more was that no one had thought to inform him of it. "You said my general description—you mean tall, dark—"

H'nik gave the spine-rasp of amusement. "Not quite. It was said that the source of our answers lay within 'a soft, wet foreigner whose roots have neither filaments nor pores but which carry its weight all the same; a foreigner who will glow both hot as a noon lizard and cold as a dark stone; a foreigner who will come to us from the farthest star, taking only a single step to complete the journey; and—it goes on at considerable length; with each phrase as vague as the last. Shall I continue?"

"No." It disappointed him: almost any mammalian Flinger could fit it. "It is sort of general, isn't it?"

"Rather," said H'nik.

Feighan sighed. But he would remember the prophecy for Gina, who loved that sort of thing. "Anyway. Now that I'm one of you, you'll tell me about the Far Being, right?"

"Ah? Yes, on the Abbot's instructions, I did state that, did I not? Very well, then. The Abbot instructs me now to state that once we know, we shall share our information with you."

"But I thought—"

"Brother I'ghra's questions have been deemed essential to our understanding of the Far Being Retzglaran—which is to say that, until you have answered them, we will not even hint that our knowledge of the Far Being Retzglaran is anything but woefully inadequate. So if you will be so kind—"

"Oh, all right." Stepping forward, he bowed again, careful to avoid its half-meter-long short spines. "How do you do, Brother I'ghra?"

"It does not speak your language."

"Oh?" He sidled closer to H'nik. "Then I can ask you this without insulting anybody—is it capable of questioning me? I mean, I thought that a matted-out Actuni like I'ghra is, ah . . ."

"Senile?" H'nik chuckled again. "Yes, yes, mentation—as opposed to meditation—and mobility lie in direct proportion to each other. But these are ritual questions, devised centuries ago by one more, let us say, intellectually capable than itself; it has merely memorized them."

"Okay." With a shrug, he turned back. "Fire away."

I'ghra's spines twitched: a guitarist strumming a minor key chord.

"It asks," said H'nik, "if—if—excuse me, the archaic form of our language is difficult, and not easily translated into contemporary English. I must request amplification." Lengthily it conversed with I'ghra. Then: "Did the stomach-foot's abduction of yourself cause jubilation?"

"Stomach-foot?" Confused, he frowned—then snapped his fingers. "Oh! The gastropod." He stopped, and gaped at the ravaged hulk before him. *Centuries ago they knew about the gastropod?* "H'nik, how'd you know *that?*"

"It is part of the prophecy, McGill Feighan—but please, answer before I'ghra dozes off."

"Ah . . . yeah, sorry . . . 'jubilation?' . . . boy, that's a good one; I mean, I was a day old, but . . . later on, my parents said, ah—" For a moment he was three again: supine on the couch by the holo. While his father rattled cookie bags in the kitchen, his mother sneaked a sip from the green bottle she kept wedged in the cushions of her chair. The warm wet spread through his diapers; the smell reached him a moment later. Paralyzed since the gastropod had released him, he could not call out. He would have to wait for the touch, and the look of disgust.

Feighan shuddered, and cleared his throat. "Actually, it caused a lot of trouble in a lot of ways—especially since nobody knew why it did what it did."

H'nik translated, and I'ghra spoke again. H'nik queried it sharply; it sawed out a reply that sounded identical to its initial formulation of the question. H'nik said, "I am not certain of how to communicate this in the terms of your culture: 'Does the dew of the divinity swell the rind of your stock'?"

"I have no idea what that means. How can I answer it?"

"Although we no longer use the term in conversation, 'the dew of the divinity' was once used to refer to the largesse of the gods, as it were; it has a meaning similar but not identical to your own 'divine providence.' As for 'the rind of your stock,' well . . . I must confess, McGill Feighan, that I translated that one literally; it is a term we do not use at all today, a term with which I must admit I am not familiar. I suspect it to be an archaic idiom referring to, ah, the health or prosperity of your—what is your Terran phrase for *skwirun'k?* Ah, your kinfolk."

"In other words—" Bitterness welled from a reservoir he had not even known he contained. "—did the Far Being's intercession enrich me and my family?"

"Yes, why, yes, that would perhaps be a—"

"No. No, my family—" The faces flipped past his mind's eye like holos in an album: Patrick Sean Feighan's smile; Nicole Buongiorno's merry brown eyes; and Rothono and Greystein and Nadia and . . . "No. They're all dead. The Organization. Which got interested in me because of the Far Being."

H'nik relayed the answer and I'ghra spoke again. This time the translation came swiftly, if not fluently: "Have you been told the why of your losses?"

He bit his lip. "No. And—"

H'nik's sharp guttural brought a long slow lament from I'ghra that the Abbot repeated. H'nik started, then twisted about, apparently to remonstrate with its superior. The Abbot paid it no mind. Uprooting itself and spinning around, the Abbot moved toward the library entrance with speed surprising in one as ungainly as an Actuni. Dirt flew; the other monks laid down their spines. As it ran it sang the lament over and over again.

Feighan said, "What was that all about?"

"Your answers have upset a balance ages old. Eighteen thousand years of searching have ended with a few words between a matmind and an ani—a Terran."

"What are you *talking* about?"

"The Abbot is now proclaiming that we know beyond a doubt the essential nature of the Far Being Retzglaran."

He studied the monk closely. Its spines drooped and its tone was more muted than usual. "So what are you unhappy about? Shouldn't this be your big day?"

"You speak out of turn, acolyte!"

The other's vehemence took him aback. "Ah—"

"Forgive me," it said quickly. "I should not have spoken so harshly, even though your impertinence does warrant a reprimand. . ." It shuffled its roots about, rippling the soil. "I am a scholar, Acolyte McGill Feighan, an historian as well as a theologian. I have invested three centuries of effort in the extension of a thesis which you have severed in your answers to three questions . . ."

"With all due respect, I don't understand."

"Your information has led I'ghra and the Abbot to a conclusion that the Abbot is now announcing as Revealed Truth: that the Far Being Retzglaran is evil."

"Evil?" He shook his head. "But—"

"The announcement will cause an uproar, for all true believers must accept Revealed Truth as soon as they hear it. This is only the fourth of all Revealed Truths, and the other three are that God planted the universe, that Actuni are meant to suffer, and that Actuni must pray at God's favored hour every day."

"But why—"

"Because the dawn prayers believe to the tips of their roots that the Far Being Retzglaran is *good!*" It jabbed its long spine at the highlanders arrayed north of the library, and then at the crests and ridges that folded back upon themselves in all directions. "The peakroots will never, ever, accept this as Revealed Truth. A time of schism lies ahead—schism, and taps."

"H'nik, I don't—"

"I would discuss it with you later, when we have the time

and the privacy to explore the reputed logic behind the deduction, but for now, I have duties to which I must attend. Perhaps tomorrow?"

"Tomorrow?" That frustrated him. He wanted to talk about it right then and there—but he had to admit that since H'nik had taken the news so poorly, any discussion would waste both their time. The monk would probably just keep on complaining and worrying. But still—the Far Being Retzglaran evil? It did not make sense! "Oh, all right. Should I look for you?"

"On this planet, at least, you are easier to recognize—I will look for you." It headed out of the library without another word.

Feighan moved to I'ghra's eastern flank, there to hide from the late-day sun in the shade of its trunk. He needed to think: *This changes all the ground rules, and for once in my life I better stop and really work things out instead of just plunging ahead. I do that too often, and it always lands me in trouble. And what better place for meditation than a library?*

All around him, the matted-out monks chanted the Fourth Revealed Truth. They sang out of tune, not having had centuries to rehearse it. Their off-key wailings made his teeth hurt; no way could he ponder productively there. Wincing, he scanned the horizons, and wondered where—"Ah-hah!"

PING

The winds of the Crown whipped about him, driving snow into his face and eyes. He ran before the wind till the edge of the high plateau plummeted away from him; careful of his footing, he peered down the cliff-face. A thousand meters below, a ledge jutted into sunlight.

PING

The shelf extended twelve meters out, and ran for thirty-five. Its rock was warm; its air, chill. His Talent twinged, then quieted. He sat, crossing his legs and propping up his chin in his cupped hands. The sun beat on his face—it was barely noon at this longitude.

Below, in an arid highland valley, farmers tended their crops. Tiny, grey-green pincushions, they moved from point of blue to point of green, pausing, fussing. An updraft carried the scrape of their voices all the way to Feighan's ledge.

Then he realized he heard not the farmers, but two other Actuni. One stood on a boulder at the east end of the fields, and the other on a terrace at the west. He squinted. They were shaking, bouncing; their spines flashed in the light so often that each looked to be wearing a rainbow.

While he wondered what they were doing, his stomach rumbled. "Oh, damn—I forgot dinner."

A voice next to him said, "Well, you're a Flinger—pop back to New York for a burger and fries."

For a moment he thought his heart had stopped. He gasped—turned his head—and stared at the fist-sized black rock half a meter away. *I been out in the sun too long, that's what it is . . .*

"Look closer, fool."

He prodded the rock's slickness, then hefted it. Turning it over revealed a meshwork grille set into its underside. "A radio?"

"Such powers of deduction!"

"Who are you?"

"Milford Hommroummy, of course."

He—*PING*—teleported the rock radio into Actu's sun. "Whew!" But before he could relax, something tweaked his Talent gently.

Hommroummy said, "Wait! This is not a trap. Just hear me out."

He scrabbled through the loose stones, looking for one with a speaker. "Oh, sure, you're such a good buddy."

"Hardly that—but we must talk."

"Why? What do you want?"

"You."

"Drop dead." Sunlight glinted off chrome. He closed his eyes—

"Wait! It has taken us quite some time to find you; I'd rather our efforts did not go for naught."

He opened his eyes, keeping his Talent hair-triggered so he could Fling out in a snap. "Why should I listen to you?"

"You're an outcast, Feighan, unwanted by your own people. Exiled to the most barren planet in the Network, you bake in the sun and—"

"What—do—you—want?"

"You. We shall pay you well."

"I don't want your money."

"But you have none of your own, have you?"

He clenched his jaws. "You know—"

"We shall commence our relationship by having your trust

fund returned to you in its entirety—would that not please you?"

In the valley, the orators still sawed away while their audience kept its distance. Feighan wished suddenly for a leafy glade, with a waterfall and ferns lacing out beneath broadbranched trees. If he had the trust fund back, he could buy a place like that... "No," he said quietly. "I'd rather be poor than get it back that way."

"Feighan, we ask so little! One Fling a day, no more. Sometimes it would be only an intraplanetary Fling—New York to Shanghai, let us say—although to be honest, most would be interstellar. Is that too much for us to ask? Considering what we offer?"

"Forget it." He lifted the radio.

"Ah, Feighan, this is your opportunity, man!"

"No."

The voice drew back, growing colder and sharper. "Perhaps, then, there is one last thing I can offer you which would change your mind."

"You can't offer me a thing, Hommroummy."

"No?"

"No." The wind blew hot across his face.

Hommroummy chuckled: dryly, humorless. "I offer you your life."

He stiffened. Dust spattered his cheek, abrading it. Below, the orators clambered down from their podia. They trundled across the fields to meet each other. Their long spines led them like lances. "Hommroummy—"

"For years we have sought to capture you alive and unharmed, because those were Gryll's orders. It has recently changed them."

"What?" He hunched forward, watching the Actuni.

"Sign with us, Feighan, or die. We shall never again attempt to capture you alive."

"But you can't kill me! I'm—"

"A Flinger? Of course you are. But surely you don't think we would send a man to meet you in the street and throttle you with his bare hands, do you?"

"Well—" The orators collided; a huge spark cracked. A hoarse wail spiraled up to him. "I credit you with more subtlety than that."

"Good. Beware, then, of poison in your water—bombs in

your mail—and snipers in the sun."

"Huh?" He shook the radio. "What?"

A bullet grazed his cheek, and ricocheted off the cliff to his rear.

Below, the dead orator tumbled onto its side.

PING

Still holding the radio, Feighan materialized outside the tent.

"You see?" said Hommroummy. "You have till tomorrow morning to decide. And then—" His chuckle rasped like the Actuni's death cry. "And then you die."

▪ **Chapter XVII** ▪

Hommroummy spun his swivel chair around. The cockpit insulation muffled the engines to a numb whisper, and passed almost no vibration. "Well done," he said. "Very well done."

"I told you it would work." Slouching in his seat, Davis grinned.

"And your man has no idea what he's doing?"

"He thinks it's a wildlife project." He snorted. "The only problem with indoctrinating them so thoroughly is that they believe anything—and damn near anybody. Can't seem to get one without the other."

"You did hear what I said to Feighan, I trust?" Hommroummy's caterpillar eyebrows lifted.

"Yes. A very nice squeeze. Now I see why you wanted him alive; he could be extremely useful."

To the pilot, Hommroummy said, "Take us down."

To Davis he said, "I have been informed that the lizard has been tagged, as well. Before you take off again, make certain that our technicians have rewired the detectors to accept that beacon, as well."

"A fail-safe?" At Hommroummy's nod, he inclined his head slightly. Things were becoming exciting. *Very* good. They're ours, now."

Hommroummy smiled like a shark spotting dinner.

• Chapter XVIII •

Slumped in the shade of a basalt outcropping some ten meters from the foot of the next terrace, he let the heat bake the moisture out of his body, and the sulphurous air foul his lungs. What difference did it make if he died of dehydration? What difference did it make if he died, period?

Hommroummy sure called it right—I am *an exile.* The US government had stripped him of his wealth, and would seize anything he ever earned again; if he went home he would be an indentured servant. The North American Consortium—his friends, his colleagues—had taken his job, and would not return it until he submitted to their brainwashing. And no one else on Earth would hire an enemy of the two most powerful hierarchies on the planet. Or off Earth, either, because elsewhere in the Network the FNC would voice the NAC's grievances, and scare alien employers away.

Oh, God, it hurts! He had a Talent—a wonderful, nearly miraculous Talent—which he could not exercise to its fullest. Oh, he could Fling monks all around Actu—even sneak back home once in a while, if he were careful—but that would barely tap the potential of the Talent. The ability to teleport across a hundred light years had to have been the Creator's gift to the entire galaxy—and here he could not use it in the way the Creator had wanted, the way the Talent itself wanted. A dolphin in a goldfish bowl, he could have an ocean—if he would be a tuna.

He almost laughed, then. Milford Hommroummy had just given him a new reason to resist the behavior modification: physical survival. Hommroummy had agents everywhere. If Feighan submitted to the b-mod, he would never emerge from the PsychSection alive. Someone would see to that.

Assuming, of course, he could *enter* the PsychSection alive.

And to top it all off, the Far Being Retzglaran—the beacon of his life since childhood—the being that even before Actu he had suspected might be God—turned out to be evil, as well as divine.

He could not stand it.

Depression settled over him like a poison mist. The glare of the setting sun, reflected off the eastern slope, blinded him. The air clawed at his throat. A bronze-shelled bug crawled out from under a rock to chew on his boot. And he did not move, because he did not care.

A mottled-green tail slapped down on the bug, squashing it flat. "That was going to bite you, McGill! What's wrong with you?"

"Nothing."

"You're just sitting there—getting sunburned again, too."

"I know." As he turned his head, the skin of his cheeks stretched, and flamed. But he did not care.

"Didja have fun at the library?" On his left wrist rustled a woven bracelet.

"Not really."

Sam looked hard at him. "Let's go home and see Gina."

"No." But he really wished they could—he missed her more every hour.

"You don't have to go to work, do you?"

"No. Where'd you get the bracelet?"

"K'rach'a gave it to me." Sam's tail lay still; his tongue flicked dejectedly. "You're going back to the library, huh?"

"No."

He came over to sit down beside Feighan; his tail curled around the Flinger's back. "Then what's the matter?"

"Ah—" He waved a hand. "Nothing. Everything. I don't know."

"I know what you mean."

Feighan lifted an eyebrow. "You do?"

"Yeah. I feel that way, too. I don't like it here."

"Really?"

"It'd be okay if it were just the heat—I like the heat, you know," he said with a three-year-old's solemnity. "But it's so dry! There ought to be like an ocean or something, so we could go and get wet and cool off."

"Dew doesn't make it, huh?"

"Uh-uh." Dejected, he dropped his head, and pressed his snout to his chest. "McGill, I wanna go home!"

"We can't, kid."

"Sure we can, you just have to Fling us back."

"Yeah, but then they'll catch me, and—"

"That's not it."

"What?"

Sam got to his feet. As he glared at Feighan, the shadows of dusk distorted his features, making his eyes pools of alien fire. "You don't wanna go home, that's what it is. You don't care about me or about how I feel and so you're making us stay here and I hate you! I hate you!" Tail arched, he spun, and rushed into the tent. Through the flaps came muffled sobs.

Stung and stiff and sunburned, Feighan got up. His body hurt almost as much as his soul. Already more depressed than he could remember ever having been, he now had a child to soothe. He took a step toward the tent—but stopped. Sam needed privacy; he needed time in which his anger could cool. So Feighan sat back down. His butt protested; his back found the basalt too hot. He shook his head.

Hommroummy's radio lay on the ground beside him, mute and gritty to the touch. He picked it up. Holding it next to his ear, he shook it. Nothing rattled. He wondered if its microphone were "live," and listening to all that he and Sam had said to each other. It would be just Hommroummy's style, and it somehow made the whole fight worse. Some things should not be overheard.

Pebbles clinked on the other side of the basalt outcropping. He tensed, instinctively suspecting a sneak attack by the Organization—but Gryll had changed its standing orders. From attempted capture he was safe. Assassination, now . . . but he had till morning.

Shadow climbed the far slope as the sun slipped beyond the ridge. Feighan sighed his relief. Things would not cool for hours—not with the airborne dust's greenhouse effect, and the barren terrain's release of the heat absorbed during the day— but at least he could stop squinting. *Next time I go back for water, I should get a pair of sunglasses* . . . A cinder landed in his right eye. *Sungoggles!*

Prickers scraped stone. He looked over his shoulder, but his eye was watering; he could not see. "Hi," he said, hoping H'nik had come to discuss the Fourth Revealed Truth. "Let me just—"

A dry, abrasive *something* pinched the top of his left ear.

Startled, he tried to scramble to his feet, but could not break its hold.

It clamped down hard. Grinding, it sucked at his ear.

He screamed in panic and in pain. Frantically he jerked his head—and the top of his ear tore away. Blood ran through his sideburns and down his neck. It spattered on the backs of his hands.

But he was free. Lunging away from the outcropping, he dove. The coarse soil scraped his palms. Somersaulting, he bounced to his feet, striking a martial arts pose with his weight balanced and his arms held high and stiff.

On the basalt stood an Actuni, its roots stained with Feighan's blood. Between them extruded the pale blind snake that was the mouth of its symbiote.

Shock washed through him. "K'rach'a?" It carried away the fright, diluted the ache, and cleared a space for rage. "WHAT THE HELL DO YOU THINK YOU'RE DOING?"

Its lower end belched softly.

That pushed him beyond reason. With a grunt, he hoisted a rock the size of his head. Holding it high, he ran forward. A meter from the monk's long spine, he stopped, and hurled the stone.

It smashed into K'rach'a's central ocular aureole, and knocked the monk backwards off the outcropping. It landed upside down between jagged rocks. Its roots wiggled; its mouth retracted.

The mouth looked like an anus with teeth.

And its tongue darted out to lick up a splotch of blood.

He stood above it, panting. With almost no thought and even less effort he could Fling the beast into the heart of Actu's sun—and he wanted to—but he forced the desire down. His heart beat so fast and loud that it drowned out the feeble scrapings of the downed monk. His fists clenched and unclenched on their own. Teeth gritted, he forced himself to draw the deepest breath he could—and to hold it for as long as possible.

Then he said, "You bastard!"

"Sorry about that, Feighan," said K'rach'a. "My inner half got the better of me. With these torn-up roots of mine, I can't move quick enough to catch the beetles, and—and things got out of control, I guess. Honest, Feighan, I'm sorry about that, and I won't let it happen again."

"Damn straight you won't," he said, still seething.

"If you could just tip me over so I could get myself right side up, I'd appreciate it a lot—we're very sensitive to gravity, you know, and I'm starting to feel pretty confused."

"I told you it wanted to eat us."

He whirled around to point a shaking finger at his three-year-old ward. "You! You *knew* what was going to happen, and you didn't say a word!"

"Why should I?" Sam pouted. "You're mean and I hate you and I'm glad it ate your ear!"

"Hey, Feighan, you want to give me a hand here? I'm getting awful dizzy."

"Shut up," he said. "I'll get you out of there when I'm good and ready. And as for you, young man—"

"I'm not a man, I'm a Rhanghan, and that's different, you said so yourself."

He grabbed Sam's left arm and marched him over to a boulder of convenient height.

"You wouldn't!" All Sam's eyelids flew open as Feighan seated himself.

"Watch me." Releasing Sam's arm, he grabbed both the child's left legs and hauled him onto his lap. He ducked the flailing tail. "You bite me, kid, or claw me, or slap me with that damn tail, you're in *real* trouble." He slapped Sam's hindquarters hard. His palm stung.

"OWW! Oh, McGill, I'm sorry, I won't do it again, please! I'm sorry, I'm sorry, really, please, don't spank me again, please?"

He brought his hand down again. The child squirmed desperately. Sam's hide was so tough that it was like spanking a moving suitcase—Feighan had to be one of the few parents alive who could truthfully say, "This is going to hurt me more than it does you." But he delivered a third blow, anyway, because one should never teach a child that a few tears will save him from deserved punishment. Then he said, "All right, you can get down now, but you better not do it again."

Sam scrambled off. "I won't, McGill. I didn't know it would hurt you that bad."

He was careful not to reveal how his hand felt. "I think I understand—you were trying to show me that I needed you, right?"

"Uh-huh." He sniffed. A slow nictitation forced out large moist drops that rolled down either side of his snout. "I thought if you got scared, you'd be friends with me again, and take me home."

Feighan had his doubts about the sincerity of those tears, but not about Sam's words. "I sort of thought that's what it was. But we *can't* go home, not to live, and it's *not* because I don't love you. I do, Sam. You're my very best friend—"

"I thought Greystein was your best friend."

"Grey—" The name caught in his throat; he had to turn his head and cough. "Greystein's dead."

"You mean you stop being friends with someone when he's dead?"

"It's sort of complicated to explain—"

"Hey, Feighan, would you get a move on? My sap's flowing in the wrong direction; if this keeps up much longer I'll be growing roots out the top of my head."

Exasperated, he shut his eyes, as if by closing them and wishing hard he could make all the bad go away. Then he sighed. "Excuse me, Sam, but I'd better get K'rach'a right-side up or it'll never quiet down."

"You gonna spank it, too?"

"An Actuni?"

Sam made a face. "Yeah, I forgot . . . but what are you gonna do? You've got to teach K'rach'a a lesson, right?"

"I suppose so, Sam, I suppose so . . ." He pushed himself to his feet and swayed. Dizziness swirled the world around him. For a moment he thought he would faint. He dropped into a crouch, hands on his knees, and let his head hang low. His cheeks felt clammy where they brushed his wrists.

"McGill! What's the matter?"

"I think . . ." It took an effort to speak. "I think I lost more blood than I thought I lost . . . let me just take a breath here . . ."

"Feighan, would you get the lead out? I need help over here, and I need it now."

Sam glanced once at his guardian, as if assuring himself that Feighan could stand without assistance, then raced to the outcropping. "K'rach'a, if you don't shut up, I'm gonna chew your roots off! McGill's bleeding to death and all you can do is gripe. If I hear one more word out of you, I'm gonna get real mad."

Hunched over, his vertigo slowly fading, Feighan had to chuckle. He took a few more deep breaths and slowly straightened up. This time the horizon stayed level, and the darkness in his eyes was that of twilight. He walked over to Sam and the monk.

"McGill, you should go to a hospital—forget about K'rach'a; it got itself into this mess and it should get itself out."

"It's okay, Sam—this won't take more than a minute or two." He looked at the Actuni. Even if he could lift a two-meter-tall being that had to weigh a hundred kilograms, he would not attempt it with K'rach'a: the monk had too many prickers, each of which was too long, too sharp, and too stout. He would have to use his Talent.

It was going to be tricky, though. He would have to impart sufficient angular momentum to make the other spin through about a third of a revolution—or was it rotation; he could never remember the difference—at any rate, the momentum imparted would have to flip K'rach'a back into a normal vertical position, and to do that, Feighan would have to have the monk up in the air to start with, and— He grinned.

PING

K'rach'a materialized two hundred meters up, with nothing between itself and the rocky soil but all that dusty air. It wailed as it plummeted.

Deftly, Feighan worked his Talent to shove the monk into a vertical posture. Then he waited.

For six and one-sixth seconds K'rach'a fell. The wind shrieked through its spines. At the end of the sixth second it was traveling at a velocity of thirty meters a second. It must have thought the ground was leaping up to squash it.

Feighan timed it perfectly. At the very last moment he awakened his Talent again and took from K'rach'a every bit of the momentum it had accumulated on the way down. The monk alit as lightly as if it had hopped into the air by itself. It sank its roots immediately. Its spines quivered, saying nothing intelligible but conveying overwhelming fear nonetheless. It shook as though an earthquake had struck.

Sam said, "Wow!"

"Think that taught it a lesson?"

The Rhanghan cocked his head and stared at the Actuni. "Yeah. Probably. I mean, *I* think it'd be fun, but K'rach'a doesn't look too happy, so maybe it did. How come you never do that with me?"

As he looked down at his ward, he realized that Sam was right. He had never dreamed of playing skyrocket with him, even though his own change-ringer—Jose Schwedeker, the retired Flinger who had discovered Feighan's latent Talent— had played it with him time and again when he had been a child. *But Jose did it to teach me about my powers,* he thought. *It's a Flinger game, not a kid's game....* And even as he thought it, he realized how much of a rationalization that was. "We'll try it sometime soon, okay?"

"How about right now?"

He pointed to his ear. "This is making me woozy, Sam. I sure would hate to faint just when I was supposed to catch you."

The Rhanghan looked him up and down, then shrugged.

"Tomorrow, all right?"

Sam shrugged again.

K'rach'a said, "F-feighan, I told you I was s-sorry! You didn't have to go taking that kind of revenge on me." Its shudder sounded like a bad orchestra tuning up. "My God, you sent me so high I was looking down on the Crown."

"Not hardly, K'rach'a—you weren't even higher than that ridge up there." From the far valley came a wailing. Feighan said, "Oh, no!"

Sam glanced at him. "At least tonight you'll only hear half of it."

"Huh?"

"You mean you can still hear out of that ear?"

"Better than I'd like to right now." He felt like crying. To sit in gathering gloom and listen to dusk prayers through an ear that throbbed with every beat of his heart... "Come on."

"Where?"

"Ah... Hong Kong. I know a doctor there."

Sam waddled closer. "Can we get something to eat, too. Like some good fish?"

"Sure." He shivered with adrenalin aftermath, and with worry about returning to a world from which he was a fugitive. He dared not be seen.

PING

They materialized on the landing of a fire escape. Feighan tried the door into the corridor; it was locked. "Damn." He leaned forward to listen through it, and caught himself just before he pressed his ear to the metal. "Sam, is anybody on the other side?"

The Rhanghan's flank muscles bunched as he concentrated. "Some people way down the hall, waiting for an elevator or something . . . nobody else."

PING

Their feet sank into the green wool rug of the hallway. Soft, indirect lighting put Feighan more at ease until it dawned on him that the same dimness could disguise a Feighan hunter, as well. Nervous again, he looked over his shoulder. The long hall was empty—the elevator doors *snicked* shut.

Twenty meters down on the right hand side, a brass plaque announced, "Dr. Lemuel Q. Leung, MD." He looked for a door bell. Nothing.

Sam said, "Why don't you just go in?"

"This is his apartment, not his office." Maybe a thumb pad worked into the intricate bas-relief design of the molding?

"Oh. That's why it's so quiet inside."

"Most likely. How many people?" The door could not be voice-activated, could it?

"Inside? Some—it's quiet; nobody wants to hurt us—but I can't count 'em, McGill. It's just good or bad, that's all."

"Okay." Wishing he had a full-fledged Minder like Gina to help, he rapped lightly on the mahogany.

It said, "One moment, please," in a soft female voice, and repeated the message in Cantonese, Mandarin, and Japanese.

Then it opened on a short, pudgy man in a blue silk robe he was holding shut. His jet black hair was tousled; he blinked in even that dim light.

"Hi, Lem."

He focused on Feighan and smiled—but the smile flitted away. He grabbed the Flinger's arm and yanked him inside. The door closed of its own accord.

"You've not been followed, have you? Or seen in the corridor?"

The questions heightened Feighan's anxiety. "Followed, no; seen? I don't think so. Why?"

Leung relaxed. "The inquiry agents have been round, you

know." He looked over his shoulder and said something in Cantonese. From the bedroom came the whisk of slippers on parquet floor. An ivory arm closed the connecting door.

"Nice," said Feighan, raising an eyebrow.

The other smiled broadly, but made no explanation. Then he squinted at Feighan, blinked, and spoke to the ceiling. The lights came on bright and dazzling. "I say, old chap, you've not been in a Wanchai bar fight, have you? One hardly knows which are more dangerous, the sailors or the hostesses." As he spoke, he took Feighan's jaw in his left hand and turned the Flinger's head to the right. "Nasty bit of work, here." Leung had trained at Cambridge, and was proud of his affected accent, anachronisms and all. Drunk, he did a better Brooklynese — which was how the two had met a few years earlier. Leung had spotted Feighan in a restaurant, ascertained that he was American, then asked in all seriousness if the proper idiom were "moider da bums" or "moider dem bums." The Flinger had had to confess ignorance. "The kitchen, I think."

"Huh?"

"Well, I should be a proper fool if I worked on you in my living room, what?" He spun on his heel and marched toward the far end of the room.

Feighan followed, as did Sam. The lights faded behind them while brightening before. It was like being tracked across a stage by a spotlight. "What was that you said about inquiry agents?"

Leung pulled out a chair at the formica-topped kitchen table. "Sit. Tilt your head to the right. Tsk-tsk-tsk. I presume that this large beast watching me so steadily understands that I am allowed — nay, encouraged — to touch you?"

Sam hissed. "I'm not a beast, I'm a Rhanghan, and for a Rhanghan, I'm pretty small. That's 'cause I'm only three."

Leung's jaw dropped and he took a step backwards.

Feighan chuckled. "I forgot to make the introductions — Dr. Lemuel Qun Ching Leung, meet Sam, my ward."

Leung recovered nicely. "I am most pleased to meet you, Sam," he said with a small bow. "I've not met a Rhanghan before."

"And it's nice to meet you, Dr. Leung — did McGill pronounce your name right?"

"As usual, he made a great bloody ballsup of it."

"He always does — how is it really?"

Leung pronounced it properly.

Sam echoed it tone for tone, then flicked his tongue at McGill. "That's easier than H'nik's name."

"Most impressive," said Leung in a murmur. "Have you perfect pitch, or—"

"Ah, Lem? My ear?" He pointed at it for emphasis.

"Terribly sorry, my dear chap—but torn ears are a dime a dozen, you know, while Rhanghans enter my chambers rather less frequently." He bent over to inspect Feighan's head again, then straightened up. "I'll just get my bag." He left the room through the swinging door, and re-entered before it had stopped oscillating. "A little anesthespray, and..."

He had the ear cleaned, stitched, salved, and dressed in ten minutes. "Rather good work, if I do say so myself, what?"

Feighan examined it in a mirror. "Uh-huh. Not bad for a society doctor who hasn't seen blood since he got out of med school. Thank you."

"One assumes that you'd rather the police failed to get wind of this."

"I'd really appreciate that," he said. "You were going to tell me about the inquiry agents?"

"Two sets of them dropped by for a bit of a chat. The local constabulary, of course, and then, the day before yesterday, a pair of brutish-looking fellows with bulges in the oddest of places."

The Organization, he thought. "A computer somewhere must list you as one of my acquaintances." He laughed, but weakly. "And I came to you because I was *sure* they wouldn't know about you... Did they explain why they wanted me?"

"Something about welshing on a rather large debt, I believe."

Feighan snorted. "Yeah, the court took every penny I had, and wanted a couple million more...so they're looking for me here in Hong Kong, too?"

"Assiduously."

"Then I'd better get going." He pushed himself to his feet.

"Have you a place, then?"

He nodded. For the first time in hours, the motion did not hurt. "But I'd better not tell you where—there seem to be a lot of Minders floating around, and I'd rather not put a name in your memory for a telepath to pluck."

"Marvelously sensible of you, old boy. And Sam, it has

been a pleasure and an honor to make your acquaintance; p'raps we'll meet again in the not too distant future."

"Yeah, I hope so, too, Dr. Leung."

Feighan and Leung shook hands, then—

PING

—they materialized outside their tent. Dusk prayers still screeched at the stars. The wind blew hot and dry. K'rach'a stood thirty meters away.

"McGill! You said we could get something to eat!"

"I know, and I'm sorry, but if the Hong Kong police are looking for me, I can't afford to go to a restaurant—somebody'll call the cops, and then—"

"But you promised!" When he shook his fist, his bracelet rustled fibrously.

"I said sure, we'd eat, but—" He spread his hands helplessly. "Sam—"

"You know I'd know if anybody was going to try to hurt you, and you know I'd tell you right away, so that's not the real reason. The real reason is you don't want— you want me to be miserable. I hate you!"

"Honest, Sam, that's not it. It's—" But how could he explain his anxiety to a child? Yes, Sam was extremely sensitive; yes, he could Fling them away on half a second's notice. But one sniper with a good rifle, one cop with a dart gun, and bam! Down he would go, dead, or worse. "Sam, I'm sorry. But sometimes you just have to take the bad with the good. We had a couple of good years in New York there, and we'll have good years later. Right now, though, we just have to put up with the way things are going."

The prayer of the valley came to an end, and the sudden silence rattled him. He waited for Sam to reply.

But the Rhanghan turned without a word and went into the tent.

Feighan followed. He slept poorly.

In the morning, screeching Actuni awoke him. Yawning, he pushed his head through the tent flaps and looked down into the valley. The dawn prayers encircled the monastery; their liturgy seemed a challenge, a taunt.

"Hey, Feighan!"

He looked to his right. K'rach'a stood there, the same thirty meters away it had stayed the preceding night. Apparently it had learned its lesson. "What?"

"H'nik wants you down in the monastery."

"Now?" The sun was barely over the eastern ridges. "Can't it wait?"

"No. You better get down there quick."

He yawned again; his eyes watered. "All right." He crawled back inside the tent to get his clothes on and to tell Sam where he would be, but the Rhanghan had already left. He sighed. *Maybe I should have risked a restaurant after all,* he thought. *I hate it when Sam's this way...*

Dressed, he stepped back outside. "Hey, K'rach'a."

"What can I do for you?"

"If you see Sam, tell him where I am, all right?"

"Sure thing... how's your ear?"

"Better than it was yesterday." He nodded to the monk. As an afterthought, he picked up Hommroummy's radio. If he were Greystein, he would use it to track down Hommroummy and get him—but he was no genius. He sighed wistfully, and—

PING

—materialized near the monastery hollow. "H'nik!"

Half a kilometer away, the scholar flashed its metallic bristles. "Here!"

PING

Its long spine quivered a meter from his shoulder; it made him uncomfortable. "K'rach'a said you wanted to see me?"

"Why did you not report at dawn?"

He blinked. "Ah... I didn't know I was supposed to."

"All seminarians report here at first light; arrive late again at your own peril."

He frowned. "I'm a seminarian?"

"You did say you sought entrance to the order, did you not?"

"Well, yes, but I thought there would be a ceremony or something."

"Of course not. You're a monk now. An acolyte, to be precise. That's all there is to it." For the first time since the two had met, the asperity in H'nik's voice was directed at Feighan. "It is equally easy to resign."

"No, I don't—"

"Then obey orders." It did the scuttle-and-hop that turned it around. "There is your row." It pointed with its long spine. "Weed it. And drive off any grazing lizards you see."

The line of plump-leaved blue bushes stretched for two or three hundred meters. He went to the first, which came almost to his knee. "I take out everything growing in this row but this kind of plant?"

"That's right." It moved away immediately.

He squinted down the line. The first weed glistened with dew a meter away, and the next grew three meters beyond that. *Easy*. It would probably take less than an hour. He knelt, and set to work.

Two hours later, he had covered less than fifty meters. The weeds had thorns, and roots of marvelous durability. His knees hurt; his back ached; his neck already stung from the sun. Sweat kept dripping into his eyes, blinding him. It turned the dust on his cheeks to mud.

The rock in his pocket said, "Feighan?"

He groaned. Milford Hommroummy was the last person he wanted to hear from now. "Yeah?"

"Have you come to a decision?"

He sat back, resting his scratched palms on his thighs. "Yeah."

"Well?"

After digging the radio out of his pocket, he held it to his mouth and screamed: "DROP DEAD!" Then he filled it with momentum. It shot straight up at two kilometers per second, trailing a soft mutter of disturbed air. It sparkled briefly, and was gone.

Going back to his weeding, he felt marginally better. He had needed to let off some steam. *Of course, maybe it wasn't the smartest thing in the world I could have done . . . I mean, maybe I should have tried to string him out a little longer, because now they're gonna come looking for me . . . Ah, the hell with it. I've got Sam, the Actuni, the Talent . . . It'd cost them to get me. Too much.*

Behind, a pair of Actuni chatted in their own tongue as they drew closer. He lifted his head—then stood, just in case.

When they were a meter away, one said, "McGill Feighan, we would converse with you." It had the prominent ribs and bright green skin of a highlander.

"Sure. Anything for a break from this weeding."

"We are dawn prayers, and we ask you to join us."

He shifted uncomfortably. "Well, I've just joined the order here, and . . ."

"We know that, but truly, dawn is the only acceptable time of day to pray the major liturgy."

"Ah . . ." Helpless, he spread his hands. "Theology isn't my strong point. I—"

"Do you not see? It is at dawn that the dew falls—"

"I thought it was a little before, myself."

"Admittedly the dusk prayers have a point when they maintain that twilight brings surcease from the heat of the day—but dawn brings moisture and the sun. It brings strength and wisdom. It is a beginning, not an ending, and we who would maintain the universe must dedicate ourselves to beginnings, not to endings."

"Well, that does make sense, of course, but . . . uh . . ."

"Join us. Not permanently; we could not ask such a commitment of you. But work our fields and talk to us and see if your path does not lead more directly than does theirs."

Though already heartily sick of working others' fields, he was interested in any path that might be shorter. "Tell me more."

"You of all people should join us."

He wiped his forehead, then dried his palm on his pants. "Why is that?"

"Because the Far Being Retzglaran has sent you to us."

He froze. "Why do you say that?"

"It is foretold."

He began to relax—

"You are its pawn and it has directed your life to this moment in time, this point in space. It is the Maker, the Planter, the highest form of life in the universe. It is God. And the so-called Fourth Revealed Truth is a pernicious lie spread by the dusk prayers."

He studied the other. "You say It shaped my life just so I'd get here now?"

"Yes." It rustled its bristles affirmatively.

"It littered my life with bodies just so I could wind up here?"

"The Far Being wants no one to suffer."

He snorted. "I thought that was why you Actuni were created—to suffer."

"Sadly, that is our role. But the Far Being Retzglaran did not *desire* it; it simply happened that for the universe to function, we *had* to suffer. Yet remember: it is through the intercession of the Far Being Retzglaran that we live at all."

"But—"

"Join us."

He exhaled slowly, sadly. "No. No, if the Far Being twisted my life around just to bring me here, as you claim It did, then It has to be evil, and you're wrong."

"You must join us."

"I said, no."

"We need you."

"No."

"But—"

"Just get out of here." Suddenly he shouted at them. "Leave me alone!"

They backed away, scuffling the dirt. "If you feel that way about it—"

"I do!"

"We will speak again."

"Not if I can help it."

As they came forward, he stepped aside to let them pass.

They hurried by, their roots kicking up soil as they moved. He stood, hands on hips, angry with them for disturbing him with their contradictory spiel about the goodness of the Far Being. If It made him kill Greystein, It had to be evil. They had to be wrong. They *had* to be.

Thirty meters away, they scurried over a patch of freshly turned earth.

The explosion knocked Feighan on his back. It peppered him with dirt, and pebbles, and scraps of shredded Actuni.

· Chapter XIX ·

Hommroummy's voice came through strong and static-free—
The Organization bought quality equipment. "Our ground spotter says Feighan is alive!"

He stared in bewilderment at the display screen of the detection unit. "So does this. I don't understand it."

"You turned it on too early, fool!"

"I could have sworn he was right on top of it . . ." He examined the control panel. His heart raced; his throat felt swollen on the inside. If he failed, he would die. "Wait. I don't have a reading for Avarice Two. Where is it?"

"In orbit, picking up a passenger."

If he had been in charge, he would have torn off his headphones and hurled them at the wall. But he was not. Even his advice against the land mine had been ignored. "Too far for accurate triangulation. Who ordered it away?"

Hommroummy took a while to answer. When he did, his voice was subdued. "A higher-up."

"Does this higher-up know that, because it did not notify Operations Control, it single-handedly aborted a successful strike?"

"That," said Hommroummy slowly, "is something only a madman would say to Gryll. If you value your life, forget that that thought ever occurred to you."

He scowled. "Let me know when Avarice Two is ready to go again. I will get Feighan my own way. And very, very soon."

• Chapter XX •

The line of dawn prayers enclosing the monastery pressed inward. Their piercing wail rent the air; it rang as loudly as if the sky itself had been torn in half. At the valley's south peak, a flying creature flapped its leathery wings and veered away. At the north end, loose rocks slid, raising a cloud of dust. In the middle, Feighan covered his ears—and gasped as pain shot through the left side of his head.

On his feet again, he brushed off the debris. Dust clung to a sticky smear on his right forearm. *Actuni sap,* he thought, making a sound of revulsion. It burned. The damp skin reddened and began to swell. *Oh, great—I'm allergic to it!* Within seconds, it itched so badly that it was all he could do to keep his other hand away from it. Instead, he bent down, poured dirt over it, and rubbed that off. The scouring did not relieve the irritation, but when he had finished, his skin was dry.

Then he walked forward, picking a zig-zag path through the pulpy bits of the dead Actuni's lower bodies. Their upper bodies lay fifteen or twenty meters away. The blast had dug a crater half a meter deep and three meters wide. If he had stepped there first . . . he almost vomited.

He forced himself to approach the corpses. *Why? Everywhere I go people die because of me—my parents, Rothono, Nadia . . .* the list ran to too many names. Friends and enemies alike; all dead on his account. *I didn't even know these two*

*and now they're destroyed . . . I can't take it any more. I just
can't take it . . .*

His head ached. Shoulders slumped, he turned away, re-
tracing his steps down the row he had weeded. The coarse soil
crunched under his boots. *Such a stupid way to try to get me!
There was no guarantee I'd be there first—hell, there was no
guarantee I'd ever get there!* And yet The Organization had
tried it anyway . . . *or was it Hommroummy? He's usually more
subtle. He knows Sam could have sensed the danger, just like
he sensed the bomb in the courtroom . . .* He groaned. *I couldn't
have two sets of enemies, could I? Please. Tell me I couldn't.*

Dozens of Actuni thumped across the fields toward him.
Bristles fluttering, K'rach'a and H'nik led the way. As soon
as they were within earshot, K'rach'a shouted, "Feighan! What
in tarnation is going on out here? What did you do to those
two old fools?"

He waited for them to draw nearer. The air stunk of chlo-
rophyll; he stifled a sneeze. "I didn't do anything. They stepped
on a land mine."

"Speak sense, acolyte," said H'nik. "Explain to us how you
know it was a land mine, and then explain to us how such a
device could have come to lie beneath the soil of Actu."

He spread his hands wide. "What else could it have been?
I was watching them the whole time. Nothing fell on them,
like a bomb or an artillery shell. It wasn't *in* one of them,
because if you look you'll see—" He gagged on the memory.
"The damage is all to their lower bodies. There's a hole in the
ground. The dirt and—the dirt flew up. It had to be a mine."

"But what was it doing there?"

He inhaled deeply, and let it out slowly. "I think it was
there for me."

"You?" Scuttling closer, H'nik twisted from side to side so
that all three of its ocular aureoles could survey him. "Did you
not leave all that nonsense behind?"

"I thought I had," he said unhappily, "but it looks like it
followed me."

K'rach'a advanced, long spine twitching. "Who planted the
mine?"

"I don't know!" Hands on his hips, he glared at the monk
which had tried to eat him. "It was somebody who knew I'd
be working this row, that's for sure. And it had to be somebody
who has it in for me."

"That sounds like an accusation, Feighan." It leveled its long spine.

He readied his Talent. "Does it? Then maybe it is. Maybe I do suspect you—after all, you're the only one around who's tried to hurt me." *Gina—where are you when I need you?*

H'nik moved between them. "Silence, acolyte. It was K'rach'a's inner half which hungered for you; now, having tasted you, it knows better. And K'rach'a itself would cause you no harm."

The dry wind parched his throat. "Then—"

"Silence, I said! The dawn prayers approach, and it will be difficult indeed to convince them that you did not deprive them of their leadership deliberately. You will leave while K'rach'a reasons with them."

The oncoming green wall had more sharp points than a dagger factory. "All right." Besides, he was too tired to argue anyway. "I'll be at my tent."

"One moment, Acolyte McGill Feighan."

"What do you want, H'nik?"

"You have not been excused from your duties. You will teleport the two of us to Iixa Ha'ghu."

He rolled his eyes to the hazy sky. "H'nik, I—"

"Do what it tells you, Feighan," said K'rach'a.

"All right, but I don't know where Ixy Hag is."

"Then we shall travel in line-of-sight jumps. Make the eastern ridge your first destination."

PING

Twenty minutes later, they reached the valley called Iixa. Barren slopes poured into it, sulking dark even in the bright sun. Lava had flowed there in recent times, and what soil there was lay beneath a smooth black shell. H'nik said, "Do you see that flat ledge halfway down the volcano?"

"Yeah."

"Respect your superiors, acolyte."

"Yes," he said through gritted teeth. "I do see it."

"Then take us there."

PING

The ledge faced south. It caught the sun's heat and held it like a miser. The rock warmed Feighan's feet even through his boots. "Here we are." He was ready to drop.

H'nik ignored him. It bustled across the ledge to a quarter-size Actuni at the very rear.

Curious, Feighan followed.

H'nik rustled its spines furiously. After a very long pause, the small one replied. And they began to talk.

Hot, tired, and aching in head and arms, Feighan grew bored quickly. To him, listening to two aliens converse in their own language was barely more interesting than watching bubbles form in a glass of tap water. Half-wishing he had studied Actuni, he wandered away.

The ledge stretched a hundred meters long by thirty deep; except for the dwarf native, it was lifeless. Only one fissure marred the smooth, dark rock, and it was through that that the small one had sprouted. Feighan walked to the edge.

In the very bottom of the valley, where ashfall and gravel had made a kind of soil, perhaps a score of Actuni worked struggling fields. He squinted down. Thin lines of blue traced a grid on the dirt—the succulent he had been weeding earlier. He wondered which part they ate. The leaves? Did it have pulpy fruit like the Actuni, or just small, dry seeds...he frowned, thinking, *Wait a minute. They said they don't have children, but if they have fruit...maybe it's all sterile? Still, you'd think...*

"Acolyte!"

He spun around. "Yes?"

"Prepare to depart."

"Okay. Is your friend coming?"

H'nik made the bristle shake of negation. "It is not my friend; rather, it is my genetic identical."

"Your twin?"

"My clone. Almost six of your centuries ago, I was drowsing here in the sun when Iixa erupted. The noise awoke me, but it was too late. Hot lava inundated me. Having no other choice, I tapped down."

Feighan shaded his eyes. "I thought you didn't remember your past lives."

"Only the last one, the one whose ending forced the present life's beginning. To continue, when I budded back up—"

"Through the lava?" He stamped it with his heel; the jar ran up his spine and hurt his head.

"Of course. One emerges through one's old brain case, which is usually where the rock is weakest. But the fissure was narrow and the bud bruised itself, triggering the branching process. As the senior, I had first access to available nutrients—

and the soil here is poor. G'raxa never got quite enough . . . Your word is 'retarded.' "

"But it seems to talk okay."

"The first time I visited New York, I spoke English poorly; in fact, I was there as a language student. On one occasion, I spent perhaps forty-five minutes engaged in a most pleasant conversation with a parrot. I did not know it merely repeated that which it had heard before . . . G'raxa is the same. Interestingly enough, Brother I'ghra maintains that in the time before the Day of Burning Water, all Actuni were as stunted mentally as my clone. One wonders about that, of course, but I'ghra is the only one among us who has actual memories of the period. Perhaps it is correct."

Feighan looked at the malnourished Actuni. It seemed shriveled, pathetic. "But you managed to develop normally, even in the poor soil, huh?"

"Hardly. When I broke free of the death root I was barely the size G'raxa is now, though I was close to fifty-five years old. I was so small that I had not even tried to find mobility— I clung to the root and drew from it as much nourishment as I could. Had a large stone not rolled across us one evening, snapping me off, I would in all likelihood still be attached— and by now I would surely be insane. I thank God every dusk for Its intercession."

"You think it was God?"

"Your own Bible says that 'not a sparrow falls . . . ,' yes?"

"Well—"

"Come. Surely it is safe for us to return to the monastery."

"All right." He glanced over to G'raxa and waved good-bye. So it was a retarded dwarf. It could still see.

PING

They materialized on the edge of the basin. Yawning, Feighan looked across. An energy tunic glistened; two Terran faces turned to him; something tugged his Talent. He blinked. They were gone.

"H'nik!"

"Yes, acolyte?"

"Who—" He was shaking. One of them had looked like Greystein. Or was he cracking up from guilt at last? "Who were those two Terrans?"

"What Terrans?" Slowly, it made its way down into the hollow. "Remain wh—I apologize. You are now a monk, and hence allowed to enter the sacred precincts."

He pointed to the other side. "When we Flopped here, there were two Terrans standing over there. Who were they?"

"I see no one there now."

"I know that—one was a Flinger." He was positive. And it was not a guilt-born vision, either, because he no longer felt guilty. Sad, yes, and lonely, too. But not guilty.

"The day has been stressful, Acolyte McGill Feighan. Return to your tent for a short rest. Report back to me in half an hour."

"Wait a minute. I want to know who those Terrans were."

H'nik's lower spines rubbed in exasperation. "Are you determined to harass me? K'rach'a!"

The other stood some thirty meters away. It scuttled about to face them, but did not speak.

"K'rach'a, the acolyte maintains that two Terrans were visiting the monastery when we arrived. Do you know anything of that?"

"He's been out in the sun too long again."

"Do you see, acolyte? Your perceptions are impaired."

"Crap."

H'nik made the scrape of resignation. "Is that the 'I know you're lying to me, so cut it out' word?"

"You got it." His head throbbed; massaging his temples did not help.

"As I thought . . . acolyte, it is remarkably unwise to insult your superiors in the order."

K'rach'a said, "Apologize, Feighan."

He felt crowded by the two large monks. "Why should I? I know what I saw."

"Should the Abbot learn of your insults to K'rach'a and myself, it would demand your immediate expulsion from the order—and of course, it being the Abbot, it would see its demands granted. You would be expelled."

Grouchy from heat and exhaustion, he said, "So? Why should I worry about that? You said I could leave the order any time I wanted."

K'rach'a spoke. "It works like this, Feighan. You can quit any time you want—walk away, no hard feelings on either side. But if you get thrown out, it means you're so screwed-up that the order would be committing a sin if it let you wander around loose—so everybody gets together and makes sure you tap down." It paused reflectively. "See, that gives you a fresh start in life."

He took a step backward, and almost turned his ankle on a loose stone. "How do you make sure somebody taps down?"

"Burn it out, how else?" Its long spine twitched.

"But I can't tap down!"

"That would be your problem, acolyte, not ours." H'nik advanced on him. "We have yet to hear you tender your apologies."

"Okay. I'm sorry. Now: Who were the Terrans?"

"There were no Terrans, acolyte, and should you persist in your impertinence, you will face expulsion."

"Then I quit!"

"Ah?" H'nik tilted back slightly on its roots. "As you would prefer, McGill Feighan, but I feel it incumbent upon me to point out that now that you have resigned from our order, we will find it sadly necessary to ask you to leave the planet."

He sagged. "That's not real fair, H'nik—you know I don't have anywhere else to go."

"Would that be a request to re-enter the order?"

He clamped his jaws shut and held his breath; after a long slow count to twenty he exhaled. "Yes. Yes, H'nik, it is a request to re-enter the order."

"Your request is accepted, acolyte. Return to your quarters until the hallucinations have faded, then report back here."

"All right." He found it distasteful to have to obey. While recognizing that he had no choice, he refused to be submissive; if they wanted him to do their bidding, they would have to accept his sullenness.

"Fifteen minutes should suffice, should it not, acolyte?"

"Yeah."

PING

"Hi, McGill! I didn't expect you back so early."

He sat in the shade of the basalt outcropping next to Sam. "I didn't either, but I've been told that I'm suffering from hallucinations and delusions and various other mental afflictions that require me to rest."

"You sound pretty angry."

"I am."

"I got an idea that ought to cheer you up." Sam's tongue flickered happily. "Let's go to Hideaway for the afternoon! They have good sun and the ocean and we can cool off, maybe stop somewhere else first for a picnic basket—" He broke off to stare at his guardian. "Why not?"

Feighan shook his throbbing head ever-so-slightly. "Sam, it's a great idea, but I have to go back to work in just a few minutes."

"You're working more here than you did back home."

"Tell me about it." He folded his arms and looked down into the valley. He smelled stale even to himself. "Did you see a couple of Terrans at the monastery a while ago?"

Eyes widening, Sam lifted his head. "Is that what it was?"

"I thought you had good vision—you're always bragging about it."

"McGill, I wasn't looking. Just I felt something . . . funny."

"Like what? Danger?" He was sitting on a sharp pebble, but was too discouraged to move.

"It was too far away. Just a—a feeling."

"What kind of feeling?"

"I don't know. A—" The three-year-old rippled the fins of his backbone.

"Well, try, will you?"

Sam held out his hands. "McGill, I am trying, but—"

"Jesus." He slapped a flat rock. "Was it somebody trying to hurt me, or not?"

"McGill, I don't know!"

He snorted. "Thanks."

After a moment of sulky silence, the child said, "Why are you mad at me?"

"I'm not mad at you."

"You are too."

"I am not!"

Sam hissed. "You're mean, you know that?"

"Dammit, I am not, I just—"

"You're mean and nasty and I hate you!" He scrambled to his feet and sped for the tent. "Leave me alone!"

Feighan let his head roll back against the basalt. Overhead the sky hung cloudless but hazy. He wished that just once it would rain, good and hard, to clear all the junk from the air so he could look up into crystalline blue sky stretching into eternity without a flaw. *Rain? Sure. Santa Claus brings it . . .*

The fifteen-minute respite had ended; he had to go back to work. Using the outcropping for support, he hauled himself to his feet. His muscles complained stiffly; his head pounded like a jagged-voiced drum. And every motion hurt his ear.

PING

"Here I am, H'nik. What do you want?"

"Beyond the library field lies a patch of land that requires clearing if we are to extend the library into it, as we have planned."

"Uh-huh." Nodding, he waited for instructions.

"Did I fail to make myself clear?"

"I'm afraid so. What do you want me to do?"

Pointing with its long spine, it said, "Go clear the field."

"Pardon?"

"Clear it. Remove the rocks and boulders. Grade—"

"Boulders?" He squinted at the monk, who seemed to be shimmering in the sunlight. The heat was affecting him, after all.

"Boulders. Remove them." It twisted back and forth on its roots so all three of its eyes could focus on him sequentially. "Then you may rest for the remainder of the day, as long as you understand that it is my compassion which permits you to idle away valuable hours, and not any action on your part."

With a muttered, "Sure," he headed for the field H'nik had pointed out.

Things were just not going the way he had thought they would. He had expected that joining the order would change things for the better, that he would be entering into a fellowship, a fraternity of loving, caring beings who would ease his hurts and teach him the path to serenity. Instead, H'nik barked orders, and K'rach'a treated him with derision, and the only thing he had learned was that the Far Being was evil—and that was something that he wished he had never heard, no matter how much sense it made . . .

The new field had to be twenty-five hundred square meters, and on first glance, a boulder jutted up from each of those square meters. "Oh, God!" A mere examination of the area drenched him with sweat; what would the actual labor do?

He soon found out. Bending for those rocks he could lift, he piled them up and teleported them out to the badlands, then straightened to rub the small of his back. He felt like a sponge which the hand of the sun was squeezing dry. Dizzy from the heat and exertion, he looked longingly up the slope to the green speck that was their tent. With just a little bit of effort, he could Fling right up there, chug some water, pop a salt tablet . . .

The effort was too great. Wobbly, he sat down abruptly.

A bullet whizzed past his head. Mica chips flew as it smacked into a rock and ricocheted away.

Feighan reacted on instinct.

PING

He stood at the front of their tent, scanning the far ridge for the sniper. Actu blurred visibility. "Sam!" He needed the Rhanghan's sense, both physical and para-physical. "Hey, Sam!" Licking the salt off his upper lip, he squinted as hard as he could, but veils of haze draped the western crest. "Sam, I need you! Hey, Sam!"

It struck him that to stand erect before the only tent in the valley made him extremely vulnerable. A trickle of sweat ran down his neck. He dropped to his knees, and stuck his head through the flaps to see if Sam were inside sleeping.

The tent was empty—except for a dark card on his pillow: a recording chip. Worried, now, he scrambled inside, dug through the pile of camping gear for the player, and popped the chip in.

"Good-bye, McGill." The Rhanghan's voice was full of melodramatic self-pity. "You don't want me, so I won't bother you any more. I'm leaving."

"Sam!" Heedless of danger, he ran outside. No Sam. Nowhere. He loved the kid more than anybody in the universe, except maybe Gina; if anything happened to him . . . He jumped onto a boulder for better perspective, but it made no difference. No matter how he twisted and squinted and shaded his eyes, he could not spot mottled green skin anywhere. And the ground—barren, dry, and rocky—bore no tracks.

"Sam!"

His mind *twitched*. He frowned: somebody had used the Talent nearby.

Who? And why? And—but instinct said *get out quick!*

PING

Standing on the lip of the monastery basin, he looked back up to his tent. Nothing. He began to feel foolish for having been so jumpy. H'nik was shuffling toward him, presumably to bawl him out. He was already starting to formulate an explanation that would satisfy the monk without embarrassing himself too greatly.

His tentsite fountained in a spray of rocks and dirt. Moments later, a muffled roar rolled down the slope. Gravel rained over the valley. Jaw agape, he stood immobilized while the wind worried the cloud of dust that was all that remained.

The Organization was on the attack.

▪ **Chapter XXI** ▪

He gaped at the blue light on the screen. Another miss! Hommroummy would not excuse it. The sweat ran down his neck; his collar sopped it up. What was he going to say? He—

"Davis." Hommroummy's voice whispered coldly in his earphones. "Davis, I—" He cleared his throat. "I find myself in the distasteful position of having to apologize."

"Apo-apologize?" His breath came harshly enough to blur his boss' voice. "Wh-what do you mean?"

"Our ground observer reported that she had a clear shot at Feighan. Her marksmanship has always been superior. I granted permission to fire. She missed."

He sagged back in his swivel chair, giddy with relief. "Youm—you mean he got nervous and jumpy because he was dodging a sniper?"

Hommroummy cleared his throat again. "Yes."

"I see." He inhaled deeply. Exhaling, he felt in command once more. "Well, kindly tell your sniper to hold her fire. *I* shall dispose of Feighan. And then I'll burn the lizard." He looked forward to that. He had hated Sam for a good long time. "But if ground fire keeps them on the move—"

"It won't," snapped Hommroummy. "Now get him!"

"With pleasure."

· Chapter XXII ·

Anger finally freed Feighan from the paralysis of shock. Clenching his fists, he strode up to the oncoming H'nik. "All right. You told me before there were no Terrans on Actu—"

"You speak with disrespect, acolyte. Need I remind you—"

"At this point, all you can remind me of is that you lied. And every time I think of that, I get mad." He kicked dirt on its roots. "Maybe K'rach'a told you what I do when I get mad? Quit stalling. Where are the Terrans?"

"When I relate this conversation to the Abbot—"

"If you don't answer me pretty soon you won't be relating any conversations to anybody—you'll be squatting in a field trying to grow new bristles. Now." He wiped sweat off his forehead, and dried his hand on his pants. "Somebody just Flung an explosive charge into my tent. Actuni don't have the technology—or the *physi*ology—to make that kind of of time bomb. Who did?"

The monk backed off; the top of its barrel leaned away from Feighan's intensity. "I have no knowledge of this, acolyte, and I find your implicit accusations reprehensible in the extreme. To suggest that clergy—"

"Who would know?" He stalked after it.

"No one. There are no Terrans on this planet except for yourself, and that is a situation which will soon be remedied." Its long spine snapped into the locking position; it quivered as the monk shuffled about to aim it at Feighan. "You have caused me annoyance enough, Acolyte McGill Feighan."

He narrowed his eyes. Surely H'nik knew better than to—

The monk charged.

Gravel flew as its roots churned the soil. Its spines waved, circled, then interwove to form the fibrous equivalent of chain mail; only the ocular and the long spines jutted out. All four pointed straight at Feighan. Between its roots dangled the symbiote's mouth; it made soft slurping noises. H'nik advanced on him at a good ten centimeters per second.

Feighan laughed. Backpedaling a fast five meters, he waited. *What am I going to do? I really don't want to hurt this guy too badly—I mean, it's got answers I need, for one thing—but I can't let it think it can scare me.* The problem was, it was like fighting a legless bull, and where is the challenge—the honor—in that?

Then he snickered. He found a weathered grey rock that fit comfortably into the palm of his hand. After retreating three more steps to give himself room, he crouched slightly, and held the rock in both hands at about chest level. Then he moved, swinging the rock back underhand and bringing it forward to roll it along the ground just exactly like a bowling ball aimed at H'nik's roots—

The uneven surface caught the stone, ramped it into the air, bumped it to the right and to the left, then channeled it right into H'nik.

The monk toppled forward. Its long spine jabbed the soil, sinking in to half its length. With a furious wriggle of its roots it tried to right itself, but the long spine had penetrated too deeply, and the angle was all wrong.

He sauntered over. "You seem to be having problems here, H'nik. Need a hand?"

A field of crickets *chirruped* as it untangled its coat of spines. They slashed up and down; if Feighan came any closer they would rake his skin. "I order you to put me upright, acolyte."

Its tone irked him. "You don't understand. I don't *take* orders from you any more. If you want my help, you'll have to ask for—"

"I ask your help, acolyte!"

"—it, and you'll have to help me, in return." While he

waited for it to answer, he looked around, half-expecting another attack. The other monks and the farmers ignored them, though; the only sound came from the library, still chanting the Fourth Revealed Truth, and from the dawn prayers massed outside the monastery. The scene was so pastoral that it raised the hairs on his neck—it was too placid to be real.

"Very well," said H'nik. "Assist me into an upright position, and I will tell you what I know."

"Uh-uh. Tell me first. *Then* I lift you up."

"When the Abbot hears of—" It stopped, sighed, and said, "No. The Abbot will never hear of this, for I am violating my vow to keep it secret."

He had no sympathy. "Talk."

"I know very little," it said with audible reluctance. "The Abbot, with K'rach'a translating, conducted the negotiations for the order, and it excluded me from most of the discussions. To the best of my knowledge, they have settled into Ng'ha Ha'ghu—the second valley north of here—which is useless to us because its volcano erupted only a few years ago, and coated all the land with lava to a depth of two or even three of your meters. For their purposes, it is adequate: the lava provides a landing pad for their rockets—"

"They're using shuttle craft?" He clutched his stomach. The Organization usually relied on Flingers—except within a few days travel of a major base. His throat suddenly dried and constricted. If Actu were close to a sector headquarters, ten thousand Organization gunmen could be within range right now.

"Yes. And their craft have made many, many trips."

"But why are they here?"

All its bristles twitched violently. "Did you know, Acolyte McGill Feighan, that tapping down releases into our dying pulp a hormone which, dried and purified, is hallucinogenic to Rehmal? Cumulatively toxic, too, of course—and hence most illegal—but quite pleasurable. And therefore profitable."

He groaned. "And you say their camp is the second valley north of here?"

"Yes."

"All right." He started to prepare his Talent to extricate H'nik, then stopped. "Wait a minute—those two Terrans I saw a couple of hours ago—were they from that camp?"

"No." It scraped its spines hesitantly. "That is, I do not

believe so; one of them was your Director Davis. He said he had information that your life was in danger and that we should direct you to him. The Abbot said that you were not on the planet."

Davis? Had he changed his mind? "Why did the Abbot lie?"

"Because it suspected the motives of your Director, and decided that inasmuch as you had become a member of our order, you deserved the protection of our order. So it lied—and just look at how you have repaid it!"

Ignoring the outburst, Feighan said, "Hold still a minute." He closed his eyes—concentrated on the fallen Actuni—visualized—felt—knew—

PING

Still horizontal, H'nik materialized ten meters up, and began immediately to rotate. It fell, squalling in fright even while the momentum Feighan had applied brought it into true vertical. He caught it just before it hit—and let it settle down soft and easy. "All right?"

"Ye-yes. I . . ." It shook itself, fluffing out its bristles, and in the process recovered its arrogance. "Yes." It turned to trundle toward the monastery.

"You could say thank you," he called after it.

Without stopping it said, "Yes, I could—but I won't."

He was tempted to teach it how to play skyrocket for real, but decided that that would be juvenile—as well as a waste of his time and strength. Grimacing, he focused on the cliff at the head of the valley.

PING

He stood on a small plateau. Its north end tumbled into a gorge so long and skinny that it looked like a dry fjord; its far slope ran like a frozen black river. For a few minutes he rested on a sun-warmed rock while the hot wind rustled his hair. Suddenly he shivered: *I forgot about Sam! What if he goes back to the tent? He*—He swallowed hard. *Migod. What if he can't go back to the tent? What if he made that tape because he had to? Because The Organization had grabbed him?*

Tired or not, he had to go on now.

PING

He materialized on top of the lava flow just as the plateau to the south exploded. *How the hell did they know I was there?* Instinctively, he looked for a helicopter or an observation balloon or even a glider—but the sky overhead stretched hazy and empty from horizon to horizon.

He glanced down. He stood on the lip of a crater perhaps half a kilometer wide. At its bottom, steam rose through fissures in the lava; here and there magma gleamed a dull red. *No, I don't think I'll cross this on foot . . .*

PING

Behind him the crater belched. He yawned. Even short hops could sap his strength. *I really ought to wait at least ten minutes, recharge myself . . .* but ahead, men and machines swarmed over a smooth valley floor, and he feared that any delay could doom Sam.

Haze filled the valley, a giant amphitheater two or three kilometers in diameter. All the way at the other end, sheet-metal buildings nestled against the bare, gentle slope. He could not even count them, much less see anything useful. Stifling another yawn, he—

PING

—Flung himself to the northern rim, and looked back to The Organization's outpost on Actu.

A gout of flame enveloped his last resting place. Three seconds later, the roar of the explosion reached him. *What is going on? How can they home in on me so quickly? Ah, Grey-stein, Greystein, you could tell me, if only—*

Obviously, he could not afford to stay in one place for more than a minute or two. He squinted down through the smoke. Seven buildings. The largest was clearly a shuttle hangar; Sam would never be imprisoned there. None of the other buildings' windows looked to have bars—but then, the windows themselves were nearly invisible. He would have to get closer.

PING

Pulse pounding in his ears, he leaned against the window frame for support, pressing his face to the glass. A row of cots stretched from one end of the building to the other; each had a locker at its foot. Every bed was made, with its sheets and blankets pulled so taut and tucked so tight that it seemed to quiver. A door in the right wall opened. Out stepped a man with wet hair, wearing a towel knotted about his waist.

"Attention all personnel!" Jaw dropping, Feighan looked up—to the speaker mounted on the ten-meter pole in the center of the compound.

"Attention all personnel! Hostile loose in the area! Draw weapons; shoot on sight. Hostile is a tall, dark-haired Flinger—

shoot on sight. Hostile is extremely dangerous—shoot on sight."

A well-Flung stone would silence the speaker, but Feighan would need every Fling he had in him just to survive. He had none to spare for annoying distractions.

The man inside dropped his towel and ran for his locker, from which he pulled an automatic rifle. After checking the clip, he sprinted stark naked for the front door of the barracks.

Feighan dashed for the rear door of the next building. He had barely opened it before a small *krrumph* sounded behind him—exactly where he had been standing a moment before. Glass shattered; smoke dissipated.

This is serious! Somebody knows where I am all the time, and that's spooky. He ducked inside, hoping that he was being tracked visually, and not telepathically.

Long fluorescents glared down on four-meter-tall rows of shelves bearing canned goods, sacks of flour and dried peas, boxes of breakfast cereal... he moved to the other end of the storeroom, tiptoeing because voices came through the door there. He could not make out the words until he had pressed his good ear to the flimsy wood:

"—air-conditioning, damn planet's bad efuckingnough but when you got these muthing stoves turning this whole damn place into a oven, I got a good mind—"

"You really got a good mind, Jimboy, you going to keep your thoughts to youself. You say anything to Mr. Hommroummy, he find you something a lot hardern just cooking for the team."

He stole away, not needing to hear more, thinking, *No way they'd lock Sam up in the messhall, too many people around, too vulnerable...three down, four to go.* As he reached the back door, another anti-personnel bomb went *krrumph*. The cook screamed. His shriek clogged into a gurgle. The other said, "Jim—?" and retched loudly.

Panting, Feighan slipped outside. *Well, it's not visual, that's for sure, must be telepathic unless I've got some kind of homing beacon stuck on me, but where—* He ran his hands down his body, pressing his clothes tight against his skin so he could feel for suspicious bumps or bulges. All was normal. He scowled. He had wasted at least thirty seconds frisking himself. He ran for the next building.

The storeroom's back door exploded. A piece of wood

thunked his left ear; he yelped in pain. Out front a voice shouted, "He's back there! Let's go!"

He twisted the handle hard and tumbled inside, pulling the door shut as he turned to—

—to face Milford Hommroummy. The hard old man perched on the edge of a grey metal desk. He cradled an automatic rifle. His grin spread as his trigger finger tightened and—

—flames raged across Feighan's mind.

PING

Stunned, he shivered. The image of Actu's sun still burned in his brain. *Jesus, that was too damn close. But I did it!* Yet he could not pause to savor his victory, his vengeance. He took a step, stopped, trembled—*My God, after all these years . . . I don't believe it . . . Milford Hommroummy is dead!*—then sped into Hommroummy's office, where he yanked open closet doors and shouted "Sam!"

As he passed a window, the round brown face of a guard peered in. Her eyebrows shot up. She snapped her rifle into the firing position—

He lunged away. Glass burst. A thousand holes appeared in the opposite wall. From that side of the building came the cry of a wounded man.

He hurried through Hommroummy's living quarters as another *krrumph* slashed the office with shrapnel, and filled it with smoke. Nothing. No cages, no locked doors, no saurians bound and gagged behind the couch . . . He cracked the front door a centimeter and peeped out. Dozens of armed guards were converging on him. He had to use his Talent, exhausted as it was, because he had to escape, he had to search—

PING

—the building farthest from Hommroummy's. The running guards had their backs to him, now. One of them kicked in the door he had just left. Grateful, he turned the front doorknob of this building and practically jumped inside. Sweat dripped from his forehead into his eyes, blinding him to—

"Hi, McGill. Haven't seen you around, lately. You here to give me a hand?"

His heart almost stopped. Moving slowly, expecting bullets but finding the voice familiar, he wiped his eyes. And trembled with abrupt relief. The speaker was another Flinger from the

New York Building, an older man whom Feighan knew but could not name. "Hi, uh—"

"Harry." He stroked his bald head. "Don't feel bad, I'm lousy on names myself; only reason I remember yours is because Jose and I were buddies, and I've sort of taken an interest from a distance, if you know what I mean."

He blinked. "Uh, yeah, it's real good seeing you, Harry, but I'm not quite sure just what's going on, so—"

Harry threw his hands up into the air. "On this planet it's impossible to tell what's going on—d'jou come straight from New York, or you been here a while? Hey, how's Gina? You know, she's one of my favoritest ladies. You two make a great couple."

"I've been here a while." If the pattern held, another bomb would explode any second. He crossed to the far side of the room and stood behind a desk with a thick front panel of white-marbled epoxy-glass.

"Then you've heard those damn tremors out there." I tell you, McGill, I don't know how I'm supposed to clean up this epidemic—"

"What epidemic?" He rolled the desk chair to one side so he could drop unhindered if he had to.

"They didn't tell you anything, did they?" He pointed to a stack of oblong metal boxes painted a flat green. "That's a wind-spread fumigant there. Davis is up in orbit right now tracking a flock of infected birds; every time it settles down I set the timer for about thirty seconds and Fling it to the coordinates Davis gives me. When it goes off—"

"Wait a minute. You Fling to coordinates?"

The older man blushed. "Well, not coordinates, really—my computer takes the real coordinates and gives me distance and direction." He patted the device in his breast pocket fondly. "You can do that, can't you?"

"Uh-*uh*." The skill impressed him, even though it had been used nearly to kill him. Then his eyes widened. Along the opposite wall ran a line of drums labeled "Caution—Herbicide."

"You know, McGill, I didn't think you could do it, which is why I'm surprised they sent you here. Far as I know, only six Terrans can do it—Rii—edsch are real good at it, of course—but I was pretty sure you weren't one of us. Boy, I don't know why they sent you, then, even though it's real good to see you again. Have a seat. Davis should be calling down any minute now. The flock's been up a long time. Hope it comes down close. I'm only accurate to about ten klicks; past that I'm wild."

Feighan wondered how Harry would react to an order to "fumigate" the office he was sitting in—*But he's not all there; he'd probably just shrug and go ahead and do it and Jesus, Davis must be going crazy up there trying to figure out how to handle this* . . . He realized then just how he would handle it if he were in Davis' position. Leaping to his feet—

The door flew open and a machine gun—

PING

—they materialized on top of the cliff at the north end of the valley, but most of Harry's blood and all of Harry's skull had stayed behind. Feighan turned away from the bullet-torn figure and vomited. *Ah, Jesus, Harry, you didn't deserve that at all . . . you didn't know what you were doing and you wound up shot by the people you were helping . . .*

He wiped his mouth on the back of his wrist and wished he could rinse it out. Down below, the metal roof flipped off the building in which Harry had been working. It rose into the air, turning end over end, glinting in the sunlight. Smoke poured from the interior; two adjoining walls collapsed. A huge roar reached Feighan a second later.

Musta machine-gunned the time bombs, too . . .

At least he could rest. *No more explosions, thank God.* He needed to catch his breath; he had been Flinging too hard, too fast, too often . . . as he sat, resolutely ignoring the corpse behind him, he wondered how Davis was tracking him. *I could swear there's no beacon on me . . .* on the off chance, he tugged off his boots and scrutinized their heels. Both were so worn down that nothing could have remained within and undetected. His fatigue was lifting.

With a yawn and a stretch, he stood. *First things first.* Clenching his jaw, he looked at Harry's body.

PING

Actu's sun vaporized it instantly, and scattered its atoms to mingle with those of Milford Hommroummy. *Maybe I should have Flung him to a different star—a good Flinger buried with Hommroummy . . . never thought I'd get that chance . . . hard to believe he's out of my life permanently, he's been chasing me so many years now . . . about time, though. Small repayment on very large debts.*

Then he turned about to study the outpost in the valley, trying to remember which buildings he had searched and which might still imprison Sam. Mentally he marked the ones he thought he had entered. *Why didn't I go through them in a line? Is that one the mess hall? I can't see a thing from here . . . no, that's Hommroummy's, so that's the mess hall, so . . .*

He waited till the crowd of milling guards left one door unwatched, then—

PING

—grabbed its knob, hot from the sun; twisted it and stepped inside. A single glance: half a dozen jacked-up jeeps and spare parts dangling from every wall: a motor pool. That left the building next door.

He peered out the window. The guards had extinguished the fire in Harry's building and were spreading out again. They held their weapons at the ready and their heads swiveled ceaselessly. *Dammit, how*— He snapped his fingers at the answer.

He went to the closet. A pair of grease-stained coveralls hung inside; he pulled them on and zipped them up over his energy tunic. Patches and splashes of color showed through, but palely. *Got to be a cap, a hat, a towel*— A dirty black beret lay on the floor. A size too large, it tilted over his bandaged ear and flopped down across his forehead. He wiped his hands on the coverall and then rubbed them on his face. *It's the best I can do.*

Holding his breath, he opened the back door—but caught himself and returned to the tool bench for a wrench. Then he went out, flipping the wrench as he walked, hoping nobody would stop him on general principles.

No one did.

The last building housed the generators. A deep thrum of electricity made the hairs of his body stand on end. A brief search turned up nothing.

He did not know whether to be angry or relieved. *Here I've gone and risked my neck to find the kid and he's nowhere around. Hommroummy didn't grab him. That means he did run away. Just wait till I get my hands on him. He won't sit down for a week. . . .* but he had to break his anger with a chuckle, because Sam never sat down anyway . . .

PING

The south slope of the valley offered a good view of the base and its landing strips. He wanted to destroy the installation without killing too many people—those below were hardly your upright citizen types, but then, neither was he their judge or jury. But first he ripped off the beret and slipped out of the coveralls. To wear them a second more would have overloaded his skin. *Why don't mechanics ever wash their work clothes?*

Squatting, he contemplated his options. He could slap a hundred-kilo rock into the generator at maybe twenty meters a second—knock out all their power and communications, probably. And do the same with the motor pool, but bring the boulder in from above to collapse the roof and dig a crater and really ruin everything. Or—

A beam of light stabbed his eye. He looked up. A gleaming fuselage winked at him. *Somebody coming in for a landing?* The flash of light swelled into a shuttle craft—*No, a fighter!* It dove at him. Not at the runway, at him! He stood and squinted. Yes. No way it could land at that angle. It—

Smoke enveloped its stubby wings, then blew back as rockets leaped away. He shook his head, not believing—

PING

On the northern cliff, he turned around. A mini-nova burst on the far slope as the rockets slammed home. The valley trembled. Loose rocks clattered and slid. Flames spewed from the impact site; for a moment, Feighan doubted his eyesight. *Fire on bare rock?* Then the mountain quivered and a fissure opened in its north face. It ran from top to bottom in a giant, ragged zig-zag that widened and gaped and—

The volcano coughed.

White-hot magma gushed from the fissure, which yawned wider with each passing second. Molten lava splashed the valley floor a kilometer away from its source; hot gravel spattered even near Feighan.

In the base, people were scurrying for the landing pad, where a shuttle crew readied its craft for take-off. One high-speed stone through the fuel tanks would—

Images of greasy smoke and charred metal quickened his pulse, his breath, and made him feel superbly potent—then he spurned them, as he would the come-ons of a whore. He had to.

They were his enemies, yes, and evil too, and he would not

save them, but deliberately to strand them in a bowl filling with the planet's hot blood was more than he had any right to do.

Again the volcano coughed. A ten-ton spray of basalt soared across the valley. A man-sized chunk punched a hole through the shuttle's right wing. Feighan shrugged.

A hot pebble glanced off his shoulder; it was time to leave. He looked around one last time—and threw up his hands in disbelief.

The fighter had returned in silence, knifing ahead of its own soundwave. Its rockets, already launched, would strike in a second. He staggered backward—

PING

—and bumped into one of the cliffs of the Crown. He had come to the ledge where he had spoken to Milford Homm-roummy, and he had come there because the fighter could have struck the monastery too swiftly. Feighan needed time to breathe and to plan.

Preparing to relax in the sun for the first time in what had to be hours, he sat—and gawked. A giant balloon was tethered to the ledge. Blue and gold, it bobbed in the stiff breeze. It flew a white flag.

"What the hell?" He grabbed for a pebble.

"Feighan." A speaker attached to the underside of the balloon synthesized the voice. "Fear not. Truce."

Instinct said, "Flee!" but he was tired. And curious, too. "Who are you?"

"Gryll."

His heart raced as he scrambled to his feet. "Gryll of The Organization?" Clutching the pebble so tightly that its sharp edges bit into his palm, he readied his Talent. If anything happened, he could scatter the gas-being to the winds of Actu. "What do you want?"

"Truce talks. Peace treaty."

"I told Hommroummy, I am not going to work for you no matter what you offer—or threaten."

"Would you consider mutual non-aggression pact?"

"What?" He squinted against the glare.

"After twenty-two years of effort, have come to reluctant conclusion that you are too well protected. Wisest course is to stop throwing good money after bad. Concentrate efforts on more profitable investments. Competition is over."

"Why should I believe you?"

The breeze pushed it toward the rocks; a small propeller on its rear whirred into brief life. "Hope is that you scoff. That you stay on guard. That you sleep poorly for rest of your life. Would be inadequate revenge for loss of Hommroummy, but any vengeance better than none. Scoff. Avoid dark alleys. Trust no one. Give some return for billion dollar investment."

"This is insane!" He sat down slowly, but did not release the pebble.

"More like return to sanity. Have been obsessed with you for twenty-two Terran years; sector profits dropped accordingly. Suspect intervention of your protector, my enemy— 'Whom the gods would destroy, they first make mad.' Superiors most displeased."

"Let me get this straight." Staring at Gryll, he noticed idly that blue and gold were the colors of the gases, not of the balloon itself. They swirled in and out of each other, never mixing. He wondered how. "You're going to leave me alone from now on because you've spent so much time and money chasing me that it's hurt your profits and gotten your boss on your back?"

"Approximately."

"How can I trust you?"

"Don't. Yield some pleasure, at least."

He jiggled the pebble in his open hand. "So why shouldn't I destroy you right now?"

"Can't. Mass 950 kilograms even without prop: more than you can Fling. And pebble trick futile—balloon skin my skin; instantaneous chemical reaction between body-gas and Actuni atmosphere."

"I don't believe you."

"Try."

He did. At the instant of puncture he caught a whiff of something foul, but the hole puckered up and sealed immediately. That shook him. Fully alert, striving to keep his voice calm and even, he said, "All right. Tell me about this mutual non-aggression pact you want."

"Simple. No attacks in either direction. Self-defense acceptable."

"In other words, you won't be hunting me any more?"

"If you abide by agreement as well."

"That includes calling off your man Davis?"

"Davis? Free-lance, mercenary. Not subordinate; merely temporary ally of convenience. Dispose of as you see fit."

He slapped his thigh in anger. "*I* should dispose of him? You sicced him on me; you call him off!"

"False. Davis had own motives for attacking you. Launched own attacks before alliance formalized."

Feighan leaned forward, interested now. "What were his motives?"

"Never discussed." It spun a quarter-turn on its tether, then returned to its original position. "Must go, but will offer two small tokens of good faith: first, Rhanghan carries tracer unknowingly, and Davis will kill it. Second, you carry beacon as well."

He sagged back against the sun-heated cliff. "I knew it! Where is it?"

"Tunic-energizing implant. Decommission and beacon falls silent."

He touched his collarbone, behind which lay the implant. "How do I decommission it?"

"Tunic generated by silicon chip powered by nervous system. Break connection between chip and container, and beacon shuts off."

"How do I know you're not lying?"

"Don't. Impaling you on dilemma offers one small consolation for red-ink balance sheet. Choice is yours."

He scratched a shoulder blade on the rock's rough face. "Dammit . . . do you know where Sam is?"

"Rhanghan?"

"Yes."

"Yes."

"Where?" He bounced to his feet and walked over to Gryll. "Where is he? Tell me!"

"No. Second small consolation. Mutual non-aggression pact establishes relationship as not enemies. Says nothing about friendship. Good-bye." Its mooring line parted abruptly. With a whirr of its tail propeller, it scooted away on the wind.

Frustrated, Feighan kicked a stone over the edge; it raised a small dust cloud in the valley below. *Can I trust it?* He touched his collarbone again. *If I mess with this, will it blow up on me? Jesus, what am I going to do?*

Light flashed on metal. He lifted his head. The fighter zoomed straight at him, again so close that he had no time to take it down, he had to—

PING

—get out. The library monks chanted the Holy. He stepped into the shade of Brother I'ghra, knowing he could not stay for long . . . unless he did something about the implant.

From the periphery of the monastery came the shouts and sizzles of schism. He cocked his head, listened for a while, then decided he would not even investigate. He would let H'nik, K'rach'a, and the Abbot handle it. It was their responsibility.

Sitting, leaning against I'ghra's bare trunk, he fingered his collarbone. He knew where the tunic implant was; he knew exactly what it looked like. If he closed his eyes—concentrated on that plastic horse-capsule with the two metal contacts— visualized the integrated circuit within both as it should be and as it would look were it twisted half-way around within its shell—felt how it should happen—knew how to do it—

PING

He had time for one throat-tearing scream before pain knocked him unconscious.

▪ **Chapter XXIII** ▪

The blue light vanished from the screen. "Dammit!"

"Where to now, sir?" said the pilot over his shoulder.

"Let me think." Feighan had caught on to the implant. But how? And how had a dumb Flinger shut it off? Davis mopped his forehead. "How many hours fuel do we have?"

The pilot glanced at a gauge. "At least forty, sir."

"You are leaving us enough to reach the orbiter, aren't you?"

"Of course." His tone said, *Do I look suicidal?*

Both Harry and Hommroummy had severed contact. He would have to nail Feighan by himself, with rockets. He wished the pilots were better, though. Those rocket runs over the base had been sloppy.

One green light remained on his screen. It glowed small and steady. He nodded. "Let's go for the green."

"Do we blow it away, sir?"

"Y—" He stopped to think. "No. Not yet. Let's use it as bait. You do have good visuals here?"

"Yes, sir. The best."

"All right. Notify Avarice Two of our plans, and let's go."

He would get Feighan. He would.

· Chapter XXIV ·

Unconscious, he dreamed. Around him the library chanted the Holy; the music seeped into his dreams to shape them, color them, and give them direction.

Bronzed by the sun, he lay on a black sand beach talking to Greystein. Sam frolicked in the wavelets, shrieking with delight when they splashed on his snout. Only Gina was missing—and he missed her. He was saying, "I'm sorry I had to kill you, but it was you or me—I mean, it was pure self-defense, if you hadn't tried to kill me first, well, you know . . ."

Greystein, paler than usual, tapped the hole in his chest. "McGill, McGill, my young daffodil, I really don't mind. Events transpired exactly as you say they did; your rationalization not only attempts to clear you of guilt, it actually does exonerate you! Besides—so many times I'm confronted by someone who calls me a heartless bastard that I really appreciate the chance to open my shirt and say, 'You're absolutely right!' Wonderful to see the looks on their faces, simply wonderful . . ."

Dragging his tail, Sam came up to the blanket. "Where'd the water go?"

"What do you mea—" Feighan stopped, stunned. The ocean had vanished. Brownish-red dust coated the empty sea-bed, transforming it into a rusty mixing bowl. Away off, a smear of green retreated to the horizon. "My God! What's happening?"

Greystein shrugged. "Somebody pulled the plug."

"Yeah, but—where is it going?"

"Let's go take a look."

"That's got to be ten klicks, at least—that's an awful long walk."

Greystein and Sam shared a look of mutual exasperation. "Do you want to tell him, Sam, or should I?"

"You better; he never listens to me."

"McGill, there is about you an attribute that sets you apart from most of the human race, not to mention all the various and sundry alien races floating here and there around the Galaxy. A rather unique Talent, it is unusually useful in a situation such as this. Not to put too fine a point on it, you're a Flinger, you chucklehead, and you can teleport us out there!"

He looked down at his clothes. Blue shirt, white pants, black boots . . . "I can't be a Flinger, I don't have a tunic. Why don't you teleport us? You have a tunic."

"Ah, but I'm not a Flinger, either—I'm a Rogue! It means I'm heartless. And this is definitely not my job; I'm just along for the ride."

He groaned. "All right. But I warn you, if it doesn't work, don't blame me, because I don't have a tunic. Come to think of it, I don't have a job, either. But I'll give it a try." He closed his eyes, and—

PING

"See?" said Greystein. "No muss, no fuss; not a hump or a bump: maybe you lost your shirt of many colors, Joe, but you haven't lost your Master's Talent. And here's the last of the sea."

He pointed to a large pond, in which waded perhaps ten million dwarf Actuni, shouting at each other while they sucked up the water.

"I can't understand them," said Feighan.

Sam flickered his tongue in mock-disgust. Waving to the two nearest Actuni, he said, "The one on the right's saying, 'Grr! Rgr!' And the other one's saying, 'Krch?'"

"'Krch.'"

"'Gng-rrg?'"

"'Ka.'"

"'Ka kr grr rrg?'"

"'Krkrkr—ca!'" It locked its long spine into place, then charged the other, which quickly readied its own weapon. Wet sand spattered as they clumped toward impact; the others in the pond turned and watched.

On they came, never swerving, holding course till spines stabbed rinds and lanced on through. Sap spurted. Roots knotted for better purchase. The spines penetrated deeper and deeper and—sizzled at simultaneous discharge. Their prickers drooped. Their tap roots thumped into the drying sea-bed. Their barrels, still twined in fatal embrace, tore free of their stumps and fell over.

"Jesus," said Feighan softly. He shook his head, then stopped abruptly. All the water had vanished. He squinted into the burning sun. The Actuni had left nothing behind but ten million fleshless brain cases already rusting into powder. "Greystein, do you believe that? They're *all* dead. Greystein?" He turned. He was alone. He spun on his heel through 360°, searching for any sign of life or friend or ward—

A plume of smoke rose on the horizon.

"There they are." He closed his eyes—

*   *

In disbelief he studied his feet. Or rather, the stumps of his legs. They had sunk hawser-thick roots through the dusty soil, down through the clay and the gravel and the vast sheet of basalt thirty meters below, down to the subterranean aquifer which maintained the deathroots of all the dead Actuni in the area. Maintained, not nourished. Feighan could draw so little water that his hands began to shrivel. His ears withered up and fell off. "Help!" He threw back his head and screamed it to the blazing sun. "Help!"

The smudge on the horizon bellied into a cloud. Not smoke, but dust. Kicked up by a massive vehicle or a buffalo stampede or an ochre gastropod that had to stretch at least a hundred meters long as it raced across the desert.

He waited patiently, wondering only if the sun would set before the gastropod reached him. Not that he would mind—the sun would rise again in the morning—but animals who come calling on vegetables get upset if their hosts nod off when photosynthesis shuts down for the night . . .

It wheezed to a halt a few meters away from his branches. "Hello, McGill. Long time no see. Sorry to hear that the trust fund got confiscated, but some things simply can not be foreseen."

"What's going on here?"

It swiveled its huge snail-head, as if surveying its surroundings for the first time. "Oh, yes, well . . . time-lapse holography, you know; it actually took a good many eons for things to reach this point. Surprising that the Far Being let it get so out of hand, but in my master's defense, I must point out that its attention had been occupied elsewhere for rather longer."

"You're not making any sense! None of this makes sense! I'm a human, not a—" He scowled at his leaves, but did not recognize them. "A maple."

"Actually, you look more like a son-of-a-birch to me, heh-heh. You're not laughing—did I get the idiom wrong?"

"It's not funny, dammit! I'm trapped here and there's not enough water."

"That's because it's all locked up in the deathroots of the Actuni—but don't you worry, we're providing more."

"We?"

Its ochre deepened into red. "I do exaggerate . . . the Far Being is going to provide the water." It twisted one eye-stalk to stare at the sun. "Should be on its way now—I'd get out of here real quick if I were you."

"What? How the hell am I supposed to get out of here when my roots go forty-five meters down?"

It made a noise of sympathy, a warm slurping sort of sound. "In that case, it's been a real pleasure, and—"

"Wait a minute! What's going to happen?"

"Oh, didn't I say? The Far Being is sending down some water—in the form of some very large icesteroids."

"Asteroids? But—"

"*Ice*steroids. Balls of frozen water. Say, ten kilometers in diameter, each. It's not going to turn this place into a rain forest, but it'll keep the Actuni going for another few million years—once things settle down."

"Pardon?"

"Well, you can't expect to drop huge icesteroids into a gravity well without major repercussions. It's going to shake this old planet up, let me tell you that. Anyway, I really must run, and McGill, it has been wonderful seeing you again." With that, it rippled about and humped back to the horizon.

Feighan called, "Hey, wait! Come on, don't leave me here! Take me—"

The sky caught fire as the first asteroid entered the atmosphere. It streaked from west to east. A sonic boom knocked the leaves off his branches. Denuded, he trembled in the wind of its passage.

Disappearing beyond the curve of the horizon, into the night side, the asteroid struck—

Searing light blinded him. Things that hissed and spat plopped into the sand all around. Reflected heat warmed his trunk. The ground shook, slowly at first—

The noise of a billion bombs roared by.

The ground heaved him free, savaging his roots. A fissure opened. He toppled half into it.

And then the fireball washed over him. It torched his twigs; it scorched his limbs. Flames crackled all over his bark—and he could not put them out.

He died.

He awoke in the full glare of the sun, and for a moment could not figure out why. *I mean, I'm dead.* No, he had to be alive: his head hurt; his collarbone throbbed. *Just a dream. But why am I still on fire? Oh, yeah...shadows move, and if you're asleep and don't move with them you wind up getting—* He touched his face. *Ouch damn! Sunburned again.*

From the south came a screeching as of a million rusty saws chewing through warped wood. He sat up, then groaned and lowered his aching head onto forearms crossed atop his knees. *Oh I don't need to hear that! I'd better get the cotton—* But the cotton had blown up along with the tent. The tent from which Sam had run away. Sam who had not been found yet. Sam who was in mortal danger, if Gryll's half-recollected statement were true..."Oh, my God!" His throat was so dry and dusty that the words came out ugly as a crow's squawk.

Greenness bristled in his peripheral vision. He lifted his head. "Oh, K'rach'a."

"For the dark and the dew we thank you, Master. Did you sleep well?"

He squinted at the Actuni, wondering if he had mistaken its identity—but no, it was indeed K'rach'a. The monk held a round grey rock in its roots. Odd. And what was this 'Master' stuff? "Are you feeling okay?"

"Well, sure, Master—as an individual. As Abbot of the order devoted to your worship, I'm pretty anxious about our future, though. Which is how come I've scraped up the courage to ask for your help."

"What are you talking about?" His stomach rumbled; his eyes ached from the glare. Closing them, he considered Flinging back to America for a quick breakfast. *And a shower and shave, too,* he thought, catching a whiff of himself. "Make sense, will you?"

"The infidel dawn prayers attack, Master, and they just might overrun the monastery. If they do that, they'll have the power to deny your true nature." Carefully, it set down the rock, which looked like a weather-slicked tennis ball.

"K'rach'a, who do you think I am?"

"Do you seek to test me, Master? Everybody knows you're the Far Being Re—"

"What?" He rocked to his feet and shook his head—then clutched it as pain ripped through him. His upper left torso was so swollen he could barely move that arm. *"Who* do you think I am?"

"The Far Being Retzglaran, Master—or do you prefer another title?" it said anxiously. "I'ghra remembered your pattern, but didn't say you might want another name."

The monk's broken eyespine must have confused it. "I'm McGill Feighan."

Its barrel rocked from side to side; its roots churned the soil. "We always said you've got the best sense of humor in the universe, Master, and you just proved it again. That was really funny. Will you help us?"

"McGill Feighan, K'rach'a." He walked over, stopping three meters in front of the partially blind monk. Pirouetting slowly, he displayed his front and his back and both profiles. "McGill Feighan—*now* do you recognize me?"

"You know, Master, I *had* thought your voice was familiar, but since you don't look a thing like Feighan, I put it down to coincidence." Suddenly it fluttered all its spines, and then flattened them against its epidermis. "Oh, Master! I humbly beseech your forgiveness! I had not realized who you were, and I just remembered that I did not treat your avatar with appropriate respect. Please, Master, I beg your forgiveness, but if you think I'm not worthy, only say the word and I'll tap down to start a new cycle, so maybe next time I'll pick up the understanding, the insight, I so clearly lack in this."

Am I still asleep? But except for K'rach'a, none of his surroundings had the surreal touch so common to dreams. *Nah—I've just gone crazy, that's all.* He patted his chest. Other than the hematoma around the implant, his body had surely not changed overnight—but his fingers looked different.

He frowned. Holding his hands out to arm's length, he examined them in the strong sun. No, palms up or palms down, they looked all right. So why, when he brought them in close, did they suddenly— He snapped his fingers as the answer came. *The tunic's gone! And that changed my infrared emission pattern. My new pattern must look like the Far Being's, so when I'ghra saw me . . .* And though the thought frightened him—for if the Far Being Retzglaran's worshippers could mistake Feighan for It, so could Its enemies—it also relieved him, vastly. He was not crazy, nor was K'rach'a.

And for the moment, at least, he was God. He started to smile, then stopped: *If the Far Being were truly divine, It— uh-oh!* "K'rach'a, have you seen Sam?"

"The Rhanghan ward of your previous avatar?"

"Yes." He gave it a sour look.

"No."

I've got to find him before Davis homes in on him . . . no, wait a minute, Davis is probably way the hell up in that damn fighter, keeping an eye on Sam with a computer telescope or something, and as soon as I show up near the kid *kapowie*. Hmm . . . so maybe Sam is safe for a little while, at least until I get there . . . Hmmmm . . .

"Master, please! Will you help us?" One of its roots curled around the grey rock it had set down earlier.

He raised an eyebrow. "Tell me, K'rach'a—your faction believes in my evil, correct?"

"Yes, Master."

"And the lot of you are, of course, aware that should you have made a mistake in your assessment of my nature, such a mistake would be a grievous offense to me."

Sand clumps crumbled as its roots shivered. "Yes, M-master."

"Then tell me, plainly and simply, why you think I am evil."

Its spines whirled in agitation. "Because you condemned us to life, Master. To an arid, sunbaked existence in which our only joys are the relief of night and a sip of the morning dew. If you were good, if you loved us, you would have let us die during the Great Drought. You wouldn't have given us just enough water to stay alive. Nobody else in the Network puts up with such misery and suffering. If you were good, you would have let us die! That's why we know you're evil."

"I see." He scratched his chin. His whiskers scraped his fingers. "And tell me, how did I provide the water?"

"Is this another test, Master?"

"It's certainly another question."

It rotated its barrel 40° right and then 40° left, back and forth and back, so it could study him through its functioning flank eyes. It seemed suspicious—but fearful, too. "As you well know, Master, you dropped the water on us from the sky. It burned as it fell, and it struck the world like a huge rock spit up by the biggest volcano of all time—and then some. Just the noise it made going by stripped off our spines; the quakes smashed our roots. Most of us died right then, not from thirst but from all those quakes."

"Do you know this because you remember it?"

"Me? I'm K'rach'a, not I'ghra, who last tapped down on the Day of Burning Water. What I know is what I heard from I'ghra while I was a library monk."

He nodded. The Far Being *had* dropped icesteroids into the atmosphere to provide . . . *Wait a minute, if they were ten klicks in diameter, lessee now, God I wish Oscar were here, he'd eat this up in a second, but it's 4/3·pi·r³ = lemme see, now* . . . He could not work it out in his head, so he lowered himself to his haunches and fingered the numerals into the sand. *Five hundred cubic kilometers of water in* one *of those mothers? That'd put five hundred square klicks one klick underwater, or 500,000 one meter under, and the Far Being—* "How many separate balls of water did I drop?"

"I knew this was a test," said K'rach'a fretfully. "I apologize, Master, but I never paid much attention to the details since so many of the other library monks knew them so well. Eight, I think. Maybe twelve."

Feighan sighed. Suddenly, a great deal made sense to him. And if he still did not understand the Far Being's essence, at least he knew that the Far Being was not God.

For a true God makes miracles, not messes. A God of omni/ ubi attributes inclines toward the elegance of creation, rather than the brute force manipulation of large masses. And a God with wisdom and power who nonetheless has a weakness for the pyrotechnic would certainly not miscalculate the trajectories of the relief supplies.

Unless, of course, It were malevolent . . .

No! he thought. *No, I can't believe it. I refuse to believe it. True evil would have let them die, or it would have extorted payment for continued life, but it wouldn't have acted like a clumsy Good Samaritan . . . No, the Far Being can't be evil.*

And then he shivered. While he had convinced himself that It was neither divine nor evil, he had also glimpsed Its power: It could juggle eight or twelve asteroids each the volume of a good-sized lake.

He opened his mouth to explain it all to K'rach'a, but closed it again immediately. Discussion now would be futile. The monk was too obviously attentive only to the screeches shrilling out of the valley.

"Let's go see about your uprising," he said instead.

"This way, Master." Seizing the round grey rock, it turned to lead him, but he said—

PING

—"My way's quicker," and stepped onto the lip of the terrace overlooking the monastery valley. He sucked air past in teeth in surprise.

Marching roots had trampled the neat fields from the monastery hollow to the far south end of the valley. The cause of the devastation massed in the middle: perhaps three thousand Actuni, arrayed in two long opposing lines. Two meters in front of the southern column, a wide white stripe had been painted on the soil. He squinted through the haze, leaning into the noise from below as though it were as tangible as the wind. All three rows, two green and one white, stretched as straight as laser beams. Each ran from one terraced slope to the other: easily two kilometers.

"I can't see a thing from up here." He fingernailed gunk out of the corner of his right eye. "Where's your Abbot?"

"In the library." It pointed back to where they had come from.

"Is it hiding, or what?"

"When the dawn prayers opened their attack, it decided today would be a good time to go into retirement. It toddled back and matted out."

"Who's in charge, then?"

"I am, Master." It tilted its barrel forward in a prickly parody of a bow.

"Hmm! That's quite a promotion, K'rach'a."

"Thank you, Master."

PING

They stood between the approaching lines. Now Feighan could see. *Talk about Birnham Wood to Dunsinane* . . . for the Actuni of either camp stood as close as possible to the individuals on either side of them, and interlocked spines with them. The row of vegetation ran bristly and unbroken along the entire front. Behind each column milled single Actuni, apparently waiting to take the place of any forward warriors who fell in battle.

Forty meters separated them, but hours would pass before they clashed. They did not advance as units; rather, the individual on the eastern end took one small step forward, and then its immediate neighbor went exactly as far, and so on all the way to the extreme western end, where that one took *two* steps—one to straighten out the row, the next to advance it— and that salient would ripple back through the line to the east end.

That, thought Feighan, *is the silliest battle formation since Yorktown. Although, they're probably not too eager to get on with the killing, even if they are screaming like banshees* . . . A silence fell over the valley.

"They recognize you, Master," said K'rach'a.

That should make things easier. "Find out, please, who's in charge of the dawn prayers."

Before K'rach'a could scrape out the question, a familiar voice rasped, "I am, Your Excellence."

"H'nik!" He scanned the line. The voice had come from somewhere in its middle— *Ah, there it is!* He strode up to the monk, while K'rach'a stayed north of the white stripe painted in the soil. "H'nik, I'm surprised. I thought you were a dusk prayer."

"I was, Your Excellence—"

So H'nik "sees" me as the Far Being, too.

"—until their dogma and my researches came into ineluctable collision."

"You no longer believe me to be evil?"

"No, Your Excellence. Once I did, but no more."

"What changed your mind?"

"Never have I found proof that you have ever acted with other than the best of intentions, Your Excellence. Evil has followed you, yes, but it does so because your existence is both a reproach to it, and a threat. Your followers could stamp it out, if they so chose. You are not evil."

"Master, will you let it malign you like that?" said K'rach'a. Then it paused, scraped a few spines thoughtfully, and set down the grey stone. It scuffed the soil with its stumpy roots. "Is malign the right word? H'nik's saying good things about you, and that's praise, but the good things are exactly what you stand against, so... why are we speaking English, anyway?"

"Because I prefer to," said Feighan firmly.

"I am sorry to have questioned you, Master, I did not mean—"

"K'rach'a," said H'nik, "you are wrong! And only the beneficence of the Far Being Retzglaran keeps It from striking you down for slander."

"No, it *is* evil."

"It is *not* evil."

"It is, too."

"Is not!"

"Is so!"

"Hey!" said Feighan. "What is this? You people are going to go to war over whether or not I'm good or evil, and you don't even think to ask me which I am?"

H'nik twisted about on its roots. "Ah, Your Excellence, with all due respect... I do not need to ask, for I know the truth. Did I need to ask, then it might be conceivable that you were evil, in which case it would be in your nature to tell me that you are good, in order to delude me. And were you now to state that you are, indeed, good, K'rach'a here would refuse to believe you, and would prefer, instead, to believe that you were lying to me to sow the seeds of confusion. Am I not right, K'rach'a?"

"The peakroot's right, Master. As usual, of course, it got so busy passing dust that it missed the main point, though. See, Master, we're not fighting over whether you're good or evil—we're fighting over which of us gets the monastery."

"What?"

"Yes, Master. The important point isn't *which* of us is right—because one of us will always be right, and the other will always be wrong—what matters is that one of us *is* right. And one of us must be. As long as the right one keeps on praying, the universe stays alive, and we've done our duty.

Now, we can pray anywhere—we can keep the universe alive from anywhere—but whoever runs the monastery is top dog, politically speaking."

Feighan scowled. "Don't you have a theocracy?"

"Of *course* we do! The monks are in charge, we run things. But see, Master, the one in charge gets more grace." It crept forward and sat on the small grey rock.

I don't believe this. He threw up his hands. "There will be no war, do you hear me? I forbid it."

H'nik clacked two dorsal spines together. "Ahh, Your Excellence, this is not truly your decision to make, I am afraid. It is, of course, another sign of your goodness, that you wish to spare us the horrors, the agonies, of the battlefield—but you must remember that our role *is* to suffer." It stepped forward then as the salient in its line reached it and passed on.

"This is crazy," said Feighan in a mutter.

"Yes, Master, H'nik *is* crazy, and that's why we beseech your help. Wipe these heretics out for us—toss 'em back up above the frostline where they belong—please?"

"No!"

"In that case, Your Excellence, *we* beseech your assistance. We would be most appreciative if you were to snap your fingers and turn the opposing line into, say, berry bushes, to replace those it has trampled."

"I'm telling you, you're not going to fight."

"Sorry, Master." K'rach'a shifted about to return to its own side. It had tucked the rock out of sight among its roots. "But if you won't kick those guys out for us, we'll just have to do it ourselves. Can't have heretics running the monastery."

Frustrated, he spun on his heel and paced toward the dusk prayers. White crystals crunched under his boot. Puzzled, he dropped to one knee, pinched some onto his palm, and sniffed them. They had a strange, sharply chemical odor. *What the— ohmigod, those drums in Harry's building!* Rising, he hurried back to H'nik. "You have to stop."

"Have we not discussed this completely then, Your Excellence?"

"That stuff on the ground there—" He pointed. "You see it?"

"The cool, coarse substance?"

"Yes. That's herbicide—poison—it'll kill you if you walk through it. You *have* to stop."

"I am sorry, Your Excellence, but we are willing to die for our faith. Excuse me." It moved twenty centimeters forward. Another six steps and it would be rooting in the herbicide.

"Please, H'nik!"

"Our duty is clear."

PING

He stood on the lowest terrace of the valley's western slope. Turning around, he glared at the massed Actuni. There had to be a way to stop the battle before the dawn prayers crossed the line.

But how? There were fifteen hundred on each side! If he tried Flinging the dawn prayers to safety, he would collapse— or they would reach the poison—long before he had saved more than a few of them. Even if he could Fling seven at a time . . . He spat on the rocky soil. No way.

What about a warning? A shot across their bows, so to speak? Say he took a big rock and gave it enough momentum to act like a cannonball . . . Velocities and trajectories came effortlessly—instinctively, almost; he had spent so many years working with them that he calculated them as an outfielder does his throws.

Boulders littered the terrace. He glanced at the nearest and *PING* moved it just a meter, to make sure he could handle it. After a short rest, he concentrated on where he would make it materialize and what sort of momentum he would impart to it.

He took a breath—

PING

—the boulder appeared at the west end of the dawn prayers' line and promptly headed east. Displaced air clapped in behind it like a roll of miniature thunder. Its surface heated from friction and began to redden, but it crossed the valley in two swift seconds and slammed into the opposite terrace with enough force to blast a hole in its wall.

Both lines continued to ripple as they advanced.

I think I've just invented a siege gun, thought Feighan in disgust, *but it looks like a rotten anti-personnel device . . .*

The problem was, H'nik knew that he would not send the boulder careening through its line—his intent was to prevent sapshed, not cause it. And so they would continue to march forward, confident that he would not hurt them.

What he needed was something that would shake them up, terrify them, and simultaneously prevent them from sinking one root into that tainted soil.

But what could he use? He looked around. Rocks. Sand. Hazy air. He ran wildly through a list of things he could find on Earth and Fling back to Actu: Gasoline, spill it out and draw a line of fire; a brick wall, lay it and watch them butt up against it; tons of excelsior, pour them atop the herbicide and watch the Actuni wade into the fluffy whiteness... *Oh, crap, I can't think of anything decent, gotta pull a solution out of thin air like this... thin air... air?*

It was worth a try.

He concentrated on the air before him. He squinted his eyes and imagined a sphere—*Darn, it weighs two grams a liter, 500 liters a kilo times 900 is something like 450,000 liters times a thousandth of a cubic meter is 450 cubic meters*... Moving gingerly, he squatted to work the math out in the sand. *Nine meters in diameter? My God, that's the size of a small house!* He imagined a sphere nine meters in diameter, composed entirely of air. He visualized it floating, its bottom about three meters off the ground. He concentrated on that. He triggered his Talent. He pulled from the Energy Dimension enough momentum to give it a slight upward velocity of about one kilometer a second and—

PING

Flames burst and leaped away. A sonic boom threw him onto his butt, then rumbled into the distance. As it sped across the valley, it blew the Actuni back and down like nicked bowling pins. The lines lost all semblance of order. Some smaller Actuni wound up five and even eight meters from where they had started.

He crossed his legs. His swollen shoulder hurt, but he laughed as the fireball slapped into the opposite terrace. It dislodged more of the retaining wall, and ignited the plants at its base.

Chuckling, not really caring that he could barely hear himself, he got to his feet and brushed dust off his clothes. *Boy, that oughta show 'em.*

All across the valley floor, Actuni were digging their roots into the soil and levering themselves erect. Most had broken dozens of spines. Though he felt bad about that, the damage would have been worse if they had collided with each other.

And then, to his utter disbelief, the Actuni marched forward to reform the battle lines.

PING

He stood one terrace higher up the slope. Catching his breath, he waited for them to mesh spines so that he could—

PING

Fire streaked across the sky, trailing a thunderclap that once again hurled the Actuni roots over crown like a row of cards brushed by a gale. Smoke wisped up from scorched berry bushes, and against the eastern slope the flames doubled in size.

His ears hurt. As did the rest of him. But he nonetheless picked H'nik out of the crowd and—

PING

"Well, H'nik?"

The monk wobbled, almost stabbing Feighan in the side. More than half its rear spines had snapped off; several roots leaked glittering sap. "Your Excellence?"

"I believe I told you not to fight?" He crossed his arms and looked stern.

"Yes, your Excellence, you did."

"And yet you attempted to disobey."

"Yes, Your Excellence."

"You have witnessed my reaction?"

"Yes, Your Excellence."

"Do I need to repeat it?"

The monk shuddered. "Your Excellence, why is it that you direct your rage only at me? We who pray at dawn would honor you properly if you would but let us seize the monastery."

"You would honor me by forcing those who pray at dusk to tap down?"

"It would give them a fresh start in life, Your Excellence."

PING

K'rach'a looked even more woebegone than H'nik. It staggered about, seemingly dazed by its new perspective. The grey rock rolled from its grip, and lay before them. "Please, Master, enough is enough! I beg you, no more."

"Will you stop fighting?"

"If they stop attacking, Master—but if they won't, then we'll have to defend the monastery."

"Even if I give you specific orders *not* to defend the monastery?"

"Why in the world would you want to do that, Master?"

"Because I don't want you killing each other!"

It grabbed the round stone. "Master, I'm afraid we'd have to pretend we didn't hear that order—"

PING

Force Ten winds threw granular snow in their eyes; Feighan gasped at the thinness of the air. "All right!" He shrieked to make himself heard. "Do you two want to walk home from here? Or can you settle this without going to war."

Both monks trembled. K'rach'a said, "You mean if we don't negotiate you leave us here?"

"That's right."

"Well, maybe we can work something out . . . what do you think, heretic?"

"The name is H'nik, infidel, but yes, perhaps, if we were to sit down together and discuss things reasonably, we might be able to—"

PING

The snow melted in the hot air; both monks hummed appreciatively as their skin soaked up the moisture. On the plain below, the leaderless armies milled about, waiting for a command to regroup—or to disperse.

Feighan said, "It's only a suggestion, but your people, H'nik, seem to function better in the day than they do at night—"

"Well, of course, Your Excellence. We are mountain-bred."

"Uh-huh. And yours, K'rach'a, seem to do better at night—"

"Naturally, since we're from the lowlands."

It still made no sense to him, but he let it pass. "All right, then! Let me suggest that the dusk prayers run the monastery at night, and the dawn prayers have it during the day. What could be simpler?"

"We'll see," said K'rach'a.

PING

The steady dry winds of the Badlands teased his hair. He needed a shower and shampoo so badly he could scream. Something long and cold to drink would be nice, too. But he forced himself to be patient, and to say to the native at his side,

"K'rach'a, you tried to poison H'nik and its people."

"Never, Master, it was those Terrans the Abbot—"

"Crap. It wasn't the Abbot, it was you. This very moment you're carrying one of their transmitters, disguised as a rock. What were you going to do, call them in if the poison didn't work?"

K'rach'a wiggled until it squeezed the radio in a coil of root. "Exactly," it said. "And that's what they're doing right now—killing all the dawn prayers. I don't care if you are the Far Being Retzglaran, you're wrong—and they're tapping down."

"Sorry, K'rach'a." He gave the radio enough momentum to break it out of the monk's grip. It fell to the ground a few meters away. He walked over and stepped on it. Delicate components *crunch*ed. "There was a slight eruption in that valley a while ago. They won't be killing anybody. They're all dead."

Its bristles twanged. "But—"

"Too bad. Have a nice walk home."

PING

"Back so soon?" said H'nik.

"The dusk prayers are going to need a new leader."

"Ah?" It twisted about on its roots to broaden its field of vision. "Ah."

"K'rach'a was working for The Organization."

"I rather thought so. The Crown?"

"The Badlands." He wondered how many years would pass before K'rach'a showed up again. If it did at all.

"Excellent choice, Your Excellence."

"Thank you." The words were parching in his throat again. "Now you can go down and tell your troops to go home, yes?"

"Of course."

But before he put it back on the battlefield, he said, "H'nik—have you seen Sam?"

It tilted its barrel sideways. "The small Rhanghan?"

"Yes."

"Why, yes. The last I saw of him, he was on the ledge with my clone—"

PING

Sun shimmered off the ledge. "Sam?"

"McGill!" He emerged from a small fissure in the cliff face. "Didjou bring your canteen—McGill! Danger!" He spun and pointed upwards.

The fighter came screaming out of the sky, sunlight sparkling on its stubby wings. Smoke billowed as it launched its rockets.

He almost Flung them to safety—but the clone was matted out, and its roots held far too much soil for him to get the three of them off the ledge.

"McGill, do something!"

Two rockets, four, six— He could not detonate each of them in time to— *Wait*. He concentrated—

"McGill!"

"Quiet, Sam." He imagined again that massive sphere of air, and visualized it appearing ten meters from the nose of the lead rocket with a velocity of three kilometers per second and—

PING

"Cover your ears!"

The sky caught fire. One instant later the flames outburned the sun as the superheated air swallowed the rockets and ignited them. A half-second later it gulped down the fighter and gave its luminance to the dusk.

The sonic boom hit like a massive fist. Feighan flew backwards. Slamming into the cliff face, he grunted in pain. Sam dug his claws into the crack in the ledge, and then slipped his tail in as an additional anchor. The clone squawked in fear.

Then came the roars of the exploding rockets—and the huge hollow bellow of the bursting fighter. The echoes rattled down through the hills. Hot metal fell like misty rain.

And then it was quiet.

Feighan tried to get up. Broken ribs grated together; his shoulder screamed. He groaned aloud.

"McGill! Are you okay, McGill, oh please be okay, McGill?"

"Yeah, Sam, I just—" He winced as he levered himself to his feet. "I just hurt my back, that's all. How about you?"

"Who was that? Hommroummy? Who?"

"Davis. Hommroummy's dead. So's Davis, now..." He looked out across the ridges and the slopes, but the fighter had broken into parts too small to see.

"Does that mean we can go home?"

He cocked his head. "I'm not sure. Maybe...I'll have to check. But if Davis really was waging a private war...maybe we can, Sam. Maybe we can..."

"Before we do, though, there's something I've got to check at the library."

He could not help smiling. *"You* want to visit the library?"

"Uh-huh. 'Cause then I can tell the Actuni how to have babies again."

· Chapter XXV ·

Gryll counted its losses. Eighteen survivors from the base, out of the one hundred thirty-seven stationed there, plus however many were alive in the one aircraft spiraling up to the orbiter now . . . its gases roiled.

It would have a most difficult time explaining this to its superior. One hundred employees and perhaps a third of a billion fancies down the drain. No, find another idiom; its superior was not Terran . . . ah, a third of a billion shed in the sun . . .

And the planet itself was a write-off, too. After this fiasco they would not be permitted to return for generations. Which meant that thousands of customers on Rehma would be forced to learn to live without the palliatives The Organization had been providing . . .

Madness, pure and simple. If it had not tangled with the Far Being, it would be showing a profit at that moment. But it had. So it showed a loss. And it regretted its foolishness immensely.

One had to recoup. Regather, reorganize . . . Hommroummy was gone, too; he required a successor . . .

The last lifeboat off Actu drew near to the orbiter. Gryll watched it on the screen. It would have a long conversation with those beings. And it would not punish them for failure— after all, they had survived.

Perhaps they were immune?

▪ Chapter XXVI ▪

On the ledge, Feighan had to laugh. "You really think you can teach plants a hundred times older than you are how to make babies?"

"I know I can, McGill." Sam folded his arms across his chest and lifted his chin haughtily. "I been thinking about it for a long time, and now I know I can show them how to do it again."

He reached out to scratch his ward between the ears. "If you're so confident, kid, how come you have to visit the library first?"

"A little farther back, ah, ah, ahhhh . . . thank you. I missed you, McGill. I'm sorry I ran away." His tongue flicked Feighan's wrist. "You need a bath."

"Even I knew that. So how come—"

"Because I gotta check something. A little bit of history. Please, can we, McGill? It won't take long, honest."

"Fine by me. You ready?"

"Can we go to the tent, first, though? I'm real thirsty."

He rubbed his jaw. Stubble scraped his fingers.

"You sound like G'raxa! So can we get the water?"

"You speak Actuni these days?" he asked in surprise.

"Yeah, it's easy. But puh-leeze, McGill, I'm so thirsty!"

"The problem, kid, is that the tent and the water tank got blown into a billion pieces—"

"Oh, yeah..." Sam shuffled his front feet. "Yeah, I saw that."

"The Flinger Building has some water, though—let's go there."

"Okay." He turned to wave good-bye to H'nik's clone.

"Wait a minute." He took Sam's left arm, and slid the bracelet off his wrist. "I think—" He squeezed it. A metallic lump hid in its middle. "Uh-huh. This is a signal beacon. It's how they found us."

"Yeah?" Sam tugged it out of his fingers, sniffed it, then threw it over the edge. "I didn't like K'rach'a anyway."

PING

As they entered the one-story stone building, Feighan cast a suspicious eye at the sagging ceiling. It had not yet collapsed. *Probably waiting for me to come back and get underneath it,* he thought.

Sam scampered ahead, tongue lashing the air as he tried to smell water. Feighan plodded behind, feeling stiff and sore and much older than his ward. *At least Davis is finished, and Homm-roummy too, though I can hardly believe that... or that K'rach'a would poison the dawn prayers just to keep control of the monastery... hope it has a nice long walk home... people!*

As he thought about it, he realized he had racked up an acceptable score for a mere seven days on the planet: the destruction of an Organization outpost; the healing of a schism and concomitant prevention of a religious war; the death of two people who could have ruined Terra; *I even weeded fifty meters of garden row, cleared boulders out of a field... and got used to what I did to Greystein...*

Around the corner of the white corridor, Sam yelped in outraged surprise. A moment later a Terran male shouted, "Dammit!"

Oh God! Tired as he was, he broke into a run. *Anybody* *pant* *hurts Sam* *pant* *he dies!*

And then his ward said, "I'm sorry, but you scared me, grabbing my tail like that. You oughta know better!"

Puffing, Feighan slowed down and listened.

"Well, I reckon it is my fault, Sam. How many teeth you got there, anyway? Felt like about a million."

Walking Mule? He swung around the corner. Sure enough, standing there with Sam—and wrapping a red kerchief around his bloody right wrist—was the Senior Flinger from the New York Building.

"Walking Mule!" He said it with joy and affection, but instantly wondered if he should have. They had parted on less than good terms. "Ah . . . fancy meeting you here."

The AmerInd's smile made his eyes crinkle. "How do, McGill. Gina sends her love. Say, you look like you've been rode hard and put away wet. Can you help me on this?" He raised his forearm. "Can't do a hospital job working one-handed . . ." He sniffed. "I'd appreciate it if you stayed down-wind of me, boy."

He tied the kerchief's loose ends together. "Actu doesn't have all that many bathhouses, you know?" Then he backed off to eye the older man carefully. "So what brings you here?"

"You do." His smile vanished. "What happened to your tunic?"

"I had to shut it off." Quickly, he explained why.

"You and me are going to have to have a lo-o-ong talk, McGill."

"I'm not so sure we will." Something green and prickly flashed behind Walking Mule; he looked over the other's shoulder. "H'nik? How'd you get up here so quickly?"

The monk made the scrape of amusement. "I hurried."

Sam said something in Actuni.

H'nik rustled its bristles in amazement. "That is most impressive, young Sam. You have learned our language most rapidly."

Again the Rhanghan resorted to the native tongue.

"Your accent is flawless," said H'nik, "but your manners are not. Please speak in English so that McGill Feighan and Walking Mule can understand you."

Feighan raised his eyebrows: forty-five minutes earlier, H'nik had been taking him for the Far Being, and calling him "Your Excellency." Now it was back to McGill Feighan, but the tunic implant had not yet been fixed. What was going on?

"I shall explain momentarily," said the monk.

He lurched forward, almost elbowing Walking Mule aside. "Wha—?"

H'nik had already turned back to Sam. "There is a water dispenser down the hall and to your left, but it is heavily locked. Perhaps I had better escort you." It scuttled about to face in the opposite direction. "Let us proceed."

"That's one hell of a neat eetie there." Walking Mule held his wounded wrist in his left hand. "Must have been a real pleasure getting to know it."

Feighan made a face. "It just trotted out its company manners."

"Like that, huh? Remind me to stay company, then."

Feighan leaned his right shoulder—the uninjured one—against the wall. "So why did you come to this oven?"

"Like I said, it's on your account. You really believe Gryll's going to lay off you?"

"Uh-huh," he sighed. "Well, I can hope, can't I?"

"Let's mosey on down to the dispenser while we talk; looks like you could use some of that water, too."

He yawned as he gave up the support of the building. "Not a bad idea. But you're still stalling."

"Well—" He drawled it out so it sounded like "Way-ull." "It appears as though the good Director Davis has up and disappeared on us, you see, and considering some of the things he had instigated, initiated, and authorized before he did his Invisible Man trick, the Board of Directors thought it might be a good idea to take a careful look at *all* the things he's been doing."

Feighan stifled another yawn with the palm of his hand. "It's only been a couple of days, hasn't it? Why would they get that suspicious that quickly?"

Walking Mule twitched his dark eyebrows. "I know you don't have a whole lot of faith in the system, McGill, and I'm not so sure I can blame you for it, but some of us have been a little on the curious side ever since he started putting the screws to Greystein."

What he wanted to say was, *Goddammit, you could have gotten curious in time to keep him from screwing Greystein—* but then, if he himself had had faith, he would have waited before hounding his roommate to his death . . . Something pricked behind his eyelids, then, and it was not dust. Nor was it guilt. "Okay," he said. "But still. He must have covered himself, must have said he was taking a couple of days to go fishing or something. Why didn't the Board buy it?"

"A combination of things." Around another corner, to their left, a door stood ajar. Inside, Sam and H'nik rasped away in Actuni. "That's one sharp kid you've got there, McGill. You must be proud as hell of him."

He gave the Senior Flinger a wry look. "To tell you the truth, there are times I'd rather strangle him."

"Since I have a couple of kids of my own, I can't say as how I'd blame you, but if the temptation ever gets too much, remember, just about the last thing you want is to start an interstellar incident." He winked.

"Hey, McGill!" called Sam.

He stepped into the small, high-ceilinged room. Next to a scintillating panel in the wall, Sam held a plastic cup of water. H'nik stood next to him; its roots spasmed now and then. "Did you leave some for me?" said Feighan.

"Yeah, there's plenty. Let me get you some. Watch!" He reached high up the wall, and pressed a soft bronze plaque. Behind the panel, something whirred. Something else splashed. A moment later, it retracted to reveal another plastic cup, filled to the brim with sparkling water. "Here you go." He snatched it up and went to pass it to Feighan, but he jiggled it, and spilled some on the floor.

"Aahhh!" said H'nik. Its roots slapped down in the puddle. Which dried.

"Thank you," said Feighan. Cold and clean, it tasted like liquid heaven.

"You know what else, McGill?"

"What?"

"I told H'nik about how they could have babies again—I didn't need to go to the library 'cause it knew the answer I wanted—and—"

"Wait a minute. What was it you wanted to know?"

Sam flashed him a most superior look. "If they used to have bees, of course. Back before the Great Drought. And they did! But they all died, and that's how come—well, not really how come." His tail drooped.

Feighan looked from the monk to his ward. "You just hooked me; don't stop now."

Sam shrugged. "See, I figured, since they didn't have bees any more, they couldn't ponnilate—pottilane?"

"Pollinate?"

"Yeah, that's it! I figured they couldn't pollinate each other like they're supposed to, and that all they had to do was get some from home. Only H'nik . . ." He looked up to the Actuni. "You tell it; I still don't understand it too well."

"There is really very little to tell. Needless to say, your

Terran bees would not survive in our environment, but should we desire pollinating agents, the Network entomologists and geneticists could surely provide us with something appropriate."

Feighan nodded. "They could probably make you something almost identical to your old bee."

"The key point, however, is that we do not desire 'bees.'"

Sam said, "I thought it was because they stung, but H'nik said no."

"As McGill Feighan probably understands, the Great Drought came upon us gradually, but one of its proximate causes was overpopulation. We quite literally drank our planet dry."

Walking Mule pressed the bronze dispenser plaque. While he waited, he said, "That's a good line, H'nik, but it does seem a bit improbable."

"You must remember our deathroot. When we tap down, we return our barrels to the environment—but we keep the root. A new bud forms off it, and slowly reincorporates the deathroot into itself. Thus, whereas on your planet you continually recycle all elements, here we recycle only a portion of the elements which compose one being. Now, if that being has thousands of offsprings, as we can, you will see that in not too many generations the world can be drastically overpopulated. Remember that no offspring ever die, either. And neither do their offspring. Before the Great Drought, I have been told, it was virtually impossible to drop root without encountering a dormant deathroot waiting for the moisture to bud. Think of that in terms of your own planet. Think of being unable to walk without disturbing the bones of your ancestors. Think of how it would be if those bones never decayed, but always ate just enough of your food to maintain themselves. Famine would be your constant companion—as drought was, ours."

Feighan refilled his cup—and looked at it uncomfortably. "So what you're saying is, your childlessness is a conscious decision on your parts?"

"Exactly. The extinction of the 'bees' has made it easier to implement, but wind and close physical contact and occasionally other insects do serve as pollinating agents. Self-pollination is not unknown, either. So not all our seeds are sterile."

"So you *do* have babies!" said Sam.

"No, young Sam. For we have learned to eat our own fruit

as soon as it falls. Not only is it nutritious, it prevents accidents."

The three-year-old turned to Feighan. "Can you believe that, McGill? They don't want kids!"

"Speaking as a parent," he said, "I don't find that at all hard to believe."

"Oh." Sam backed up a step. "You mean 'cause kids cause trouble?"

"Uh-huh." He advanced on his ward, made the most threatening face he could, and spread his hands into a circle just wide enough to fit around the Rhanghan's neck. "They sulk and they complain and they run away—" He grabbed Sam under the arms and hoisted him into the air. It hurt his shoulder, but he did not care. He pushed his nose up against Sam's snout so he could glare at him eye-to-eye. "And they worry hell out of the people who love them."

Sam nictitated slowly. "So how come you're not mad at me?"

"I'm too tired. *Tomorrow* I'll be mad at you." He set him down.

"What if I'm real good?"

"Then I probably won't be mad."

He clapped his hands together. "Okay! Then tomorrow I'll be real good." Tail swinging from side to side, he whisked across the room. "Hey, Walking Mule, you ever seen an Actuni fence?"

The Senior Flinger looked down with a smile on his seamed face. "Can't say as I have, Sam. How come?"

"'Cause H'nik wants to talk to McGill in private for a minute, and there's a real neat fence outside, so let's go." He seized Walking Mule's hand and dragged him to the door.

"Guess I'll talk to you in a few minutes, McGill," he said, before the Rhanghan pulled him out of sight.

Chuckling, Feighan told the monk, "Three-year-olds are *not* known for their discretion."

"How true. But then, I do not embarrass easily. I wished to say farewell. It is almost time for me to leave. And I wished to thank you, McGill Feighan."

The other's use of his real name reminded him: "Say, H'nik—back in the valley you were calling me 'Your Excellence.' I, ah—"

"Does the descent from godhood disappoint you?" It scraped

its spines for the sound of amusement. "I used that title because the others believed it to be true. It would not have served our purposes if I had occasioned doubt."

Puzzled, he frowned. "I'm not too sure what you mean. You recognized me without the tunic? Why didn't the others?"

"Oh, no—without the tunic your pattern was, indeed, identical to the Far Being's—which is as it was intended to be."

He crushed the plastic cup, blinking as he did so. "Intended to be?"

"Why ever do you think the gastropod ingested you, McGill Feighan?"

He looked around for a chair to collapse into. Finding none, he squatted, leaning back against the wall. "Wait a minute. You're saying that the gastropod swallowed me to change my emissions pattern so that when I came here and turned off my tunic I'd look like the Far Being?"

"Among other things."

"But why?" He almost wailed it—it made no sense!

"Only the intervention of the Far Being Retzglaran could have prevented a horrifying schism that would eventually have resulted in the tapping down of millions of my people. Agents of The Organization would have collected the discarded husks, processed them, and sold the purified drug on Rehma. The quantity would have been sufficient to addict half that planet, and subsequently poison those addicts. Both Actu and Rehma would have collapsed utterly, their civilizations destroyed."

"Jesus." He whistled softly. "Two whole planets, wiped out? But in that case, why didn't the Far Being Itself come?"

"It is busy elsewhere, attempting, if I remember correctly, to prevent an eight-planet war of teleportation scheduled to occur sometime next century. Which is why It delegated us to handle this problem."

"It saw this coming twenty-two years ago?"

"Oh, much longer than that."

"How did It do it?"

It rattled its bristles. "I have not the faintest idea, McGill Feighan. I am an employee of the Far Being Retzglaran, not the Far Being Itself. I really must be leaving." It made for the door.

"Wait!" He had a billion questions; it could not just leave them unanswered. "You've seen the Far Being?"

"In a manner of speaking, yes."

"Where is It?"

"Wherever It wants to be."

"What does It look like?"

"Ahh . . . rather like you, with your tunic off . . . but only to another Actuni. I have not the faintest idea of how it would appear to a Terran." It edged closer to the door. "And now—"

"Please, H'nik!" On his feet, he stretched out his arms. "Did It—has It been—oh, I don't know how to phrase it. I mean, I'm here because It wanted me to be here. Does It make me do things, or—"

"Do you ask if It caused you to kill your friend?"

"Among other things."

"No. Your friend caused you to kill him."

"And I caused him to cause me . . . but what about—"

"It sees the paths you walk, the branches you might take. Sometimes It will snip off a branch, to force you to grow in another direction, but you are not Its puppet. Were you, you would be no use to It."

It was halfway through the door. "One last question: is It— is It God?"

H'nik paused. "No," it said at last. "No, It is not God—but It is good, indeed, it is. Good-bye, McGill Feighan." And it disappeared.

His Talent twinged; his jaw dropped. *H'nik was a Flinger all along?*

Dazed, happy, and trying to comprehend some of what he had just been told, he ambled down the long corridor to the terrace, where he found Sam instructing Walking Mule on the predatory habits of the grazing lizard.

The Senior Flinger said, "You look blissed out—something H'nik said?"

He nodded, and sat on top of the low stone wall. *After all these years I got some answers! Holy— It almost makes it worthwhile . . .*

"You want to talk about it?"

"Ah . . . no, not yet." The glare hurt his eyes, but he kept on smiling.

"Sam was telling me what you did to Davis—real neat trick, there, McGill. When we get back home, you'll have to show it to us. Flashy."

"You don't get good flames unless there's a lot of dust in the—" He cocked his head. "Was that a roundabout way of asking me to come back?"

"Yup. I never did finish telling you what we found."

"So tell."

Walking Mule made himself comfortable on the wall next to Feighan. "To begin with, Davis told his staff he was going to spend a week in Kansas City, checking out some new steak-houses. The mistake was that Gina Maccari was there when he said it. She got suspicious; said he didn't 'feel' right."

It was nice to hear that after unwittingly helping Davis to nail Greystein, she had used her Talent against the Director. "Uh-huh. And that?"

"Well, Harry Lipsiento disappeared, too. Didn't make his shift, and if you know Harry—"

"I met him about ten minutes before he died." He sketched in Harry's fate.

"Damn shame." He sighed heavily. "Well, the Board got concerned, got a warrant, and searched Davis' place. Found a small fortune in exotic jewels—not stolen, understand, but definitely smuggled. Damnedest thing: he kept them in his refrigerator, in an empty gooseliver can. So they suspended him without pay *in absentia*. If he'd shown up, they'd have given him a hearing, but he probably would have gotten, um, canned in the long run."

"So who's the new Director going to be?"

Walking Mule grinned.

Despite the glare, Feighan's eyes widened. "You?"

"Yup."

He slapped the older man on the back. "Congratulations!"

"Thank you kindly. It's more like a sentence than a promotion, but it's high time the NAC had a Director who understood what Flinging's all about, you know? I think I can do some good things in the job...truth to tell, McGill, I've already made a start."

"How's that?"

"Well, with the Board's written permission, I canceled every executive order Davis issued—on the grounds that we didn't know when he went off the rails, and every one of his orders ought to be double-checked for craziness or corruption before it was implemented." He winked broadly.

"I get the feeling you're trying to tell me something, Walking Mule, but I am too damn tired to work it out for myself. What is it?"

"Well, hell, McGill, you ought to spot it! One of his orders was for you to report for behavior modification."

He sat up straight. "And that's been canceled, too?"

"Yup."

He started to beam. "And it's not going to be reissued?"

A cloud passed over Walking Mule's face. "Well . . ."

"Ah, hell!"

"Hold on there, McGill. I didn't say it would be reissued. Just I find myself in a delicate sort of position. See, I've been indoctrinated just like every other Flinger—well, like almost every other Fl—no, let's not say that. That's a question I am never going to ask you on my own."

"Thanks for that," he said with a grunt.

"But see, if I get orders, I have to follow them."

He squinted at the new Director. "Which means—?"

"Well, the way I figure it—and Sam, you keen-eared, big-mouthed little critter, if you ever repeat this to anyone, I'll have your tongue for a flyswatter—the way I figure it is, the people who need *re*-indoctrination are the people who don't do their jobs. As I recall it, you were Number One on the rating list just about every month. So it seems like you were doing your job. Which, if you follow my logic right on through to the bitter end, makes it seem like about the last thing in the world you need is *re*-indoctrination. If you get my drift."

Relaxing, he smiled. "I think I do, Walking Mule. Thank you." He held out his hand.

Walking Mule took it. "But I've got to warn you, McGill— if I'm ever ordered to order you to report to PsychSection, I will obey. Because I will *have* to." The older man's gaze searched Feighan's face. "You do understand?"

"Yes," he said. "But we'll worry about that when it branches off our paths, all right?" He was pretty sure that if it ever did, Something would be there to offer an alternative.

"All right, boy! Let's get ourselves on home." He stood, and slapped the dust off his pants. "Oh, speaking of that— once I canceled Davis' orders, I sent our lawyer back to court. Oscar, the penthouse, and the trust fund are all yours again."

"I don't think," said Feighan slowly, "that I can ever live there again."

"Well—" Walking Mule patted him on the shoulder. "I can understand that. There are other places to live—and hotels to stay in in the meantime. So what say we get on back now? I need a drink."

"And McGill," said Sam, wrinkling his nose, "needs a shower."

PING

· Chapter XXVII ·

Gryll floated in the alkali flaying tank. It hated it, but it could not bear confinement within that "skin" of its a moment longer. Skin was convenient for wandering through the atmospheres of certain planets, but it aggravated one after a while.

At least it had company. "Seem qualified for position. Vacancy must be filled. You want?"

"Yes," he said, "yes, I do want it. Badly."

"Silly statement. Weakens bargaining position. Start tomorrow?"

"That's fine by me."

"First couple years, watched constantly till competence proven."

"I have no problem with that—you will find I'm very, very competent."

"Job's yours."

"Thank you." And Nathaniel Davis smiled.